I0724758

DON'T MISS THESE OTHER
SPELLBINDING NOVELS BY NYT & USA
TODAY BESTSELLING AUTHOR DONNA
GRANT

CONTEMPORARY PARANORMAL

DRAGON KINGS

(Spin off series from *DARK KINGS SERIES*)

Dragon Revealed (novella)

Dragon Mine

REAPER SERIES

Dark Alpha's Claim

Dark Alpha's Embrace

Dark Alpha's Demand

Dark Alpha's Lover

Tall Dark Deadly Alpha Bundle

Dark Alpha's Night

Dark Alpha's Awakening

Dark Alpha's Redemption

Dark Alpha's Temptation

Dark Alpha's Caress

Dark Alpha's Obsession

Inferno

Whisky and Wishes (novella)

Heart of Gold

Of Fire and Flame (novella)

DARK WARRIORS

Midnight's Master

Midnight's Lover

Midnight's Seduction

Midnight's Warrior

Midnight's Kiss

Midnight's Captive

Midnight's Temptation

Midnight's Promise

Midnight's Surrender (novella)

Dark Warrior Box Set

CHIASSON SERIES

Wild Fever

Wild Dream

Wild Need

Wild Flame

Wild Rapture

LARUE SERIES

Moon Kissed

Moon Thrall

Moon Struck

Moon Bound

HISTORICAL PARANORMAL

THE KINDRED

Everkin

Eversong

Everwylde

Everbound

Evernight

Everspell

DARK SWORD

Dangerous Highlander

Forbidden Highlander

Wicked Highlander

Untamed Highlander

Shadow Highlander

Darkest Highlander

Dark Sword Box Set

ROGUES OF SCOTLAND

The Craving

The Hunger

The Tempted

The Seduced

Rogues of Scotland Box Set

THE SHIELDS

A Dark Guardian

A Kind of Magic

A Dark Seduction

A Forbidden Temptation

A Warrior's Heart

Mystic Trinity (connected)

DRUIDS GLEN

Highland Mist

Highland Nights

Highland Dawn

Highland Fires

Highland Magic

Mystic Trinity (connected)

SISTERS OF MAGIC

Shadow Magic

Echoes of Magic

Dangerous Magic

Sisters of Magic Boxed Set

THE ROYAL CHRONICLES NOVELLA SERIES

Prince of Desire

Prince of Seduction

Prince of Love

Prince of Passion

Royal Chronicles Box Set

Mystic Trinity (connected)

MILITARY ROMANCE / ROMANTIC SUSPENSE

SONS OF TEXAS

The Hero

The Protector

The Legend

The Defender

The Guardian

LaRue Series, Book 1: Moon Kissed

The Royal Chronicles Series, Book 1: Prince of Desire

Check out Donna Grant's Online Store,
www.donnagrant.com/shop, for autographed books, character
themed goodies, and more!

ROYAL CHRONICLES COMPLETE BOX SET

DONNA GRANT

ROYAL CHRONICLES BOX SET
© 2013 by DL Grant, LLC
Excerpt from *Mystic Trinity* copyright © 2011 by Donna Grant
Cover Design © 2021 by Charity Hendry

ISBN-13: 9781942017776
Available in ebook and print editions

www.DonnaGrant.com
www.MotherofDragonsBooks.com

PRINCE OF DESIRE

Four brothers, a secret kingdom, and an ancient curse.

Lucian, a prince of a secret kingdom, must find his mate and return with her to Drahcir before time runs out. He's unprepared for Isabelle and the insatiable appetite he has for her. But will the passion they feel be enough to convince her to venture to a hidden kingdom where magic is a way of life?

Isabelle has resigned herself to her life until a fascinating, devilishly handsome Lucian walks into her life. He shows her desire and adventure that shakes the foundations of her world. She can't live without him, but can she give up the life she knows for one she can't begin to imagine?

Summer, 1268
Somewhere in the Highlands of Scotland

After years of searching, he had finally found her.

After weeks of watching, he would now have her.

Lucian Sinclair inhaled the cool, crisp air of the Highlands. He had waited for this day for as long as he could remember. Ever since his father, King Urises, had told his sons they must find their mates before the fifth moon of the Harvest year, Lucian had prepared.

Drahcir, his homeland, was deep in the heart of the Ben Nevis Mountains. A land so secret that no one knew of its existence, and it was essential to its survival that it continue that way.

Centuries ago, a scorned Fae princess cursed their small kingdom. Since that black day, the princes and princesses of the royal house had been forced to seek their eternal mates and convince them to return to the kingdom, or the city and its occupants would cease to exist.

Already Lucian had spent nearly two years searching for his mate, but now that he had found her, he wanted to make sure he trod slowly in approaching her. Thankfully, time moved slower in his hidden city, allowing him the time needed to accomplish his mission.

He watched as she finished cleaning the tables in the small tavern, her glorious brown hair hanging down her back in a thick braid. Her laughter drifted to him through the open window as she and the owner's wife talked and put the last chair atop the table. It hit him square in the chest and settled into his skin.

She said something and turned her head so that her face was in profile, giving him a view of her slender neck and easy smile. She was small, her body holding all the womanly curves he could want. Her aura, which had led him to her, glowed bright and solid despite her meager living and tired body.

Soon he would take her away from all this. Very soon.

His hand flexed on the hilt of his sword as she opened the door to the tavern, casting her in the warm glow from within. Her face was heart-shaped, her forehead high, her chin stubborn. Dark brows arched over her wide, midnight-blue eyes. Her lips were wide and full, a wicked temptation for a man such as Lucian.

He held his desire in check and watched as she waved good-bye to the owners and walked from the tavern. She came within inches of him as he hid in the shadows. He reached out and touched the end of her braid that hung to her hip as she walked past. Lucian waited until she ventured down the road that led to her tiny cottage before he whistled for his stallion. His horse came immediately.

It was everything Lucian could do not to snatch her up

and carry her away with him to Drahcir as he hurried to mount his horse. She must enter the gates of the kingdom willingly or all would be lost. Many times he cursed the rule the Fae had put into place, but his family was bound to it just as they were bound to the hidden city.

He kept a firm hand on the reins as Elad pranced beneath him, eager for a run. Lucian counted to ten, then loosened the reins to give the stallion his head. He loved the night and everything about it, the velvety darkness and the brightness of the moon, the sounds and the peace.

He traveled almost halfway to his mate's cottage when he heard the male laughter…and then the ear-piercing, soul-shredding scream.

Without a doubt, the yell belonged to his mate. With a growl, he unsheathed his sword and nudged the stallion into a run.

The wind whipped at his hair and cloak as the ground raced beneath Lucian. His blood froze in his veins as he realized because he had been so careful to give his mate time, he might have sent her to her death.

What Lucian saw when he came upon the group made him explode into an ice-cold fury. Four burly, filthy men surrounded his mate. Three held her while another unlaced his trousers.

The need for retribution consumed, overcome Lucian. He leaned low over his mount and charged them, narrowly missing his mate, but he wasn't a famed horseman for nothing.

It was just the surprise he needed to scatter the men. He wheeled Elad around by using his knees and waited, rage settling his body into cold, biting calculation. He, like his three brothers, was known to have a temper. But Lucian didn't explode in his wrath. He was like the snow and ice that hid his kingdom—chilly in his regard, remote in his dealings, and lethal in his intent.

He narrowed his gaze on the attackers, his heart pounding a dull *thud thud* as they looked around trying to locate him. Sitting atop the black stallion with his black cloak, he blended into the darkness, becoming one with the night.

Lucian would use it to his advantage. He'd never feared the night. Instead, he'd embraced it, welcomed it…learned it. As if, somehow, fate had known it would come down to this day, this very night, when he would need it for his mate.

He spared a glance at his woman. She had scrambled against a tree, molded to the trunk as if she could blend into it. Her eyes were wide, her chest heaving, but his mate wasn't given to hysterics. To his delight, there was murder in her gaze as she stared at the men who had dared to do her harm.

Her gaze shifted, searching for him. Lucian wanted to tell her everything would be all right, but he didn't want to give away his position quite yet. He'd comfort her when it was over. For now, he had men that needed to be shown a lesson.

Elad pawed the ground with one hoof, sensing Lucian's need for retaliation. "No' yet," he leaned low over the horse's neck and whispered.

"Where is the bastard?" one of the attackers demanded of his comrades.

One came out of the trees not far from Lucian's mate. "All I saw was the damned horse."

"There was a man," the third said as he got to his feet from his prone position on the ground.

"Aye, lads. One man. Against us four."

This last of the brigands was obviously the leader of the small ramshackle group. Easy enough to take down, Lucian thought. He could prolong the men's pain, exacting his judgment on them. Or he could end it quickly and get to his mate.

It wasn't a difficult decision to make.

Lucian smiled when all four men noticed him. He gave a little bow of his head, mocking them. The leader motioned one of his men to attack. Lucian didn't even move Elad. Instead, he kicked out his right leg, landing the toe of his boot square against the man's nose, smashing bone instantly.

The man howled and fell to the ground with his hands over his face. The smell of blood permeated the air. Lucian stared at the other three, waiting for their next move. He didn't have to wait long as all three attacked at once. Out of the corner of his eye, he spotted his mate still standing sentry by the tree.

Isabelle knew she should run and never look back, but she couldn't take her eyes off the huge man on horseback. Even in the darkness, with only the full moon for light, he was intimidating and powerful, ominous and lethal. Yet, the fools who tried to rape her continued to assault him.

She stared, spellbound and more than a little awestruck, as he used his feet, sword, shield, and horse to defeat the remaining three men. A smile pulled at her lips as she looked at the four men writhing on the ground moaning in pain. He hadn't killed them. Mercy from such a daunting male? She wasn't so sure she could've been so forgiving. True, they hadn't actually raped her, but that was only because her savior had reached her in time.

And just who was the dark man on the horse?

Her attention was diverted by one of the men being helped to his feet by his friends.

"Serves them right," she whispered.

And then her rescuer turned toward her.

Isabelle drew in a slow, deep breath to calm her heart, which still felt like it would beat out of her chest. She knew these woods, and she could lose him in them if necessary. She'd spent hours in the forest as a child. Every nook and cranny was locked in her memory.

She should be afraid, yet the man on horseback didn't make a move. That was the only thing that kept her still. She wanted to thank him for what he'd done. But she also wanted to know the face that went with such a fascinating body. The dark and his cloak hid most of him, but only a man with finely honed muscles could move as quickly and fluidly as he had.

His cloak was thrown over one shoulder, and with the moonlight, she saw it was cloth of fine quality. Even if she hadn't seen his clothing, she would know by his mount that he wasn't a peasant. Besides, peasants couldn't fight as he had.

"Thank you," she said, after swallowing twice to wet her mouth.

He bowed his dark head before dismounting. The four men were attempting to leave, but he stepped in front of them and wiped the blood from his sword on one of their tunics. Once it was sheathed, he walked around them, seemingly forgetting them, and looked at her. "Are you injured? Did they harm you?"

The deep treble of his voice surrounded her, enchanted her. Soothed her. She slowly shook her head, unable to find her voice with the emotions he caused swirling around her. The attack was almost forgotten as he filled her senses, drowning her in his masculinity and strength.

Even without seeing his face, she was charmed, utterly fascinated.

"I am not here to harm you," he said leisurely, as if speaking to a child or a frightened animal.

In truth, Isabelle was terrified. More than she cared to admit. She had lived in the small village all her life and never once came upon any ruffians who would do her harm, until tonight. And though she should be glad someone was there to aid her, he was a stranger.

Through all of that and her unusual reaction to him, she realized his speech was that of not just a noble, but also very high ranking noble. The deep, seductive timbres of his voice held the Scottish brogue, but there was more to it.

"Who are you?" she asked softly.

He smiled and bowed his head as if he were introducing himself to a queen. "I am Lucian Sinclair."

As soon as he had said his name, she felt a tremor run through her, though it wasn't from terror. It was almost like…recognition. *Impossible.* Or was it? Her heart still pounded, but it wasn't from fear. It was from…Lucian.

Good manners or not, after her attack, she wasn't eager to trust anyone. "A stranger to our small village? Where do you hail from?"

"A land far from here."

"I hear your brogue. You're Scottish."

A sliver of moonlight caught his grin. "Oh, aye."

There was nothing left to ask him other than to leave,

but she knew he wasn't about to do that. She had no weapon. Her only defense was the forest, and though he was on foot now, he could mount his great horse and catch her before she was able to sufficiently use the forest to her advantage.

"Let me take you home," he said, and took a step toward her, his hand outstretched.

Isabelle didn't move. She had seen firsthand how quick and deadly he was with his sword and body. He was a dangerous man, a stranger, and if she wasn't careful, she might find that she had stepped from a group of attackers to one man who could do more damage than the four before him.

Though she could see part of his face from the light of the moon, the smile did not diminish the power emanating from him. Was he her savior or her demise? Her decision could well cost her life.

In response to her silence, he reached down and pulled a dagger from his boot. "Here," he said as he handed it to her hilt first. "Take this. If I do anything that you doona agree with, use it."

Only a fool would refuse a weapon, and Isabelle wasn't a fool. She reached out and grasped the dagger. The blade wouldn't do much damage, but it was a weapon and could very well give her the chance she needed if she had to escape.

"Good. Now, since you have had such a horrible night, why not allow me to escort you home? You may ride Elad, and I shall walk," he said, before she could issue a retort.

Isabelle looked around her. The men were slowly scurrying away, but who was to say they wouldn't return with reinforcements. She wanted to be away from here and in the shelter of her home. Safety was something she had always taken for granted in her small village. Never again would she assume she was safe. It was just another reason she hated living alone.

As always, whenever she thought of being alone, she thought of her grandparents and how much she missed them. She was tired of the loneliness, but even she knew that was all she had to look forward to for the rest of her life. The village was small, too small sometimes, for the few men to notice someone like her.

Though she knew she shouldn't trust the dark stranger, he pulled at her with invisible fingers. It was as if her body knew what her brain did not.

To her surprise she found herself saying, "All right." She moved away from the safety of the tree to the horse, and stared up at its great height.

"Let me help," Lucian said, just before his hands grasped her waist.

Isabelle barely had time to gasp before she was perched on top of the horse that had the gall to turn and look at her as if she were a nasty fly bothering him.

She was given no time to do anything but hold on as Lucian grabbed the horse's bridle and began to walk. Tension had her muscles wound tight. She waited for him to speak, and when he didn't, she became even more on edge. Who was this mysterious Lucian Sinclair? And why had he been in the village?

The sounds of the night echoed around them as the moon followed their path. She couldn't take her eyes from him. His clothes were as dark as the night, and his silence intrigued her. Lucian didn't seem to mind the darkness or the sounds as he leisurely walked down the path after she directed him which way to go.

Once more she decided to question his origins. "Where exactly do you hail from?"

"Deep in the Highlands."

Isabelle snorted, very unladylike, but some things called for a snort. Like vague answers. "Which clan do you hail from?"

For a moment, he didn't answer. He stopped and turned toward her. "I doona belong to a clan."

She studied him silently. It was apparent by his fine clothing and speech that he was of noble birth. His brogue wasn't as deep as many Scotsmen, but it was there. How she longed to see his face. "Everyone in the Highlands belongs to a clan."

He shrugged and gave her another smile before he patted Elad's great neck and resumed walking. By the way he evaded her question, she realized he wasn't likely to tell her anything more, which made her wonder at her sanity in allowing him to accompany her home.

But every time she thought of sliding to the ground and running away, she couldn't do it. Something about Lucian held her tightly, as if urging her to be patient. Patience wasn't a virtue, yet she couldn't seem to leave him.

They continued in silence, the clopping of the horse's hooves on the dirt road adding to the night's sounds. By the time they reached Isabelle's cottage, she was anxious to be rid of him and the fear he instilled.

Fear and thrilling excitement.

She hadn't thought her life dull until she'd met him. In just a few minutes time he brought into focus how gloomy her life was. He was like a full moon on a cloudless night, lighting up everything in the gray.

Shut up, she silently told herself. Just because she lived a boring life didn't mean she wanted Lucian's kind of excitement.

How do you know? You might like it.

Isabelle seriously doubted her sanity. Was it a sign that she had lived too long alone that she talked to herself? And argued with herself?

In all her years of working at the tavern, she had never feared living alone. In one night, that had changed. It would always be in the back of her mind that someone could lay in wait for her, and it would give Mr. and Mrs. MacDonald more reason to push her to move into town.

At least if she lived over the tavern she would have the MacDonalds to talk to, which just might save her sanity. But, in truth, she didn't wish to live over the tavern. She liked her home. Mostly because it was the only home she had ever known, but also because she had known love within its walls.

Her grandparents had given her all they had and worried endlessly of what would become of her once they were gone. Isabelle had never fretted much, thinking she had plenty of time before she had such a decision to make. And then the fever struck and taken her grandparents within days of each other.

They reached her cottage, and as always, she felt a pang at finding no candle burning in the window waiting for her as her grandmother had used to do. Darkness, stillness awaited her. A tremor of something profound and intense ran through her as she found Lucian staring at her.

Before she could dismount, he was there to help her. He set her on her feet and his hands lingered a heartbeat before he took a step back. Isabelle drew in a shaky breath at his nearness. She tried to see more of his face, but, with his back to the moon, only shadows met her gaze.

By the way he patiently waited, she knew he wanted something. "Would you like to water your horse?"

He shook his head.

"Do you need oats for your mount?"

Again, he shook his head.

She wasn't about to ask him to come inside. Regardless of the fact he had saved her life, he was a stranger, dangerous and unknown to her.

"Then what is it you need?" she asked, trying to keep the agitation from her voice.

"Your name."

She swallowed. It was a small thing he asked, but for some reason, she wasn't sure she wanted him to know. She glanced at the ground between them before raising her eyes back to him. Though his gaze was hidden in the shadows, she felt it on her, warm and penetrating. She caught a glimpse of a strong jaw and square chin, but that's all the moonlight allowed her to see.

How could she deny him such a simple request? And she feared what else he might ask of her, because apparently, she couldn't tell him no.

"Isabelle."

"A beautiful name for a beautiful woman."

"Would you like to come in for some tea?" She couldn't believe the words even as they left her mouth. Hadn't she just told herself she wasn't going to invite him in? Yet, here she was doing just that.

Excitement. Admit you want it.

A smile pulled at his lips, and she had the urge to see what he looked like in the light of day.

"Another time," he answered, his deep timbre raising chills along her skin. "Until next we meet," he said, and vaulted onto his mount.

Isabelle bit her lip as she watched him ride away. She didn't understand why she wished he had stayed.

"He's a stranger," she murmured as she walked into her dark cottage.

But an exciting stranger.

2

*L*ucian ground his teeth together. It had taken every ounce of control he had to walk away from Isabelle last eve. He had wanted to stay and tell her everything, but that would have frightened her off. She had already been afraid after her attack, and it was because of that attack that he was once more hiding in the shadows.

Watching her.

Desiring her.

Craving her.

His body knew she was the one, the other half of his soul. He ached to pull her into his arms and kiss her. The small touches he'd stolen while putting her on Elad and helping her dismount hadn't been nearly enough.

Nay, they'd only fanned the flames of his desire until he burned, blazed…smoldered with it.

He spent the day tracking the men who had attacked her to make sure they were no longer in the village. After that, he stayed near her cottage and followed her into the small town. He would take no chances with her life now, not after finally finding her.

His stomach growled, and with the hours ahead until she left the tavern, he knew he needed to eat. A slow smile spread across his face as he tied off Elad and walked toward the tavern.

The anticipation of seeing Isabelle again made his hands shake as he reached for the door. He pushed it open and stepped inside to the heavenly smell of roasting meat, ale, and fresh baked bread. A quick glance showed the brightly lit room to have a few men at the bar drinking while others sat at the tables eating and conversing.

Lucian found an empty table near the door and slid into the seat. His eyes raked the room until he spotted Isabelle walking from the back, her arms laden with trenchers of food. She smiled easily to the patrons and even joked with a few.

He knew the moment she spotted him. Her body jerked slightly, and her midnight-blue eyes softened in welcome. He gave her his most charming smile as she finished setting down the mugs of ale she carried, and walked toward him.

"Good evening," he said.

She swallowed and licked her lips, luscious kissable lips that he'd dreamed of sliding over his cock. "I never expected to see you again."

Lucian had to forcibly move his gaze from her lovely mouth to her beautiful midnight eyes. "I told you last night that I'd see you again."

"I know, I just didn't think you meant it."

Her words, spoken so softly, hit him right in the chest. He leaned back in the chair and regarded his mate carefully. She had an easy smile and kind eyes, but if he looked deeper, he could see there was a hurt, deep and profound, that she kept only to herself. He wanted to know what it was. More than that, he wanted her to trust him. "Are you still frightened of me?"

She started to deny it, then promptly closed her mouth. She stared at him a moment before she said, "I am. Strangers always make me nervous."

"Yet we are no longer strangers."

The smile was slow, with just a hint of sensuality, telling him she had no idea of her allure. "You're so proper. We don't have much of that around here."

He loved how her eyes sparkled mischievously when she teased. "I'm no' so proper. Shall I show you?"

Lucian prayed she said yes. He wanted so much to wind his fingers in her long hair and pull her against him. He craved to place his lips on hers and taste her, to hold her. He yearned to know his mate fully.

And claim her for his own.

Isabelle stared at the man before her. Even without seeing his entire face the night before, she'd known it was him instantly. It was his black clothes and the way he held himself. And the way he watched her.

His black gaze fairly smoldered. It sent her stomach fluttering to have such a look directed at her.

To say he was handsome would be an understatement. His thick, wavy black hair stopped just below his shoulders, with a lock falling near his right temple. A regal nose and forehead went along with his noble stance. A strong jaw line and chin, just a shadow of a beard and wide, thin lips finished off a face a sculptor could only dream of. He had eyes as black as his hair, fringed with long lashes that would have made a lesser man look feminine.

Those wide shoulders she'd glimpsed the night before in the darkness didn't prepare her for them in the cold light of day. Thick sinew corded those broad shoulders and neck. His tunic stretched tight over solid arms. And how she wished his jerkin was gone so she could get a look at his chest.

Isabelle was shocked at her reaction to him, but it was visceral, primitive. Primal. This need, this hunger that besieged her ever since she'd first caught sight of Lucian atop his huge horse.

Whoever he was, she wanted to know more of it.

Silence grew between them until she cleared her throat, noticing that he'd let her look her fill. "Are you hungry? We serve some of the best food around."

"I'm famished."

Somehow she knew he wasn't referring to food. Chills raced down her spine and her heart pounded against her ribs as his eyes moved to her mouth.

Excitement. Exhilaration.

Anticipation.

She felt those things and more, so much more she couldn't even begin to name. Isabelle had never cared for strangers, and usually kept a clear path from them. It wasn't difficult in her small village tucked away in the Highlands. No one sought out their village willingly.

Yet Lucian was here. And she couldn't seem to stay away from him.

Isabelle tucked her hand behind her back when she found herself reaching up to comb her fingers through his hair. She didn't know what was wrong with her.

"What are you serving tonight?"

"Mrs. MacDonald makes excellent haggis, but she's also made a big pot of stew that will make your mouth water."

Lucian's wide mouth pulled into a smile. "I'll take the stew and an ale."

Isabelle moved toward the kitchen to get his order. The need to return to him quickly made her nerves frazzled, and her already rapid heartbeat quickened. She told herself it was because he was different from the men in her village, but the truth was…he stirred her. It had been so long since she had found anything exciting that she was drawn to him like the flowers to the sun.

"Isabelle, lass, are you all right?" Mrs. MacDonald asked as Isabelle hurried into the kitchen.

A laugh bubbled up inside her. She was anything but all right when Lucian was around. Isabelle smoothed the strands of hair away from her face. "Another order of your stew, Mrs. MacDonald."

"Ach, I'm glad I made a big pot this time, though I fear I just might run out soon," she said as she spooned the delicious stew into a bowl. "Tell me who it is that has made your face glow."

Isabelle blinked. "Pardon?"

"You heard me, lass. I may be old, but I still remember what it was like to have a man notice me, especially when I was interested in that man."

Isabelle laughed as she grabbed a spoon. "Mrs. MacDonald, I hope you're speaking of Mr. MacDonald."

She winked as she handed Isabelle the bowl. "Of course, lass, of course. Now," she said as she walked to the door. "Point him out to me so I can tell you if he's good enough for you."

"I doubt you'll be able to tell me that."

"Why is that, dearling?"

Isabelle reached the door and stared at Lucian. "He's new to the village."

"Ah, a stranger. We don't get many of those around here. Mayhap that's just what you're needing, lass. The men left in this village aren't worth much of anything." Mrs. MacDonald leaned out and looked around the room. "'Tis the dark man by the door. I see the way his eyes search the room, as if he is looking for something." She straightened and looked at Isabelle. "Or someone."

Isabelle smiled. "Just because he's added a little excitement doesn't mean anything."

"It does if he is the same man that rescued you last night."

"He's the same man."

Mrs. MacDonald mumbled something to herself and went back to her cooking. Isabelle walked through the doorway to the bar. She set the bowl of stew down and reached for a goblet.

"We're busy tonight," Mr. MacDonald said from beside her.

"Aye. I'll sleep well, that's for sure."

"Who's the stranger?"

She knew he would ask. Mr. MacDonald always made sure to know who it was that visited his tavern. "Lucian. He's the man who saved me last eve."

His wrinkled face brightened. "Then give him his meal and ale free. Anyone who would put their own lives at risk to help you deserves no less."

Isabelle nodded and took the bowl and ale to Lucian.

"Smells delicious," Lucian said as he took the bowl.

Isabelle took a step back, making herself put distance between them. "You won't be disappointed."

"Shall I walk you home tonight?"

His question, softly spoken, sent a wave of eagerness

through her. A 'yes' was on the tip of her tongue when she paused. "Why?"

His brows lifted. "Why? Could it be that I worry for your safety?"

"Could it be that you want to take advantage of me?" she retorted.

He lowered his spoon and met her gaze with inky dark eyes. "If I had wanted to take advantage of you, I could've done that last eve."

She crossed her arms over her chest, wary because of her reaction to him. What she was feeling was so abnormal that it frightened her, alarmed her. "I don't know."

"You shouldn't be walking alone in the dark. I'll even let you keep my dagger."

She had completely forgotten to return it to him last night, but she did have it strapped to her thigh. The thought of his hand on the weapon, the same weapon that was against her bare thigh, made her blood heat. "We close up in a couple of hours if you'd like to wait."

He nodded and took a bite of the stew. "Excellent, just as you said."

She walked away, her legs wooden and her body on fire.

For the rest of the evening Isabelle felt his eyes on her. No man had ever noticed her before, and certainly no man like Lucian. He didn't just look at her, his eyes devoured her.

And she liked it.

Possibly too much.

When they finally began to close up, she watched as Lucian tried to pay Mr. MacDonald. After a few minutes, Lucian gave up and put the coins away. Isabelle grinned as she hurried to finish her duties so she could be with Lucian.

Alone.

With only the darkness and the night.

A shiver of eagerness went through her.

Lucian couldn't wait to walk Isabelle home. This time he would go inside if she invited him. This time he would speak of who he was—and where he was from.

He just prayed she was willing to listen.

"I'm done," she said as she placed the last chair atop the table.

He nodded. "Stay here while I get my horse."

When he returned, Mr. and Mrs. MacDonald stood at the door with Isabelle. "Thank you again for the delicious meal and fine ale."

"We want to thank you for happening upon our Isabelle as you did. Lord only knows what would've happened had you not been there," Mrs. MacDonald said.

Lucian refused to think about it and instead held out his hand for Isabelle. "Shall we?"

She waved good-bye to the MacDonalds, and he lifted her atop Elad before he took the reins and started into the darkness.

"How long will you be staying here?"

"Until I find what I came for." He knew that wasn't the answer she wanted, but he didn't wish to speak of such things until he could see her face.

"More evasive answers?"

He grinned into the night. She was feisty. Just what a princess of Drahcir should be. "I'll answer all your questions, just not now."

"Fair enough, I suppose."

"Tell me of you," he urged. "How long have you worked for the MacDonalds?"

He heard the smile in her voice as she said, "I started out helping with odd jobs when I was smaller and my grandparents were in the village. Then, as I got older and realized the extra coin helped, I began working whenever they needed help. It was about two years ago that I started working every day. They're very good to me."

"They love you."

"Aye, and I love them. They're my family now."

He wanted to ask about her grandparents and parents but decided to wait. Somehow he knew it wasn't the right time. All too soon they arrived at her cottage, and he wondered if she would ask him in for tea again. He halted Elad by the door and reached up to help Isabelle down.

It was a taste of rapture to be able to touch her again, even if it was just his hands on her waist. When her hands gripped his shoulders for balance he thought he heard a sharp intake of breath. Did he affect her the way she affected him?

He forced his hands to release her. He let them linger on her before his arms dropped to his sides. It was painful to know the woman who could help secure his kingdom stood before him, but knowing what it would cost her kept him from spilling everything right then. He had to take it slow.

"Thank you for escorting me home."

Lucian bowed regally. "A pleasure, for sure."

"Would you like to come in for tea?"

"I would love to. Let me see to Elad."

Isabelle bit her lip as he walked away, then spun around and rushed into the dark cottage. She walked blindly to the hearth and hastily started the fire. By the time she had water in the kettle and over the fire, she heard the door open.

She smoothed her hands down her stained brown gown. Men never made her nervous, but this one set her on edge, made her worry about things like if her hair was neat or if her gown looked good. Men of marriageable age in her tiny village were scarce, and she never caught their eyes. She had known for years that she would never have a family of her own.

Slowly, she turned to face her rescuer.

Her eyes traveled from his face to his wide shoulders. She swallowed as she imagined what he looked like without those fine black clothes of his.

"It's as if you are of the night, almost as if you belong to it."

His eyes narrowed as he cocked his head. "What do you mean?"

"You wear all black, your hair and eyes are black, and even your horse is black."

One side of his mouth pulled up in a smile. "What if I tell you that it's exactly what I am?"

"I may be a peasant, but I'm not a fool. My lord," she said, after a small hesitation to let him know she knew he was of nobility.

Lucian clenched his hands in fists as he watched her turn to the kettle. It was everything he could do to talk to her instead of crushing her to him and tasting her plump lips.

He had never believed everything his father told him. Aye, he knew he would recognize his mate, but he never expected to feel such…lust. He had thought his father told him that just to make things easier.

His eyes raked over her slender form, a form he watched from afar for too long. Now that she was so near to him, he devoured the very sight of her, from her soiled, plain gown to her long fingers that gripped the kettle handle to the profile of her face, a face that was no more peasant than he was, with her high cheekbones and stubborn chin.

When she turned and handed him a cup of tea, he looked into her midnight-blue eyes and wished he could tell her everything without the fear of her running away.

"What is it?" she asked, her brow slightly furrowed as she stared at him.

Her question drew his gaze to her mouth, a mouth of the darkest pink, full and inviting.

"Nothing," he said as he accepted the cup and sat down at the small table. "Have you always lived here?"

She nodded as she poured herself a cup. "It's the only place I've ever known."

"Are you happy here?"

She laughed as she joined him at the table. "What a strange question."

"Not so strange."

"Do you like where you live?"

Lucian sighed as he recalled his beautiful home, a home that called to him even now. "Nay, I doona like it. I love it. It's a wonderful place, and a more beautiful place I've never seen. The people are friendly, the game plentiful, and the town prosperous."

She smiled wistfully as she placed her chin on her hand. "I'd love to see such a place."

"Then I'll take you there," he said, his breath caught in his throat

She cocked her head to the side as she gave him an indulgent smile. "If you love this place so much, why did you leave?"

"I had to," he said as he glanced down at the cup. "I'm looking for someone."

She turned her blue eyes away from him and drank. "Have you searched long?"

"Nearly two winters."

"It must be someone of great importance."

"She is."

Her eyes flew up to meet his, and for a moment Lucian thought she might ask who it was he sought. Instead, she lifted her cup and took another drink.

His patience was about to run dry. But, he recalled the words his father had told him.

"Go slowly, son. Doona rush your mate. She has to realize the truth on her own. Bringing her here against her will is worse than never finding her at all."

Yet, even the reminder of his father's words didn't stop the impatience as it usually did. Now that Isabelle was here with him, he wanted to hurry back to Drahcir, convincing her on the way of just who she was. But she wouldn't believe him, and in the end he would fail, sending his beloved kingdom to doom.

"Where are your parents?" he asked, needing to turn his mind away from his quest for a moment.

"I was raised by my grandparents, who I lost last winter. My mother died giving birth to me."

"I'm sorry. And your father?"

She shrugged. "I've never met him. What of you and your family?"

"Both my parents still live. They wait expectantly for my return."

"And I suppose you cannot return until you find who you seek." At his nod, she continued. "It's your sister then?"

Lucian laughed. "I've no sister. Just three brothers. One elder and two younger."

His breath caught as she closed her eyes and smiled. "To

have siblings. It's something I've always wanted." She opened her eyes and looked at him while she flicked her braid over her shoulder. "Do you love your brothers?"

"Verra much. We'd die for each other."

She ran her finger around the rim of the cup. "Your village and your family sound almost like a dream. Do you never fight?"

Lucian chuckled, recalling the many—and various—arguments. "Loudly and frequently. It's what brothers do."

"How much longer will you search before you return to this heavenly place of yours?"

Lucian watched her closely. He knew he had to earn her trust, it was the only thing keeping him on his own side of the table. "I have another cycle of seasons before I must return."

"What will happen if you don't find this woman?"

"That's not an option I can even consider," he answered before he sipped the tea.

He lowered his gaze to her hands. One held the mug, and the other lay near his hand. He reached over and covered her hand with his. Her gaze snapped to his, but she didn't pull away.

"You've nothing holding you here. Come. Return with me to my home," he urged.

"Why?" she asked, her brows knotted. "I don't even know you. What about the woman you seek?"

Everything, Lucian's family and the kingdom itself, hinged on his next words.

"I found her."

3

*I*sabelle could only stare, dumbfounded, into Lucian's dark eyes. The world began to swim around her, and her only anchor was the mysterious, gorgeous man who held her hand.

She drew in a deep breath, wondering why she'd felt compelled to ask about the woman he searched for. Never had she thought it could be her. A beautiful maiden of noble blood, aye, but never her.

Yet, she couldn't deny the invitation to return with Lucian held promise, a potential she suddenly wanted to grab with both hands and never let go. The possibilities of her life opened before her, as if a dam had been broken by Lucian's words.

His black eyes watched her carefully, his thumb tenderly caressing the back of her hand. Her skin tingled from the contact, and the pull, the attraction she'd felt the first time she'd seen him intensified until it was a living, breathing thing in the cottage with them.

"Isabelle?" he prompted, his voice soft, a hint of uncertainty lacing his deep baritone.

Strong, stubborn, and unmovable was how she expected Lucian to be. The anxious man before her, she somehow knew, was completely opposite of who he really was.

Was he nervous waiting on her answer? More than that was a burning question she had to have answered.

"Why me? You don't know me."

He leaned closer and wrapped his other hand around hers. "Please understand, Isabelle, I want to tell you everything, but I doona want you thinking I'm daft."

"Well, I think it's a little late for that," she said, amazed that she could tease him after such a serious matter.

One side of his lips tilted in a heart-stopping smile. "It's you because I know it here," he said and touched his chest over his heart. Then he put a finger to his temple. "And here. It's a…gift…my family was given. We know our mates instantly."

She tried to swallow, finding her mouth suddenly dry. Isabelle couldn't look away from his penetrating gaze. He believed everything he said, the truth of it shining in his eyes. "Tell me of this wonderful place you come from."

He leaned back in his chair, crossing his arms over his massive chest as his eyes crinkled in the corners, as if he was pleased she asked. "It's deep in the Ben Nevis Mountains."

"Now I know you're jesting," she said as she finished laughing. "There is nothing in those mountains but wild animals, snow, and ice."

Instead of arguing with her, he continued to smile. "But what if I was right?"

"Nothing can survive in those mountains."

He leaned forward and placed his hands over hers again. For a moment, time stood still as she gazed into his dark eyes and something passed between them. It left her dazed but wanting to experience it again.

"Do you believe in magic?" he asked so solemnly that she knew he was serious.

"Nay."

He frowned and sat back once more, releasing a long breath. "That's too bad, Isabelle."

She loved the way her name rolled off his lips. Who would have thought her name could sound so wonderful? So sensual and alluring.

How strange that just the sound of her name on his lips could have her contemplating things she would never dream of doing otherwise, things that made her blood heat and her heart skip a beat.

And her body burn.

In order to try and regain some composure, she rose and faced the hearth. Either the man in her cottage was daft and needed to be put somewhere safe, or he was telling the truth.

"You want to believe me," he said near her ear, his hot breath brushing the nape of her neck.

Chills raced down her spine at his words…because they were the truth. She had no idea when he had risen from his chair. He moved as silently as a spirit, his body a hot, hard presence behind her that urged her to lean back against him, to believe in everything he said.

She had always dreamed as a little girl that there would be more to her life, that she was destined to be something… more. Her dreams had even gone so far as to make believe she would be taken away and made a princess.

"Let yourself consider the possibility." He softly took hold of her upper arms and drew her back against his chest.

His warmth spread around her, enveloping her in a cocoon that did anything but soothe her. She was all too aware of the very male, very solid man at her back. She imagined his large hands moving over her body, his arms holding her close as he kissed her, languidly, deeply. Thoroughly.

His head nudged hers aside so he could nuzzle her neck. His warm breath caused chills to race over her skin. "Come see my birthplace, Isabelle. See the splendor, the hidden beauty of it all. My parents await my return. They await you."

Her breath hitched when she was sure she felt his tongue touch her ear.

"Our city is hidden, but it thrives. You can do anything you want there, be anything you want. The gates to the city will open upon our return. We'll travel down the road paved with blue stones that leads to the castle sitting high up on the mountain. The people will come out to see us, cheering that I've returned with my mate. It's a place of magic, a place of indescribable beauty. We have seasons, but the winters are no' harsh. Game is plentiful, the grass greener, the flowers more vibrant. You've never seen such majesty before."

She closed her eyes and allowed herself to imagine a place like the one he had described and, to her astonishment, was able to envision it clearly. "I won't belong there," she whispered.

His voice, smooth and soft, replied, "You doona belong here. You belong with me in Drahcir."

Her eyes opened. It was as if Lucian knew all of her secret longings, all of the dreams she'd barely allowed herself to imagine. It frightened her at the same time it excited her. She turned in his arms and looked up at him. Her fingers itched to trace the strong line of his jaw, to know if his lips were as soft as they looked.

She inhaled and breathed in the scent of pine, sandalwood, and leather. It was a heady mix combined with a man such as Lucian. He tempted her body, and his words tempted her soul. Did she belong with him? Or did she belong in the tiny village she'd grown up in?

There was nothing holding her here. Her grandparents were gone, her friends were few, and the likelihood of her finding a husband was as slim as her tugging a star from the sky. She was tired of being alone, of having no one but herself to come home to. How she yearned to share her troubles, to have someone to eat with, to face each new day with.

Someone she climbed into bed with each night.

"I'll take you away at first light, if you let me. You need never work in a tavern again or want for anything. Please, Isabelle, believe. That's all you have to do. I'll do the rest."

The gleam in his eye was one of hope, of anticipation. He was daring her to trust him. And before she even knew what she was doing, her soul already accepted his words as truth.

His arms came up around her. "Believe."

"I don't think I can." She'd seen her reality, lived her reality for too long to do anything else. The disappointment in his black gaze was like a punch in her stomach.

She wanted to explain to him, but his nearness jumbled the words. He confused her, spun her about until she wasn't sure what was right and what was wrong. Her body craved him, longed for him.

And her soul cried out as if had found its other half.

"You're the woman I've searched for, the woman that I can no' leave here without."

His words sent a sizzle of awareness through her. He lowered his head. His hypnotic eyes held her spellbound. She lifted her hands to his chest, telling herself it was to help keep her balance, but really it was because she wanted to feel him. Even against the coolness of the leather jerkin beneath her hands, she felt the heat of him.

"Believe me," he whispered, just before his lips touched hers.

His lips were soft, yet insistent as they nibbled and kissed her mouth. She moaned softly as she let him guide her against his body and his arms wrapped securely around her. His arms were like bands of steel, his chest an unmovable force. The kisses became more urgent, deeper with every taste, and Isabelle felt herself awaken, slowly, fully. The fire started to burn, and her body trembled as she ached for more of Lucian.

Even her hands wanted more of him as they roamed over his thick chest, wide shoulders, and into his dark, silky hair. When his tongue swept into her mouth, she sighed as a rush of pure passion and excitement ran through her.

In that moment of such exquisite pleasure, she would have promised him anything.

Lucian knew he couldn't continue to kiss her and remain in control. He was amazed to find he wanted her as much as he did, yet "want" was mild compared to how he truly felt. He ached, he hungered. And only Isabelle would be able to ease him.

Just touching her was enough for him to realize what kind of future they could have. Her beauty was just one part of it. He felt the passion within her, waiting to be released. She was stubborn but kind, stalwart but sympathetic.

The fear that had taken root in him months ago when he thought to never find his mate began to loosen. The longer he kissed her, the more he knew he couldn't live without her. He…needed her.

Not just because of the stupid curse. Because she was the other half of him, the part he hadn't realized he was missing until he'd found her. He couldn't explain it, could barely comprehend it himself. There was no denying it.

He ended the kiss and inwardly smiled when he heard her groan in irritation. With his hands, he smoothed back the tendrils of hair that had come loose of her braid and tilted her head up to him.

"I know you felt what I did," he said.

She licked her swollen lips, nearly sending him to his knees with need. "Oh, aye. I felt it."

Lucian tried to control his ragged breathing. "Then you also feel the connection between us."

He held his breath as she cocked her head at his words.

For several heartbeats, she didn't speak. He feared he had gone too far, said too much too soon and had lost her forever. But it wasn't just the fear of losing his home and sending the kingdom into nothingness, it was not being able to be with Isabelle as well. Though he was just getting to know her, already he felt as if he had known her his entire life.

When she stepped out of his arms, he clenched his jaw to keep silent and let her think. It wasn't in his nature to have patience, but more was at stake than just what he wanted.

"I do feel something," she finally said.

He sighed in relief but saw the look of doubt on her face that told him she was far from convinced. How could he tell her that once they had found each other, they would forever yearn for the other, only to be whole together? He'd wanted to tell her that after they reached his kingdom, but he might have to tell her sooner.

She walked around the small kitchen, rubbing her neck. "I don't know who you are. Your likes and dislikes. What meal is your favorite? What are your vices? There are too many unknowns for me to agree to go with you tomorrow. I need time."

"Time isna something I have." After a deep breath, he sank into a chair at the table and folded his hands over his stomach as he regarded her. It was time. She needed to know everything. "Then I will tell you. All of it."

"Really?" she asked, her brows raised. She took the chair opposite him. "Then, begin. Please."

"I am a prince of my kingdom, Drahcir."

Her lips flattened, and she shook her head. "Aye, you said that name a moment ago. I've never heard of it. I thought you said you were from the Ben Nevis Mountains."

"I am. You've never heard of my kingdom because it's hidden from the world."

"By a forest or something?"

"Nay. It's a special place, Isabelle, a place that can no' be opened for just anyone. What makes it special is the people who reside within the gates of the kingdom. If the other kings, lords, and mercenaries find my home, the kingdom will be overrun with the worst kinds of people."

"And your people will be driven out, leaving Drahcir to the very people you are hiding from," she finished.

"Not hiding exactly," he said. "The kingdom has been in existence for centuries. It wasn't hidden on purpose. At one time, Drahcir was visited by people all over the world, despite its location making it difficult to get to. Now, that is what keeps it hidden."

"Why did people stop visiting your kingdom? Was there a plague?"

"Drahcir simply vanished one day. Or that's what everyone believed."

"Vanished? There is much more to your story, aye?"

"My family, the Sinclairs, have always led the kingdom. However, there was one of us that went too far."

"Which king did he anger?"

Lucian swallowed and glanced away. "Not a king. A princess."

She leaned forward eagerly. "Don't keep me waiting. I love a good tale."

"She was a princess of the Fae."

Isabelle rolled her eyes, not wanting to be taken in by the jest. She chuckled, realizing belatedly that Lucian hadn't joined her. Her smile faded as her stomach fell to her feet at the look of sincerity in his eyes. "A Fae?"

"Aye," he said earnestly. "They do exist."

This was too much to believe. First, a hidden kingdom, and now the Fae. But, no matter how much she told herself to rise and demand he leave, she couldn't. Everything about him intrigued her, but the tale, as fanciful as her best daydreams, urged her to discover more.

After a moment, Lucian continued. "The princess and my ancestor fell in love, or so the Fae thought. In truth, my ancestor merely dabbled to see if he could."

"Not a very noble gesture."

"True. He had no idea of the consequences of his actions until afterwards. Once the princess discovered his treachery, she cursed our kingdom from then until the day this world no longer exists."

Isabelle found her gaze riveted on Lucian and the sadness in his eyes. Even if she didn't believe him, he did believe it.

Every word.

"And the curse?" she asked. "What is it?"

"Every prince and princess of the Drahcir must find

their mates and return with them by a designated time. If even one fails, the kingdom will vanish. For all eternity."

Her heart hammered in her chest as she repeated his words in her head. Mate. Mate. Return to Drahcir. Vanish. Mate.

Slowly, her gaze found his and saw the truth in his eyes. "How do I know what you're saying is the truth?"

"Come here," he said, and held out his hand.

She didn't hesitate to rise and take his hand. He pulled her around the table onto his lap. Then he leaned her back until he cradled her head with one hand.

"Know the truth," he whispered, just before his mouth descended on hers.

In his sweet, intoxicating kiss, Isabelle let herself go. She then saw the veracity of his words and their bond, a bond that was forged eons ago, a bond that even death couldn't break.

Her blood heated and pooled between her legs, sending a fire through her. She squeezed her legs together in an attempt to end the growing pressure, but the movement only caused a ripple of delight to lance through her. Her nipples hardened, and her breasts swelled as she wished for his hands to move over her body.

With one touch he'd turned her into a wanton. She needed his touch, his kiss. Her body was in a near fever pitch as it craved more of him. And it terrified her, alarmed her. To want someone so desperately wasn't normal, was it?

Then she forgot to care as he deepened the kiss. She wound her arms around his neck and forgot to care about anything other than the man in her arms. Doubts melted away, worries dissolved.

The only thing that mattered, the only thing that filled her mind and her heart, was Lucian.

His hand, splayed on her back, moved to her side, his fingers brushing the underside of her breasts. Isabelle gasped. The kiss turned fiery, frantic as desire took them, claimed them.

Her back arched into his hand when he cupped her aching breast. A moan, deep and low, rumbled through his chest. She wanted to run her hands over his skin, to feel the steely sinew. Isabelle pushed his jerkin over one shoulder and jerked at his tunic, pulling it up enough so she could touch him.

His stomach jumped when she laid her palm flat on his abdomen. Just as expected, his muscles rippled beneath her hand, and suddenly it wasn't enough to touch. She wanted to see him.

It took her a moment to realize Lucian had ended the kiss. Desire had taken her, seized her. He was massaging her breast while he rubbed his thumb over her hardened nipple. She squeezed her legs together and cried out from the sheer pleasure of it.

"I want you," he whispered thickly. "I want to strip you bare and spend the night loving you."

"Yes," she said, hoping, praying he did exactly as he wanted. He had to cool the fire within her. It was scorching her with its intensity.

"No' yet, my Isabelle."

"Why?" she cried out, then moaned when he pinched her nipple.

"You need to know the rest of the story."

She didn't care about the story. All she cared about was the need Lucian had fanned to life. She shook her head in answer, and instantly his hand fell away. Isabelle jerked open her eyes to find him staring at her, desire emanating from him. He did want her. The thought made her breath catch.

If he wanted to finish the story and prolong their torture, she knew she couldn't sway him otherwise. She was too inexperienced in the ways of men to know how to turn his mind away from the story and on to her.

With her breathing still labored, she finally collected her thoughts and asked, "How did you find me?"

He ran a finger down her cheek, his black gaze intense and heated. "Though the princess cursed us, another Fae took pity and gave each of us a special ability to see our mates. Mine is seeing your aura. Yours is especially bright."

She ran her hands through his silky hair, her body shaking from need. Her heart accelerated when she wiggled and felt his thick, hard arousal. "An aura? What is that exactly?"

"It's a special light around you, distinct to you alone."

"And what does it do?"

"Besides showing me who you are? Not much." He bent and placed a kiss on her neck.

She sighed at the pleasure of his kiss, and then the feel of his tongue as he tasted her skin. "Then it's worthless."

"Never," he murmured, and leaned close to her neck. "It brought me to you."

Just when she thought he would only tease her, his hot tongue snaked out and licked her again, leaving a trail of hot, wet desire across her skin.

Her sex throbbed, and her mind forgot everything but the man before her. She inhaled his exotic scent. No man had ever touched her before, but now she wanted, nay yearned, for Lucian.

She licked her lips and tried to concentrate on their conversation. "So, all you had to do was go around looking for a certain aura?"

"Hmm," he murmured as he nuzzled her skin behind her ear. "Is that no' enough?"

"More than enough."

He pulled back to look at her. "Then will you return with me?"

Isabelle saw the worry reflected in the dark depths of his eyes. She cast a glance around her small cottage. It held many memories, but she didn't want to grow old with just memories. She wanted passion and laughter, children and a husband. "As you said, there is nothing holding me here."

For a moment she worried if she was doing the right thing, then the desire coursing through her made her remember that no other man had made her feel this...special or wanted before.

He smiled and pulled her against his chest. "I vow you willna regret your decision."

This time his kiss was possessive, demanding, and erotic. It set her blood afire and singed her with its intensity. Her body cried out for more. One moment she was sitting in his lap, the next they were on her small bed, his delicious weight on top of her.

His mouth scorched a trail from her lips down her throat to her neck. Delicious sensations rippled through her body with his every touch, every kiss. It was as if he knew exactly how to touch her.

And where to touch her.

Somehow her gown was removed, leaving her only in her chemise, stockings, and shoes, but she didn't care. Lucian's touch was all she needed, all she craved. With just a flick of her feet, Isabelle kicked off her old tattered shoes and leaned her head back so his mouth could continue to do wicked, delightful things to her.

Her body was no longer her own. It belonged to Lucian,

waiting for whatever he wanted next, for what new heights he would bring her to. Never in her right mind would she have allowed a strange man into her home at night, not to mention into her bed. Yet, it seemed right to be with Lucian, almost as if it had been destined.

He rose up and kneeled beside her as his eyes roamed her body. Her nipples puckered and hardened beneath his gaze. Her breasts grew heavy and full as if she waited anxiously for his touch.

As if he knew exactly what she wanted, his hands cupped her breasts and rolled her nipples between his fingers. Flames of desire lapped at her, pulling her already burning body beneath the blaze. His fingers squeezed her nipples until the pleasure blurred with pain and she felt moisture between her legs.

And then his hands were gone. She opened her eyes to see him grip her chemise at the neck with both hands, then with one yank, ripped it in two.

Now the only thing shielding her was her thick wool stockings.

Lucian drew in a deep breath and gazed upon the perfection that was his mate. She was glorious. Her breasts were large, but not too full that they overfilled his hands. Her waist narrow, hips wide, and legs long and lean, just perfect to wrap around his waist as he thrust inside her.

His body shook with the need to bury himself in her, and her response to his touch had nearly made him lose his control several times.

He reached for her leg and lifted it toward him and placed her heel on his shoulder. Then he rolled her woolen stocking from her leg. He threw the stocking over his shoulder and gently placed her leg on the bed before he repeated the process with her other leg. He grinned as he saw his dagger strapped to her leg. He kissed the inside of her thigh and removed the sheath that held the weapon and tossed it on the floor.

Once she was completely exposed, he spread her legs and looked at her swollen and throbbing sex. He ran a finger lightly between the skin that joined her thigh and the black curls that hid her.

She sighed and opened herself further. Lucian grinned and repeated the gesture on the other side. Again and again his hands touched near her sex, but never on what ached the most. It didn't take long in her already heightened state until she was thrashing her head side to side and moaning his name and begging for release.

Lucian had her just where he wanted.

He shifted his cock, which had grown painfully hard as he teased Isabelle. Then his finger lightly grazed her swollen clit. She cried out and gripped the blanket in her fists as her back arched. Lucian repeated the move, except this time he swirled his finger around the nub before dipping a finger into her wet sheath.

It was pure torture, his control fast slipping away with each moan and cry from her lovely mouth. She was all fire and passion, and he couldn't wait to spend hours making love to her.

He took a pert nipple in his mouth and ran his tongue over the hardened peak. She groaned and ground her hips against his hand. He slipped another finger inside of her, stretching her tight sheath, her slick heat nearly his undoing.

Isabelle knew she was going to split open at any moment. The sensations running rampant through her had her body spiraling into a frenzy of desire and passion. Each lick, touch, taste of Lucian had her panting for more. She never knew she could feel such emotion, and she never wanted it to stop.

She loved the feel of his fingers inside her, but wanted more of him, all of him. Her breath locked in her throat when his hands found her breasts again. His expert fingers teased and pinched her aching nipples until she was mindless with yearning.

Then his hot tongue replaced his fingers. He began suckling and lapping at her nipples, bringing her to a point where she needed him deep inside of her. When she opened her eyes and found him feasting on her breasts, her stomach clenched, and she throbbed deep inside her sex.

Witnessing him at her breast was so…erotic she found she wanted to explore him as he had done her. With great effort, she moved her arms and pulled his head up. His black eyes were glazed with desire as they stared at her.

"My turn," she said as she pushed him up.

His fingers pinched her nipple once more, and she felt a moment's remorse. Then, with a wicked smile, he sat up and removed his leather jerkin. The neck of his tunic plunged deep giving her an ample view of his wide, sculpted chest.

She moved to him on her knees and reached for his tunic. Slowly, she pulled the garment from his trews and lifted it over his head before she tossed it carelessly to the ground.

Her breath caught in her throat at the specimen before her. He wasn't just defined, his muscles rippled and glowed bronze in the firelight. She touched his warm flesh, and sighed at the wonder of such a man.

A sizzle of awareness passed through her. She raised her gaze to Lucian and found him watching her.

"It's as if my body already knows you," she whispered.

"Because it does."

She swallowed, unsure she could comprehend just what was happening to her. Before he could say more, she leaned forward and placed a kiss on his collarbone. His quick intake of breath made her smile. She had no idea what she was doing, but her body seemed to know exactly what it wanted.

As she placed kisses along his neck and shoulders, her hands roamed at will from his thick chest to his narrow waist to his bulging arms.

And never once did he stop her.

Not even when she reached for the laces of his trews. She had never felt so in control before, and she loved it. When he rose to remove his boots and pants, she reclined on the bed watching each delicious inch of him revealed to her.

When he stood as naked as she, she sucked in her breath at the length and width of him straining forward. His rod was large, and it gave her pause to know that it would push through her maidenhead.

"You've never had a lover," he said.

She heard the excitement in his voice as she shook her head.

He leaned down until his hands were on either side of her, and his face mere inches from hers. "Good," he said, just before he claimed a kiss that curled her toes and promised delights she had only dreamed about.

The kiss drained her of everything at the same time life surged within her, growing and consuming her until all she thought about, cared about was Lucian and the fire he had started within her.

Her arms wound around his neck as she gave in to his kiss, releasing every doubt she had. His cock pressed into her stomach, its thick, hard length reminding her just what her body craved.

Yet, Lucian didn't allow her that pleasure. Instead, he

brought her body back to the frenzied peak with his fingers and mouth. She was mindless with the passion, careening out of control.

Then she felt his mouth between her legs. The cry of pleasure died in her throat as waves upon waves of bliss rolled through her. All she could do was hang on as Lucian continued his wonderful assault, her pleasure growing with each breath and lick.

And just when she was about to reach the pinnacle…he stopped.

"Nay," she cried, and reached for him.

"Easy, love," he whispered near her ear.

And then she felt the tip of him at her entrance. She opened her legs wider, eager to feel his fullness, filling her, stretching her…completing her.

Inch by agonizing inch he pushed into her. Isabelle wrapped her legs around his waist urging him on, but he ignored her. She shifted her hips and felt him sink deeper before he suddenly stopped and rotated his hips.

Isabelle sighed and ran her hands down his arms. "I need you. I need to feel all of you inside of me."

He responded by moving his hips again, rocking gently inside her. She knew he wasn't fully sheathed, but the sensations his movements caused were too good to stop. Isabelle found herself rising to the summit again. This time she wasn't going to let Lucian stop. She wanted him like she had never wanted anything in her life.

He pulled out of her and rubbed the head of his cock on her swollen sex, inciting her already trembling body. In and out he continued his torture until her body easily accepted him, anxiously awaited him.

Her body shook with anticipation. Relief from the pressing desire was just out of reach. Lucian knew how to keep her on the edge. She was breathless as she reached for him. In that instant, he drove into her, piercing her hymen.

The pain was quick and fleeting. Her state of arousal quickly pushed aside everything other than the feel of him deep inside her, of his thickness and the way he filled her —completely.

"My God," Lucian whispered in awe.

Isabelle could only stare up at him in amazement. But as wonderful as he felt, her aroused body needed relief. Her hips rocked against his, and he quickly found a tempo. His thrusts grew quick as he plunged deeper, harder inside her.

All she could do was hold him as she was swept away on a tide of pleasure so profound, so immense, it was incomprehensible. Their gazes met as her body exploded. Waves upon waves of pure delight pulsed through her, in her…around her.

Lucian watched in amazement as Isabelle's body clenched around his cock, urging him to meet his own release. Her eyes were dazed with pleasure, her body dewed by a fine sheen of sweat. Her kiss-swollen lips parted and her legs tightened. The last shred of his control snapped. With her nails digging into his back, he pumped his hips faster, sinking into her moist heat. The aftershocks of her orgasm continued to rock through her, and she clamped down with her inner muscles.

Lucian wasn't ready to end the exquisite pleasure yet though. Even when Isabelle's body stopped clenching around him, she lifted her hips and met him thrust for thrust as he plunged into her.

Sweat glistened his body as his pleasure built. When he knew he was about to give in to the desire, he stopped and leaned down to suckle at her ripe breasts. Her sighs turned into moans, her nails scouring his back. He had to grab hold and stop her from moving least he spill his seed before he was ready. And he wasn't near done with her yet.

Lucian pulled out of her long enough to move Isabelle until she was lying sideways on the bed. He stood on the side and lifted her legs until they wrapped around his waist and then he slowly entered her again. When he was fully seated, he pulled her against him until only her back rested on the bed as he began to thrust.

He knew with this being her first time she most likely wouldn't find pleasure twice, but he was going to make sure she enjoyed their coupling. He braced a hand on her stomach and let his thumb find her clit. He ceased moving his hips and slowly circled her swollen nub with his thumb. Deep inside her, he felt her clench around him.

She cried out and moved her hips, begging him for more. She screamed his name, her head thrashing side to side on the bed as her hands grabbed the blanket. Her softness met his hardness, tempting him beyond measure.

He couldn't stop looking at her, couldn't stop touching her. She was exquisite in her passion, fiery and giving. She held nothing back, and he found he couldn't either. With Isabelle, he was an open book waiting to show her, tell her everything about himself—down to his most secret wishes and desires.

"Please!" she screamed, her body trembling as he rubbed her clit faster and faster.

Lucian wasn't going to deny her. While he teased her clit, he once more began to plunge inside her going deeper, harder than before.

Just when he thought he would reach his own pleasure without her, he heard Isabelle cry out his name on a half-scream, half-moan. His satisfied inner smile lasted all of a half a heartbeat before he could no longer hold back his own orgasm. He took her hips in both his hands and lifted her slightly as he pounded inside her.

When his orgasm claimed him, he buried himself deep. Only then did he pour his seed into her, claiming her body, heart, and soul.

4

*I*sabelle woke to the most amazing feeling of contentment. She opened her eyes and found herself gazing upon Lucian's handsome face as he slept. The morning sun's rays spilled through the cracks in the shutters, falling across his face and incredible body.

She thought back over the night to see if she had regrets and was pleased to discover there were none. As she rolled to her back she felt the soreness between her legs and smiled. She had opened herself, allowed herself to do things she had never thought she would do.

And it had felt wonderful.

Slowly, so as not to wake Lucian, she rose from the bed and spotted her blood between her legs. Her virgin blood. She hastened to clean herself and found a new chemise before she dressed. Only then did she build up the fire and put another kettle of water on to heat as she walked outside to feed the chickens and Lucian's horse.

The small stable was in desperate need of repair, something she couldn't do herself, nor could she afford to hire someone to mend it for her. The meager living she made working at the tavern put food in her belly but left her with nothing to save. She knew it was only a matter of time before she had to leave the only home she knew and rent the small room in the attic of the tavern.

At least that had been her only option. Not anymore. Not since Lucian came into her life.

It wasn't that she didn't like Mr. and Mrs. MacDonald, but she was used to being on her own with no one to answer to. That would all change the moment she agreed to rent the room. But even she had to face reality, for it was closing in on her like a battering ram to a castle gate.

Last night she had agreed to go back with Lucian. It was a huge step for her to take, an adventure she wasn't sure she could take.

It's either the bleak future you know you'll have here or the adventure with Lucian. Look how he made you feel, think of the pleasure you found in his arms.

She patted Lucian's giant black horse as she passed by him to get the oats. After filling the bucket, she placed it in his stall and checked his water. Despite his size, he was a friendly fellow, and she stayed a moment to pet him. That's when she spotted Lucian's saddle. It was unusual not only in the color, which was black, but in the design. The symbols were those of the ancient Celts who used to roam Scotland.

Her hand hesitantly reached out and touched the knotwork exquisite detail, meticulous in the design. Heat met her fingertips, and she hastily jerked them away.

Magic.

Isabelle glanced around her. The word had been whispered in her ear as if someone had been standing right behind her. Yet it was only she and Elad in the stable. She swallowed and moved away from the saddle to find the horse staring intently at her, as if he were trying to tell her something.

His unblinking gaze unsettled her, and she quickly ran from the shed. She leaned against the outside of the it and tried to slow her racing heart. Her gaze found her cottage as her thoughts turned to the mysterious man inside.

"I don't believe in magic," she whispered. "I can't go with him."

Lucian rolled over with a smile on his face. His hands searched the bed for Isabelle only to come up empty. He opened his eyes to find the fire lit and a kettle on to boil. He stretched his arms over his head before he swung his legs over the bed. He had intended to make love to her again this morning, but realized she might be a little sore after the previous night. As he reached for his clothes, he spotted the marks on his arms.

His gaze was riveted on the black symbols that stretched from his elbow to his shoulder—the same symbol that was on his saddle and on his parents' arms.

The symbols that meant he was now tied to Isabelle—and she to him.

He had known it would happen, but seeing the mark meant he had nearly completed his quest. He hadn't failed his family or his people as he feared he might. The sooner he returned home, the better, which meant they needed to leave that day.

Finally, he would return to his much-loved kingdom and his family. He washed himself off and thought of his mother's smile and his father's teasing that was sure to follow his return. As he pulled on his trousers he could well imagine all three of his brothers waiting to taunt him about being the last to arrive in Drahcir with his mate.

Just as he finished fastening his jerkin, his smile slipped. Something was wrong. Isabelle was frightened and anxious, as if she were running from something. Lucian bolted for the door and jerked it open to see her dashing down the path to the village. He looked around for a threat, but found nothing. That's when he realized his mate was running from him.

For a moment, he couldn't fathom why she would suddenly bolt after the night they had shared, but he didn't allow himself more than that moment. He ran to his mount and took hold of his horse's mane. After he swung onto his back, he nudged Elad into a run. He didn't try to grab Isabelle, instead he ran Elad in front of her. Only then did he give a tug on Elad's mane to bring him to a halt.

"I must get to the tavern," she said, not meeting his gaze.

Lucian's heart felt as if it had been ripped from his chest. Where had he gone wrong? She had agreed to return with him last night. Her cries of pleasure had told him she willingly took his seed and gave him her virginity.

So what had happened?

"Why do you run from me? Do I frighten you?" he asked, praying that he was wrong.

Slowly her gaze rose to his. "Aye, you do. It was as if last night there was some type of spell on me, and this morning I saw everything as it should be."

"Meaning that you willna return with me, that you doona believe my story that I told you."

She shook her head and backed up a step.

Lucian slid from his mount. "You believed last night."

"I wasn't myself last night."

"So, you regret the passion between us."

. . .

She hesitated, and that hesitation gave him a sliver of hope. And hope was all it took to keep him going.

"Nay. I never expected to experience anything like that in my life."

The mark on Lucian's arm began to throb, signaling that what Isabelle said was the truth. She might have enjoyed the passion, but she would not leave her home. "Is there nothing I can say that will convince you my words are the truth?"

"Nay."

He felt as if someone had just hurled a dagger into his heart and twisted the blade. "Doona run from me. It's your home. I'll leave," he said, and started for the house.

There was no need to see if Elad followed him, for he always did. It was difficult for Lucian not to look at Isabelle though, to see if she watched him as he left or if there was any indecision in her eyes. He prayed she returned to the cottage so he could have one last time to convince her.

Lucian's mind raced with possible alternatives for them, but if she refused to return to Drahcir then all would be for naught. He entered the small stable that was all but falling down and grabbed his saddle. His hand smoothed over the intricate symbols that had been chiseled into the leather. He and his three brothers had each been given such a saddle upon their sixteenth summer. The saddle reminded them of the curse and all that was at stake.

He brought the saddle to Elad and began to fasten it. Out of the corner of his eye, he spotted Isabelle leaning against the doorway watching him.

"If my words and the passion between us didna convince you that what I speak is the truth, I ask your forgiveness."

"Why?"

His hands stilled. He didn't want to tell her, but it was only fair after their night together and the symbols that now marked them. He turned to look at her and drew in a deep breath.

"I didna tell you everything last eve because I hoped you meant your words. Now, I've no choice since we've shared our bodies. Not only will my kingdom cease to exist if you doona return with me, but you'll never find happiness in another man's arms."

Her eyes widened at his words. "Are you so daft that you'll resort to such hateful words just because I changed my mind?"

"I wish it were as simple as that. Look at your left arm, Isabelle."

She heaved a great sigh and crossed her arms over her chest. "Nay."

Lucian nodded his head and removed his jerkin and tunic. "Look," he said as he pointed to the symbol on his left arm. "You'll have one as well."

"It must have been there last night," she said as her arms dropped to her sides and confusion marred her stunning face.

Lucian hated the fear in her beautiful blue eyes. "You touched my body. You tell me. However, if you really want to know, check your arm."

For several heartbeats he and Isabelle stared at each other. Silently, he prayed that she would look, and then believe.

Isabelle could stand it no longer. The symbol on Lucian's arm matched the one on his saddle, the swirls and knotwork an exact replica. She didn't want to look at her arm for fear of just what she would find. And what would she do if there was a symbol that matched his? Would she then agree to go with him?

If his words were true, she would never find happiness in the arms of another man, which meant she would spend the rest of her life alone.

All because of her fear.

Before she changed her mind, she rushed into the cottage, yanking her over tunic off as she went. With a vicious jerk, she pulled her chemise down to check her arm. She gasped and fell onto the bed when she saw the black mark that ran from her elbow up to her shoulder.

"Do you believe me now?" Lucian asked from the doorway.

She slowly raised her gaze to him. "How?"

Lucian shut the door and sat beside her on the bed. "It's our mark, a mark that lets everyone know that our mates have truly been found. No matter how much you try to deny it, Isabelle, your soul knows the truth."

Never had so much doubt filled her, not even when her grandparents died and left her alone. There was no denying the mark on her arm. It was as if her soul had branded her. And in a way, that's exactly what it had done. She wasn't ready to believe Lucian, or believe in him, but apparently her soul did.

Had this happened to anyone else, she would have dismissed the mark, giving any number of explanations as to how it could have appeared. But this was her body. She knew her body, and the mark, a series of intricate knots and spirals that raced up her arm to her shoulder, had never been there before she had given herself to Lucian.

Magic or not, she was most certainly branded. The question was, did she want to put to the test the possibility that she would spend the rest of her life alone? Though she might have told herself she had expected to be alone, after a night with Lucian, she knew she would never settle for a lonely life now.

He sat patiently waiting on her response. She knew what he wanted, but her apprehension stopped her from readily agreeing to go with him.

She opened her mouth to tell him just that when his head jerked up and his body stiffened.

"What is it?" she asked, but he held up a hand to halt her words.

Three heartbeats later, there was a light knock on her door. "Mr. MacDonald," she exclaimed, and hurriedly pulled up her chemise and threw on her gown. "I was supposed to be at the tavern already."

"Dress. I'll get the door," Lucian said and rose.

As Isabelle hurried to make herself presentable, she heard Lucian's deep voice as he opened the door. "Can I help you?"

"Ah...I'm looking for Isabelle," Mr. MacDonald said, the uncertainty ringing loudly in his tone.

"She'll be with us in just a moment," Lucian said as he shut the door behind him and joined Mr. MacDonald outside.

Isabelle smiled as she ran her hands over her wild hair and hastened to put it into a braid to keep it out of her face. Her curiosity got the better of her, and she went to the window and peered at the men through the crack in the shutters.

"Is she all right?" Mr. MacDonald asked.

"She is."

Mr. MacDonald's eyes narrowed. "You have no' harmed her, have ye? I might be getting on up in years, but I can still take a man down if need be."

To give Lucian credit, he didn't laugh. Instead he

smiled. "I've in no way harmed Isabelle, and as soon as she comes outside, you'll see that for yourself."

And then Lucian looked right at her.

Isabelle jerked away from the window and blinked. How could he have known what she was doing? It troubled her more than the lie she knew she would have to tell Mr. MacDonald.

She walked to the door and found her hand shook as she reached for the handle. Mr. MacDonald's head swiveled to her as soon as she stepped outside. She gave him a smile and was relieved when he returned it.

"Isabelle, lass, we were worried about you," he said as he came towards her.

"I'm sorry. I was just about to send word to you and Mrs. MacDonald."

What few gray hairs he had on his head danced in the breeze. Though his face was wrinkled, his eyes still held an intelligent spark in them that said he could see past her lies.

"Just tell me that you're all right," he said softly. "You're like a daughter to us, lass, and we worry over you."

Isabelle looked over Mr. MacDonald's shoulder to Lucian, who stood petting Elad. She knew he heard every word. She wasn't afraid of Lucian, and if she asked, she knew he would leave.

She returned her gaze to Mr. MacDonald. "Forgive me. Will you and Mrs. MacDonald be able to handle the tavern today? I need some time to…think."

He waved away her words. "Of course. We've little Timmy. We'll put him to work."

Isabelle laughed as she thought of Timmy, the baker's son, who was always looking for something to do that would keep him away from the hot ovens. "Thank you."

For a long moment Mr. MacDonald stared at her. "Be happy," he said softly, and turned on his heel to walk away.

Isabelle watched him go. His parting remark echoed loudly in her head. Happy. What would make her happy? Would staying here working and living in the tavern with the hope of finding a husband do it? She didn't mind the hard work, it was part of life, but the loneliness ate away at her, and Mr. and Mrs. MacDonald were advanced in years. It wouldn't be long before they too left her. Then where would she be?

Happiness. It was something she had always had as long as her grandparents had been there. Up until that moment she hadn't even thought of what would make her happy, and it was a hard question to answer.

Lucian would make you happy.

Would he?

She knew without a doubt that being in his arms and the passion that was so strong between them swayed her. Yet, was it enough for her to throw caution to the wind and leave with him? For all his words and their night together, he was still a stranger.

5

*L*ucian watched Isabelle closely. There was no denying that Mr. MacDonald cared greatly for her and that she returned the emotion. It was a difficult decision she had to make, one that would have to be made very soon. He hated to press her, but he wanted to return to Drahcir as soon as possible.

"Isabelle?"

Her gaze snapped to him. "Everything is all right. I told him I needed some time to think."

She hadn't wanted to lie to the old man, so she managed to work it where she hadn't needed to.

"How much time do you need?"

"How much time do I have?"

Lucian stepped away from Elad and walked to Isabelle. He could remain with her for a few months before he had to head back to Drahcir, but he feared if he stayed she would never leave with him. It wasn't just getting to Drahcir on time. There were other threats, threats he'd do whatever he could to avoid.

"I'll give you two days."

"Two days?" she repeated, her brow furrowed in exasperation. "How can you expect me to make such a monumental decision in so short a time?"

He shrugged as hopelessness began to settle around him like iron shackles. "You know the answer. You just refuse to say it. If you have no' come to realize that now, you willna in two days, two weeks, two months, or two years."

"What you ask for is impossible," she said, and whirled around to stalk back into the cottage.

Lucian gave it all of a heartbeat before he followed her. He had seen the fire in her eyes, the anger that sparked deep within her, but if she wanted rage, he could give her fury over the injustice of his kingdom and his family.

He threw open the door and found her facing the fireplace, her arms wrapped about her waist as she stared into the flames. With a jerk of his wrist, he slammed the door and stalked toward her. If her mind wouldn't listen, perhaps there was another way he could reach her.

His hands itched to feel her satiny skin, and his body burned to be buried inside her once more. With his cock already hard and aching, he didn't push aside the desire that begged to be released. He accepted it, acknowledged it.

And welcomed it.

With a growl, he gripped Isabelle's shoulders and turned her to face him as he backed her up against a wall. Her wide midnight-blue eyes stared at him, watching him to see what he was about.

"If you willna to listen to your heart, then listen to your body," he said, just before he ravaged her mouth in a kiss meant to overwhelm, a kiss meant to shatter her.

When she returned the intensity, it set him afire, burning him from the inside out as the passion swept him, engulfed him.

Consumed him.

His grip tightened, his heart pounded. The more he had of her, the more he needed. She was the air, the sun, the moon. She was…everything. He feared he'd never have enough of her, and with that fear grew another—what if he had to return to Drahcir alone?

He pushed aside those morbid thoughts as he thrust his tongue deep into Isabelle's mouth. He expected her to resist, yet she pulled her arms out of his grasp and wound them about his neck as she sighed into his mouth.

Lucian lost all thought as his hands moved quickly and efficiently to remove her clothes until she stood naked before him. Just as quickly, he shed his own and reclaimed her sweet mouth for another intoxicating kiss.

He took her hands in his and stretched her arms to the side as he molded his body to hers. Her full breasts pressed into his chest as he continued to kiss her, taking her lips again and again in kisses that were quick and light, long and sensual, and deep and demanding.

And she responded to each one in a way that had Lucian craving her, needing her so desperately that for a moment he couldn't breathe.

His hunger for her quickly outweighed everything. So much so, that if she refused to return with him, he knew he would find it next to impossible to leave her. He was hers just as much as she was his.

Mates didn't abandon each other.

Lucian pulled away and looked down at his mate. Her lips were swollen, her lids heavy, and her eyes filled with such longing that in that moment, had she asked, he would have sworn to stay with her forever, forsaking everything.

"Lucian," she whispered, and leaned forward to rain kisses on his neck and chest.

He closed his eyes and let his head fall back. She was a temptress, a siren that lured him with her enticing face and alluring body.

"I need you," she said, and rubbed her hips against him.

Lucian hissed at the contact of her soft body against his cock. It was enough to nearly make him spill his seed.

She looked deep into his eyes. "Take me now."

It was a request he couldn't refuse.

He picked her up and carried her to the bed. As soon as she was on it, he rolled her to her stomach and began to kiss down her back to her round buttocks. His hands followed his mouth, touching every part of her.

With the slightest movement, he pulled her to her knees. He leaned over her, pressing his aching arousal against her as his hands found her breasts. As he teased her nipples, Isabelle began to move her against him.

He shifted his hips and entered her hot, wet sex. He couldn't stop the moan of satisfaction at filling her, of having her tight walls surround him. With his hands on her hips to keep her still, he plunged inside her with long, slow thrusts.

Her breathing hitched, and little cries of pleasure poured from her mouth. And each time he filled her, he was coming closer and closer to the edge of his own climax.

He reached around and found her sex and the swollen nub of her clit. With the slightest touch, he ran his thumb across it and was rewarded with a tremor that shook her. He repeated the movement and felt her clench around him.

Isabelle was under a haze of pleasure so profound that she could barely remember her own name. Each time Lucian's hands or mouth touched her, she melted. He was an expert at lovemaking and knew just where to touch her to send her spiraling into bliss.

Even now as he pumped his thick arousal in and out of her, she ached for more. She was mindless to where his hands roamed. His hips pumped faster, his thrusts began to drive into her harder, deeper. She was so close to peaking, her body flushed, her breathing ragged.

A cry tore from her throat at the pleasure that splintered through her. With just the slightest wiggle of his finger, an orgasm so intense, so incredible, consumed her. Even as her tremors began to fade, Lucian still drove within her.

He leaned over her, his breathing harsh and ragged. His hips pumped faster just before she heard him roar, and he gripped her and buried himself deep, giving his seed to her womb. Isabelle instinctively tightened around him to prolong his climax.

"Isabelle," he whispered, and collapsed on top of her before he rolled to his side, bringing her against him.

For long moments they lay silently in the aftermath of their lovemaking. Her mind was filled with Lucian. Ever since he'd come into her life, he'd turned it upside down. She'd had more excitement, more enjoyment in the past few hours than she'd had most of her life. All that was due to Lucian.

Yes, his story frightened her. She wanted to discount it, but she knew that as odd as it sounded, it was the truth. She couldn't explain how she knew, only that she did. That's what scared her the most.

She shouldn't be so sure of him. But she was.

Isabelle could still feel him inside her. Each time they came together was more pleasurable, more intense. She had never thought of herself as wicked, but when she was near Lucian all she could think about was their bodies joining again.

The rest of the world faded away, leaving only the two of

them. It made her think of possibilities, of happiness…of a future.

When he pulled out of her, she turned and looked at him. "That was…incredible."

A satisfied smile pulled at his lips. "Liked that, did you?"

"Very much," she admitted, and pulled him down next to her. "Is there more?"

He nuzzled her neck. "So very much more it would take me a lifetime to show you."

She didn't respond to his words, but they stayed with her, even as she dozed in his arms.

A lifetime.

Wasn't that what she wanted?

Yes!

Lucian held Isabelle tightly to him as her breathing evened into sleep. It was only the second time they had made love, yet it was more intense than the first. And still he hungered for her. He wanted her again, right now, but wouldn't wake her so soon.

He thought making love to her again would show her that she needed him, but all it had done was show him he couldn't live without her. He was going to have to face the truth, that if she decided against returning with him, he would have to choose whether to stay with her or return to certain death.

His family and kingdom, or his mate?

The mark on his arm, that even now glowed nearly blue, dictated that his life was in the hands of his mate. He couldn't ignore that. He was bound to his mate through each lifetime. To forsake her now would have dire consequences, but so would forsaking his family and Drahcir.

His thoughts took him to his family. He missed his family, his brothers and all their fighting, his mother and her calming effect on the family, and his father and his incredible way of knowing just what to do.

How he wished he could talk to them, to share his troubles and hear their advice. Yet he knew that was impossible. His father warned him that he might have a difficult decision to make. Lucian had been fool enough to never consider that possibility.

It was a lesson well learned, but had it come too late?

6

It was time.

Isabelle could no longer wait to give Lucian an answer. He deserved at least that from her. But even now as he brushed Elad, she still didn't know what her decision would be. She had hoped that after a full day of getting to know Lucian better she would be able to make her decision, but all it had done was confuse her even more.

There was no doubt she couldn't get enough of his body and the pleasure he gave her, but was it enough to give up her life and travel with him to a kingdom made up with the same magic that put the mark on her arm?

She stood back a moment and watched as Lucian used steady, smooth movements to brush his mount. It was obvious the time he spent with her had taken a toll on him. He hid it well, but there was no denying he was meant to be in his kingdom. He didn't belong with her, but could she let him go?

She knew the moment he realized she was there. Their eyes met over Elad's back. His black eyes were warm, welcoming. There was a small smile pulling up the corners of his sexy mouth. Her fingers longed to delve into his black locks and pull his head down for a kiss.

But the time for pleasure was over. He'd been honest with her. She could do no less for him.

"I promised you a decision," she said, her tongue thick in her mouth. How she longed to return to the night before and their exquisite lovemaking, with the decision hours away.

Lucian set down the brush and walked around the horse. "You did."

Hope—and doubt—filled his beautiful black eyes, making her heart clench. He was a warrior, a prince. He was strong, confident, and amazing. She had put that worry in his gaze. She's the one who had put the lines of strain that bracketed his mouth.

He had done so much for her. What had she done for him? She might have welcomed his touch, but she hadn't believed his story, had pushed him away when he spoke of magic. And still he remained by her side.

That's when she realized she needed to stop asking herself what she could do and ask what she *couldn't* do.

Could she allow Lucian and his kingdom to die? Could she allow him to walk out of her life with the knowledge that she would never see him again? Could she live without him?

The answer was a resounding nay.

A huge weight lifted off her shoulders as she acknowledged her answer. What a fool she'd been. Yes, he asked the impossible, but in return she would be his. She wanted to dance around and shout her answer to the world.

Instead, she smiled, her heart trembling with elation and happiness. "Will you take me with you?"

His lips parted as he simply stared at her. Lucian took a

step toward her. "Really?" he asked, his voice breathless, as if he expected her to change her mind again.

She nodded and found herself enveloped in his arms as he swung her around and around. He stopped and buried his head in her neck.

"Thank you," he whispered.

She smiled up at the sky at his words, and she could have sworn the mark on her arm sizzled.

Lucian secured a horse for Isabelle, one that was surefooted and steady. He wanted to leave immediately, fearing she might change her mind once more. But every time he asked, she just laughed and kissed him.

His heart was lighter than it had been in years. He was going home. With his mate. Isabelle had made the impossible, possible. He couldn't imagine the anxiety within her, but he was going to be beside her forever. He would help her through it all.

He smiled at his mate, his Isabelle, as she stood with Mr. and Mrs. MacDonald. That morning he'd combed her hair, hearing her sighs of pleasure. The long strands of her hair were soft as down and cool to the touch. Never had he imagined himself combing a woman's hair, but he'd found he quite enjoyed it. It was definitely something he planned to do often.

One of many things he looked forward to once they were settled in Drahcir.

He finished tying off the bag holding Isabelle's possessions to her horse. It took everything he had to stop himself from dragging her away from the MacDonalds. They were the only family she knew, and she needed to say her farewells.

"I'm going to miss you, dearling," Mrs. MacDonald said as she hugged Isabelle for the third time.

Lucian saw the moisture in Isabelle's eyes as she kissed Mrs. MacDonald's weathered cheek before turning to Mr. MacDonald.

"You were the daughter we never had, lass. I hate to see you leave, but know 'tis something you need to do," Mr. MacDonald said. "We'll be here if you ever need us. Take care of yourself."

"I will," she said.

Lucian was surprised to find Mr. MacDonald walk to him. "I better no' hear of you mistreating her."

"Never. I pledge my soul on it," Lucian answered solemnly.

Mr. MacDonald seemed satisfied with the answer as he returned to his wife and pulled her into his arms as she cried. Lucian helped Isabelle on her horse before he mounted Elad. At long last, he was finally returning home. He couldn't wait to see the gates of the kingdom or his family.

But more than that, he couldn't wait to show Isabelle her new home.

"Ready?" he turned his head and asked.

Her eyes were bright from unshed tears, but her smile was wide. "Ready."

With one last wave to the MacDonalds, Lucian nudged his horse into a walk.

The weeks of travel had been decidedly hard on Isabelle, though she made a point to never complain. Lucian made sure to travel slowly, but it was obvious he was more than eager to reach his home. She was just as anxious about meeting his family.

She heard tales of his childhood and his family, of the antics between him and his brothers. Those stories kept her laughing as she came to learn about his brothers through the stories, as well as more about him.

Isabelle had a growing respect for his parents to put up with such unruly lads. It was apparent by the way his parents disciplined the boys and the wisdom they tried to pass down that they were good people.

Lucian spoke often of how his father would spend time alone with each of the brothers riding through their small kingdom, hunting, fishing, or just walking through the village. All the while imparting some knowledge the boys needed to know about the kingdom, family, or life in general.

The king wasn't the only one to spend time alone with the boys. The queen did as well. She also had things to impart to her sons, specifically how to properly woo a woman. Isabelle knew she would have to thank the queen for that.

After another hard day of travel in the mountains, she reclined in Lucian's arms as they stared at the fire in the coziness of a cave. Her gaze was drawn to his bare arm and the intricate symbol that graced his skin.

The more time they spent together, the more she realized they had always been meant for each other. It wasn't something she could explain to anyone, more of a feeling deep within, and it was all somehow connected to the symbols. She moved her left arm near his and looked at the marks. The firelight played across their arms, but her eyes only saw the markings.

"Do they bother you?" Lucian's deep voice asked near her ear.

She smiled though he couldn't see her face. "Nay. At first they seemed strange, but now…now it's as if they have always been there."

"They have. They just needed to be awakened and brought to life."

Isabelle leaned her head back to look into his black eyes. "Like me."

His smile was devastating as he hugged her to his chest. "Just like you, my love."

"I have to admit, I'm more than a little frightened of when we reach Drahcir."

"Why is that?" he asked as he smoothed back her hair loosened from the braid and kissed her neck.

"You're royalty, Lucian," she said as she sat up and turned to face him. "I'm a commoner."

"There is nothing common about you." His eyes narrowed and he asked, "Are you afraid my family willna accept you?"

Isabelle eyes fell to the ground. "That thought has crossed my mind."

She felt his fingers under her chin and allowed him to raise her face until she looked him in the eye. "Doona," he said softly. "We doona hold to the convictions that have plagued the rest of Scotland. Royalty or commoner, it's the same in my kingdom. No one will look down upon you. You're my mate, destined to be a princess of Drahcir."

"Destiny or not, people still view outsiders as threats, and regardless of what you say, people will look at me differently because I'm not royalty."

He chuckled and ran a thumb across her cheek. "Ah, Isabelle. None of my words will ease your fears, but I'll tell you that my kingdom has had to accept outsiders every generation. It's part of our life. Believe me when I tell you the people of Drahcir will be thrilled to see you because it means they are that much closer to seeing their lives continue."

As his words sunk in, she realized just how foolish she had been. She turned and resumed her place against his chest and threaded her fingers through his. "Thank you."

"It'll be all right," he said as he nuzzled her ear.

She sighed and closed her eyes as he found a particularly sensitive spot just behind her ear. Her entire body melted against him. His hands moved to hold her breasts and soon his fingers had her nipples hard and aching. While his hands caressed and kneaded her breasts, his mouth left a trail of fire that blazed right to her core. She burned for him as she did every night and as with each time their bodies joined, the need for him grew.

Isabelle pulled out of his embrace and turned to face him as she straddled his hips. Her hand found his arousal, thick and hard, as she guided him inside her.

"By the heavens," Lucian moaned, and took hold of her hips. "I want to taste you."

She barely had time to register what his words said before she was on her back, and he knelt between her legs, licking her stomach. His hot tongue trailed from hip to hip, stopping to dip lightly into her belly button before nipping the inside of her thigh. Isabelle's lungs seized when she felt his hot breath on her sex.

Could it be? Did he really mean to kiss her…there?

No sooner did she ask herself that question than his tongue licked her sex, slow and soft.

She sighed and fisted her hands in the blankets as he settled between her legs and parted her woman's lips. She opened her eyes to see him staring at her.

"Lucian?"

"You have no idea how beautiful you are," he said, before his tongue snaked out and lightly brushed back and forth over her clit.

Isabelle bit her lip as hot, molten desires licked their wicked flames around her. Instinctively, she opened her legs wider, giving Lucian more access to her sex. Almost immediately, his tongue delved deeper, tasting her as no one ever had. Her passion was growing so fast that she knew she couldn't hold back her climax, and she wasn't ready for it to end yet.

Not until I taste him.

With great effort, she managed to sit up. At Lucian's look, she merely smiled and rolled him onto his back.

"My turn," she said, and loved the way her stomach clenched when she saw the desire in his eyes.

She gripped his cock gently, loving the feel of its heat and softness. A bead of liquid formed at his tip, and Isabelle leaned down and licked it off. Lucian's breath hissed from between his lips, but it only urged her on. The taste of him was delicious, and she wanted more.

Much more.

Growing bolder by the moment, Isabelle brought him into her mouth as she moved her hand up and down his shaft. With her free hand, she reached down and cupped his sac. She was just beginning to take him deeper when Lucian's hands gripped her waist.

Isabelle raised her head to tell him to stop when he said, "Wait."

She trusted him completely and loved anything new he

showed her, so she eagerly waited as he positioned her on top of him with her legs straddling his face and her face mere inches from his rod.

Without being told what to do, she once more brought him to her mouth, licking him from bottom to tip. She had just taken him in her mouth again when she felt his tongue moving across her clit. For a moment she couldn't move as the pleasure poured through her. To be able to receive such pleasure as she was giving it was a wonderful experience, one she intended to make sure they repeated often.

Lucian bit back a groan as Isabelle took him into her hot, wet mouth. Her sweet hands knew just were to touch and how hard or soft as she cupped his sac and moved her hand up and down his shaft. It wanted release right then, but he could tell she was fighting her own climax. He would hold off as long as she did, no matter how much it nearly killed him to do it.

His tongue darted through her sex and found her clit again. He loved the taste of her and how her body trembled each time he licked her. She was wet with desire, which only spurred his own desire to new heights.

She showed him heights of pleasure he had never known. His hands caressed over her back and rounded behind. With a smile, he dipped a finger into her sheath and felt her hot breath expel from her mouth as she moaned, deep and long.

"Want something?"

She moaned again and moved her hips against his chest. "You know I do."

"Not yet."

Lucian added a second finger and moved them inside her. This time, Isabelle whimpered and pumped her hand faster on his cock.

He closed his eyes and found her clit again as his fingers drove into her. Lucian knew her body well enough to know that he could push a bit more before she peaked. When he didn't let up his assault, she took him into her mouth and began to kiss and suck him as if her life depended upon it.

Lucian took them as far as he could before he released her and rolled her onto her back. Her eyes were glazed as she stared up at him, and he felt a rush of pride to know she was his. He pulled her to her feet before he turned her to face the wall of the cave.

"What are you doing?" she asked over her shoulder, no fear in her voice.

"Shhh," he said as he kissed her shoulder. "Trust me."

She moaned and leaned her head back against his shoulder. "I do, I'm just not sure my legs can hold me."

Lucian chuckled as he gripped his cock and found her sex. He rubbed his rod against her sensitive sex and reveled in each cry and moan that tore from her throat. When he could take it no more, he buried himself deep within her.

Isabelle gripped the cold stone of the cave as Lucian began to move within her. She wanted him hard and fast to reach her fulfillment, but she knew he would show her pleasure. With each withdrawal and thrust, she moved against him, creating more friction as the tempo increased.

She was mindless with want, her body needing release but not ready to let go yet as Lucian plunged deep within her. Their bodies were slick with sweat, and she could feel the climax building as he pumped hard and fast. She felt his hand move around her to find her sex, slick and throbbing.

His thumb moved over it once, twice…three times, and her world splintered as her orgasm claimed her, as waves upon waves of pleasure rolled through her body. And with each continued thrust of Lucian's thick arousal, he prolonged her climax until her legs could no longer hold her.

Dimly she heard a roar behind her and realized her mate had also found his release as the tip of his rod touched her womb. His seed poured inside her, and she wondered when her belly would grow round with his child—their child.

7

*L*ucian couldn't believe he was nearly home. He hadn't wanted to tell Isabelle last night that they would arrive today. He knew she was nervous, but he wanted her to get a good night's sleep, and keeping their arrival from her had given her that.

He readied their horses and turned to find her plaiting her hair. He loved her glorious mane of dark brown hair. It was thick and silky, and he enjoyed having it draped around him when they made love.

As he tightened the saddle on Isabelle's mare, he thought of their time together. They had used the travel to learn more of each other, and with each passing day, he wondered how he had ever lived without her. She had a wicked sense of humor that kept him laughing and seeing the world in an entirely different light.

His family and kingdom would be much richer with her.

He sighed and looked at the pass they would take that led to Drahcir. Home. How he had missed it, but most especially his family. A smile pulled at his lips as he imagined the homecoming with his brothers. They were a loud, rowdy lot, but they were loyal. What more could a brother ask for?

"What are you looking at?" Isabelle asked as she came to stand beside him.

"The pass home."

She stiffened beside him. "You knew this last night?"

He nodded. "I did, but felt you could use a good rest instead of staying up worrying."

"You were right, of course," she said, and chuckled while she clasped her cloak around her.

"Ready?"

"Aye," she said, and kissed him before he sat her on the mare and ventured into the snow.

They talked for hours about everything from her duties as a princess to how many children they might have. There were spots of companionable silence as well. By the time they neared the gates of Drahcir, Lucian knew whatever time he had left with her would be the most wonderful time of his life.

The entrance to Drahcir was just over the next rise. Lucian was so excited upon seeing his family again that for a moment he almost missed the frisson of warning that ran down his spine. He jerked on Elad's bridle and reached to halt Isabelle. Once she was stopped, he looked around hoping to see who, or what, endangered them.

"What is it?" Isabella whispered.

Lucian knew without a doubt that something was about to attack, he just didn't know from where. He had to get Isabelle to safety, but in the thick snow and walls of mountains, there was no place for her to hide.

"We're about to be attacked," he said casually as he leaned over and kissed her full on the mouth.

Thankfully, she stayed calm as she asked, "Who?"

"I doona know. Make sure you stay out of the way while I battle them. Take this," he said, and placed the dagger he had given her on their first night in her lap. "Keep it hidden, and use it if you must."

She nodded and gripped his hand. "I'm not going to lie and say I'm not afraid."

"I know." Lucian looked over his shoulder and saw the top of the castle through the pass. If there was anyway they could ride to the gates safely, he wouldn't hesitate, but the ground didn't allow for the horses to do more than walk up the steep slope.

He looked back to Isabelle. "I'll protect you. I didna come this far to lose you and fail my family."

No sooner had the words left his mouth than an eerie scream echoed around them. Lucian's blood froze in his veins. It had been generations since any Sinclair had come across a Tnarg. His eyes scanned the frozen area until he spotted the vile creature. Quickly, he palmed his sword and grabbed his shield. He twisted the reins until Elad now faced the Tnarg. His mount pawed the frozen earth and snorted.

Lucian looked at Isabelle. "Remember what I said. Find some cover," he warned as the Tnarg let out another loud growl.

Once he was sure Isabelle had sufficiently hidden herself, Lucian nudged Elad, and they raced toward the Tnarg. The nasty creature jumped from the cliff above them and landed with a loud thud just lengths from them.

"What do you want?" Lucian demanded.

The Tnarg smiled, revealing a mouth full of long, pointed teeth. Its beady red eyes glowed, and the short, thick reddish hair covering its entire body exuded an unmistakable vile odor. The creature stood the same height as a man, but its elongated arms and vicious claws prevented anyone from getting too close.

"I want your bride," it said, in a voice that sounded as if someone had a hand around its throat.

Lucian couldn't believe his ears. After all the searching and convincing he had done, he wasn't about to lose Isabelle to a Tnarg just moments from the gates of Drahcir and his family.

He gripped the pommel of his sword and narrowed his eyes on the Tnarg. "You'll have to come through me to get her."

"I was hoping you'd say that," the Tnarg said, just before it leapt with its thick legs.

Lucian jerked Elad to the side so the Tnarg's sharp talons wouldn't blind the horse. The second left no time for Lucian to do anything other than brace himself for impact. The force of the Tnarg slamming into him knocked the breath from his lungs as he was dragged from his horse.

It seemed an eternity from the time he was pulled off his mount until he finally landed in the thick snow. It was only the snow that saved him. And while he struggled to get his breath back, the Tnarg straddled him and lifted one of its arms. Through his haze, Lucian saw the talons extend from the Tnarg's hand and knew he had mere heartbeats to live.

He jerked up his knees and brought them against the Tnarg's back. It was enough force to knock the creature forward to land face first in the snow. Lucian rolled to his feet and looked around the snow for his sword and shield. He tamped down the panic that threatened to rise and palmed his other dagger in his boot as the Tnarg jumped to its feet.

"You plan to kill me with that?" the creature taunted.

Lucian shrugged as they circled each other. "I'll kill you any way I can."

"I can tell you that won't do anything."

Lucian didn't know if the creature was lying or not, but he refused to allow the beast to see any hint of fear. Instead, he beckoned the Tnarg. "I've had enough of this. You want a fight, come and get me."

The Tnarg cocked its head to the side. "A feisty one. You'll be a tasty snack."

Lucian dove and rolled as the Tnarg swung a meaty arm at his chest. As he hit the ground, Lucian felt his shield beneath him and quickly grabbed it as he came to his feet. When he turned to the Tnarg, the creature narrowed its eyes on his shield.

"Fine weaponry."

"Aye, it is."

The Tnarg snarled and stepped closer to him. "Where did you steal it?"

Lucian laughed. "I'm a prince of Drahcir, you filthy maggot. It was given to me as a gift."

With a loud scream the Tnarg stumbled back and bared its teeth. "You lie."

"I doona lie."

For several heartbeats Lucian and the Tnarg stared at each other. Finally, the Tnarg said, "Friend of the Fae or not, she must die."

In a blink the Tnarg had moved around Lucian and was headed toward Isabelle. Lucian shouted Isabelle's name to try and warn her as he raced after the Tnarg. He watched in horror as the Tnarg was about to reach Isabelle.

"Nay," he bellowed as he hurtled his dagger at the offending beast.

The blade embedded in the Tnarg's back, yet the

creature continued on its course to Isabelle. Lucian knew he had to turn the beast's attention from Isabelle back to himself, but without his sword he had no weapon.

Lucian dove at the Tnarg and wrapped his arms around the creature's chest. Using every muscle in his body, Lucian slammed the Tnarg against the mountain.

He turned to Isabelle and grabbed her arm as he helped her to her horse, "Take the mare and make for the pass. Doona stop and doona look back."

"Lucian," she said, but he stopped her words with his hand.

"There's no time," he said, and placed her on her mount. "I love you," he said, just before he slapped the mare on her flank.

The Tnarg screamed and tried to get around Lucian, but Lucian brought his knee up and into the creature's gut right before he planted his fist in the Tnarg's face. The beast fell back into the snow as blood gushed from its nose.

"You'll pay for that," it said.

"I warned you that you'd have to kill me first," Lucian said as the Tnarg picked itself up and glared at him. "Come slake your thirst on me."

The Tnarg laughed then, the sound menacing and evil. "I'll most certainly have your blood, but before I do, know that I'll have your bride. No matter how far she runs, she will die."

Because it had been generations since anyone had seen a Tnarg, Lucian himself only having seen drawings, he was curious as to why the beast had come out of hiding. Not to mention, he still needed his sword.

"Why?"

"Why?" the Tnarg repeated. "Why do you think?"

"Isabelle has done nothing to you. Your quarrel lies with the Sinclairs."

The Tnarg wiped the blood from its face. "She's your bride, therefore a Sinclair."

Lucian seethed with fury. The Tnarg's were vile creatures, but to attack a woman instead of a warrior—that took the lowest of the low. He stepped to his left and felt something hit the toe of his boot.

***

Isabelle's heart pounded furiously in her chest. She hadn't been able to leave Lucian alone, regardless of what he had said. He might need her. She stopped her mare on the pass and hid behind part of the mountain wall. Seeing the awful creature still didn't make it seem real to her. And it could talk.

A shudder ripped through her as she recalled it saying it wanted to kill her. Somehow it was connected to Lucian and his family, she was sure of it. Lucian had spoken of magic, and though she didn't know much about it, the creature had to come from some sort of magic.

As Lucian and the creature spoke, she fingered the dagger in her hand, ready to aid Lucian in any way. Her breath lodged in her throat as Lucian rolled and came up with his sword to face the beast.

She blinked, and Lucian and the creature attacked. Lucian's arm moved with lightning speed as he kept the beast's claws away. She had seen Lucian fight once before, but in the light of day, she saw just how excellent a warrior he was as he battled a beast made of magic.

Yet, powerful warrior or not, the monster was wearing him down. Isabelle could tell Lucian's movements slowed where the Tnarg's increased. By the resignation on Lucian's face, he knew it was simply a matter of time.

"Nay," Isabelle whispered. She could not lose Lucian after just finding him.

She rose and started down the pass. Her feet slipped on the ice and snow, and she began to fall. She kept her eyes on Lucian as she slid the rest of the way, ignoring the cuts and scrapes on her legs.

"Lucian!" she cried through her tears as she saw him crumble to the ground under the onslaught of the Tnarg's assault. She climbed to her feet, her only thought to save her mate, the man that she loved.

"Get away from him!" she cried as she raced toward the Tnarg.

The Tnarg didn't pay her any mind as it went in for the kill. Isabelle dove at the creature and buried the dagger in its arm. It screamed and threw her off as it clawed at the dagger. Isabelle's stomach fell to her feet as the Tnarg turned to her and hissed, its massive teeth bared.

And just as quickly as it had come, it was vanished.

Isabelle said a quick prayer of thanks, her heart thumbing with sickening dread in her chest. Tears gathered in her eyes at the terror she had just witnessed.

"Isabelle."

Her eyes shifted to find Lucian crawling toward her.

She cried freely now as she rose up on her knees and embraced him. "I thought I had lost you."

"You were supposed to leave," he said, his breath still coming in huge gulps.

She leaned back to look into his eyes. "I couldn't. I knew you'd need me."

He smiled then and wiped her damp hair from her face. "I did need you."

They rose to their feet, and Isabelle took inventory of him. Fortunately, he had only flesh wounds and nothing that couldn't wait to be tended to once they reached Drahcir.

"I'm fine," he said as he stilled her arms. "Are you hurt?"

She started to shake her head then felt her legs begin to sting. "Nothing that cannot wait until we reach the gates."

"Then let's go home," Lucian said.

Isabelle was more than ready now.

Lucian looked over at Isabelle and smiled as they entered the tall gilded gates of Drahcir. He never tired of looking at the city, and he could only imagine what it was like seeing it for the first time. He wanted to nudge his horse faster but held back so Isabelle could take it all in.

"You said it was beautiful, but I didn't expect this," Isabelle said as she looked around in awe.

"It's more beautiful than words. Just like you."

She turned her midnight-blue eyes on him and smiled. "You do know how to charm."

"If you follow this road, it will lead to the castle," he said, and pointed to his home high atop the mountain. He took in a deep breath and looked at the cottages and structures that lined the steep slope to the castle. He'd taken his home for granted while he'd been there, but never again would he make that mistake.

The quaint, elegant splendor could be seen from the road, from the flowers artfully planted everywhere to the precision of their symbol carved, etched, stitched, and branded on clothes, homes, weapons, saddles, and anything else they could find. Time held the kingdom in a bubble that stopped the wars and men's greed from touching them. He hated the curse, hated the pressure put on them to keep the kingdom alive, but after seeing what was outside the gates, he was almost glad it had happened.

"The knotwork is everywhere," Isabelle said, her voice low, holding a note of awe.

"It was given to us by the Fae. It's part of us, part of Drahcir. You'll find it carved in all the wood, sewn into the clothes, and etched into stone."

"A part of it is even on us," she said and cut her eyes to him.

Lucian's arm warmed as he thought of his mark and the matching one on Isabelle's arm. "Aye. If you let it, it'll become a part of you."

"I'd like nothing better." Isabelle drank in the allure and beauty of the city. "I wasn't prepared for the exquisite, quiet beauty of it all."

He chuckled and took her hand to kiss the back of it as their horses continued slowly down the street. The inhabitants began to file out of their homes and businesses in droves. They lined the street, waving and clapping, smiles of joy of on their faces.

Isabelle bit her lip, suddenly all too aware of her shabby, older clothes that were nothing like the simple, clean styles she now saw. Unlike her gown with open sides and train, the women wore gowns of solid colors with long flared sleeves and a deep border on the bottom of their skirts. She found it lovely and enchanting, so much so that she couldn't wait to get out of her soiled, stained gown and into one like theirs.

The men's clothing was just as simple and out of date as the women's. Instead of the coif, they went bareheaded. Instead of the overcoat, gauntlets, painted leather boots, and hose, they wore long tunics, trews, and tall leather boots, just as Lucian did.

It was as if Isabelle had stepped into another realm.

Her gaze moved from the people to the structures. She recognized a blacksmith's shop, a baker, and even a tailor's shop. Everything was clean and beautiful. That's when she noticed how warm she had become.

"Something wrong?" Lucian asked, a twinkle in his eyes as he waved at the people.

"I'm warm."

He smiled and reached over to help her remove the thick woolen cloak. "Though we were cursed, the city has also been blessed. Nothing could live in these mountains as cold as it is. The Fae bespelled the city to keep it warm."

"Amazing," Isabelle whispered. "So you were cursed and blessed by the Fae. Anything else you didn't tell me?"

His hearty laugh brought a smile to her lips. "There are some things that are better left experienced rather than being told."

"I've got more surprises?"

"Here's another one," he said as he stopped in front of a massive water fountain.

She could only gawk at the sheer size of the fountain and the sparkling stone it was constructed of. Isabelle eagerly went into Lucian's waiting arms as she slid off the mare. She was drawn to the fountain, unable to stay away. She ran her hand over the amazing blue rocks that formed the structure of the fountain.

"They're smooth. And I see no cracks where the stones meet up," she said, and raised her gaze to Lucian.

"Another gift from the Fae."

Isabelle turned back to the fountain and dipped her hand into the clear, cool water and brought it to her mouth. It tasted as fresh and enchanting as the city. It wasn't until she took Lucian's outstretched hand and turned to her mare that she got an up-close view of the castle.

The structure was as similar as it was different from the other castles in Scotland. The round turrets, battlements, and soaring towers mimicked the castles she knew, but the stone it was constructed of was similar to that of the fountain and shown brilliantly in the sun. There was no drawbridge, and the many stairs leading up the castle was something she had never seen before. Her gaze caught the numerous balconies overlooking the city from various chambers, and she found herself eager to investigate each room.

"Want to take a closer look?" Lucian asked in her ear.

She couldn't turn back now if she tried. She was bonded with Lucian, with Drahcir, and with its people. Isabelle threaded her hand with her mate's. "Aye. Show me all of it."

People began to follow them to the castle. The road was long and winding as it rose to the highest peak. Lucian waved and talked to the people as they passed, but he couldn't introduce Isabelle. Not before his parents met her. It was tradition.

Yet, everyone knew he'd brought home his princess.

By the time they reached the top, Isabelle was breathless, her smile bright. Lucian should have put her on Elad and rode them to the castle, but he wanted her to remember her first trip up always.

"I'm in awe of everything."

"You're no' tired?"

"I'm exhausted, but I'm too overwhelmed to notice it yet."

Lucian laughed and smoothed back tendrils of her hair that had come loose in the rough winds of the mountains. "You'll get used to it all soon enough."

She rolled her eyes and stepped out of his arms to smooth her skirts. Over her head, Lucian spotted his parents as they emerged from the castle. His chest swelled as he smiled at them. He couldn't wait to talk to both of them. There was so much he had to tell them.

In the years of his absence, his father had aged greatly. Where once his beard had been as black as the night, it was littered with gray. And his mother hadn't fared much better. Her flawless face now had lines of worry around her mouth and eyes. As soon as they spotted him, his mother began to cry and his father slowly walked to him. Lucian met his father halfway and embraced the man he had always looked up to.

"I'm so glad you've returned, son," his father said as he stepped back and gave him a once over.

Lucian's throat closed with emotion when he saw the joy and pride in his father's eyes. He smiled and moved to embrace his mother who hung back. Words weren't spoken. His mother couldn't stop crying, and his own emotion nearly choked him as he held her trembling body. Finally, Lucian moved to the side and motioned for Isabelle to come forward.

For the first time since his arrival, his mother ceased her tears and his father turned his dark eyes to Isabelle.

"Mother. Father. I'd like to introduce you to Isabelle. My mate."

"Saints be praised!" his father shouted, and pulled her

into his arms for a fierce hug before his mother pulled her away for a hug of her own.

Lucian sat back and watched his parents fuss over Isabelle, welcoming her into the family. They shared a smile, he and Isabelle, as the people of Drahcir began to cheer loudly.

"The wedding will be three days hence," his mother said as she began to walk toward the castle doors, her arm firmly locked around Isabelle.

Lucian turned to his father. "Where are Elric, Sorin, and Keiran? I expected them to greet us."

His father lowered his eyes. "You're the first to return, son."

Lucian was so stunned, he could only stare at his father. He had thought to be the last, not the first. No wonder his parents had aged so greatly in his absence. He needed to soothe their fears the only way he knew how. "They'll return, Father. I know it. You know it."

His father nodded. "Enough talk of that. Let us celebrate your return."

"Wait," Lucian said as he watched his mother and Isabelle disappear into the castle. "There's something you need to know. We were attacked."

"What?" his father exclaimed.

Lucian sighed. "It was a Tnarg, Father. It was after Isabelle."

"Ye saints," Urises said. "Are you sure? None have been encountered in...."

"Generations," Lucian supplied. "And I'm quite sure. The books that foretell our history have several depictions of the Tnargs. I used to have nightmares about the beasts. It disappeared as suddenly as it appeared after Isabelle sunk a blade into it."

"Isabelle?" the king repeated, his eyebrows raised high in his forehead.

Lucian nodded. "The beast nearly had me. She saved me."

"A fine woman you've found as your mate, Lucian. I'm happy for you." Urises ran a hand down his face. "Doona tell your mother of the attack. She's worried enough as it is."

"I hadna planned on it, and I'll make sure Isabelle doesna either."

"Was it difficult for Isabelle to leave her family?"

Lucian already missed her, even though she was only in the castle. He'd gotten used to her being by his side. "Nay. They were all dead. It was close though, Father. I wasna sure I could convince her."

"None of that matters now. You're here, Isabelle is with you, and the people rejoice. Listen to their shouts of happiness, son," he said, and looked out over the people waving and cheering still.

Lucian gave them a wave before they walked into the great hall. His gaze instantly found Isabelle. She and his mother sat in front of the massive hearth as they talked, their heads close together and smiles on both of their faces.

"Ah, it's good to see your mother smile again," his father said from beside him. "You and Isabelle will help take her mind off the others."

All of a sudden, Isabelle turned her eyes to Lucian and smiled. She said something to his mother, then rose and walked toward him. He held out his arms as she drew close and pulled her against him.

"Do you like it here?"

She tilted her head up and grinned. "It's amazing, unlike anything I could've imagined, but I would be happy anywhere as long as you were with me."

It suddenly hit him then. He had done it. He had accomplished a quest, a quest where many had depended upon him. He should be proud of that, and he was, but it paled in comparison to what he held in his arms.

"I love you," he whispered.

"And I you, my prince."

8

*I*sabelle looked out over the people of Drahcir. In just a few moments time, the wedding would commence. She still didn't know how the seamstresses had finished her gown in time. It was a gown fit for a princess.

The gold thread glittered in the deep burgundy material of her gown. The bottom had the large border that held intricate designs that were similar to the ones on her arm. There were also gems sewn on the gown—pearls, diamonds, and the most expensive of gems—garnets.

She turned to look into the mirror again. Each time she looked at the expensively gowned woman with her hair in two long plaits and wrapped in the same deep burgundy as her gown, she couldn't believe it was her reflection.

"Anxious?" asked a voice behind her.

Isabelle turned to find Morag, Lucian's mother, in the doorway. "More than you know."

"There's nothing to be worried about, dear. You and Lucian were meant for each other." Morag was tall and slender, her chestnut hair showing a few strands of silver. She held something up to Isabelle. "Now, you're going to need this."

"What is it?" Isabelle asked as Morag walked up behind her.

"Every princess of this kingdom has worn this," she said after it was placed on Isabelle's head.

Isabelle looked in the mirror and gasped as she spotted the small crown on her head.

"Wear it with pride, dear," Morag said with a smile, her brown eyes holding a kindness that still surprised Isabelle. "Now, come. It's time, and Lucian grows restless."

Isabelle followed Morag from the chamber, down the long hall and stairs to the great hall where Lucian waited for her. She drank in the sight of him in his royal finery. He still wore black, but she noticed his tunic was trimmed to match her gown. His black hair was left free to float in the breeze, and his black eyes crinkled at the corners as he smiled at her.

"A lovelier vision I've never beheld," he said as she approached and took her hands. "Shall we?"

"I've been waiting for you my entire life."

"Then you shall wait no more, my love," he said ,and guided her from the great hall.

Lucian wanted to run to the tower. After the assault from the Tnarg, he had been more than a little nervous about another attack. If he had had his way, the wedding ceremony would take place in the great hall or chapel, not on the tower for the kingdom to see. Isabelle's life was more important than tradition, but he hadn't been able to talk his parents into it.

Much to the annoyance of his parents, he had worn his sword. There was no way he would allow himself to be unprepared if there was an attack. For whatever reason, that Tnarg wanted Isabelle dead, and Lucian had a feeling it would come back until the deed was done. Whether or not the beast could get into their kingdom was left unanswered.

None of the books he'd poured over had mentioned that little—very important—fact.

By the time they reached the top of the tower he focused on his bride. He was more than ready for the ceremony to be finished. His mother had refused to allow him to spend more than a few moments in Isabelle's company since their arrival. He wanted to kiss, touch, and taste his woman, and after today no one would be able to stop him again.

The priest stood patiently awaiting them as Lucian and Isabelle came to stand before him. Below them, the entire kingdom of Drahcir was there to witness the ceremony.

Lucian felt Isabelle's hand shake on his arm, and he quickly took hold of her hand and gave her a gentle squeeze. He listened to the priest's words with half an ear as his eyes looked for any signs of an attack.

"Do you, Isabelle Ferguson, agree to take Prince Lucian Sinclair as your husband? To love, cherish, and obey?" the priest asked.

Lucian looked down at Isabelle and watched as her mouth spread into a wide grin.

"I do," she answered.

The priest then turned to Lucian. "Do you, Prince Lucian Sinclair, agree to take Isabelle Ferguson as your wife? To protect, cherish, and love?"

"I do."

The priest gave them a smile and motioned someone to him. To Lucian's surprise, a Fae moved to stand before them. The Fae's unusual, mystical blue eyes swirled in the morning sun, and his white blond hair hung down his back and was held back from his face by many tiny intricate braids.

"Lucian. Isabelle," he said. "Today is a magical day, a day that puts Drahcir one step closer to continuing. I am here as emissary from King Theron and Queen Rufina who send their approval and blessings for this union."

He drew in a deep breath and gave them a smile as he raised his hand over them and said something in what could only be the Fae's language before he lowered his arm. "Enjoy your life together," he said with a wink.

The citizens of Drahcir erupted in cheers. Lucian wasted no time in taking Isabelle into his arms and tasting her sweet lips again. "Princess Isabelle. I like it."

She giggled and smiled up at him. "I do, too, my prince."

While his mother came to congratulate them, his father moved to the edge of the tower and said, "Let the celebrating begin."

They all laughed as the music and drinking began immediately all through the kingdom.

The Fae stepped in front of Lucian as he tugged Isabelle out of the tower. "I heard you were attacked."

Lucian nodded and glanced to make sure his mother was occupied "We were."

"Who was it?"

"A Tnarg."

The Fae mumbled something that Lucian was sure was a curse of some sort. "Are you sure?"

"Absolutely. It tried to kill me, but it wanted Isabelle. It seemed verra interested that we were friends of the Fae."

Isabelle nodded as the Fae's gaze turned to her. "It didn't leave until I used Lucian's dagger on it."

"A weapon of the Fae," the Fae mumbled. "Interesting. And you say you stabbed it?"

Isabelle glanced at Lucian. "I did. It was about to kill Lucian. I had no other choice."

"Nay, you didn't," the Fae agreed. He looked from Isabelle to Lucian. "You two have no idea what you've done, do you?"

Lucian eyed the Fae. "And what exactly is it that we've done?"

"The Tnarg's only goal is to kill any, and all, men and women that the children of Sinclair claim as their own. Very few have escaped it when it has decided to venture from its lair."

Lucian pulled Isabelle against him. "Nowhere in the texts of Drahcir's history does it state what the Tnargs are for. Can you tell us?"

"I wish I could. You were very lucky."

"Aye, but will my brothers be as well?"

The Fae looked away, his swirling blue eyes troubled. "That I cannot tell you. I must go."

The words had barely left his mouth before he vanished.

"I didn't even know his name," Isabelle said.

Lucian hugged her and ran his hands down her back. He looked out of the kingdom to the gates and farther below, to the pass that led to the city. His thoughts turned to his brothers.

"They will come," Isabelle said, as if she could read his thoughts. "Your brothers will arrive soon."

He looked down into her sweet face. Her smile chased away his melancholy. "Aye, they will, my love. We Sinclairs doona give up easily."

"Thank God for that," she said.

Lucian glanced once more to the gates of the city. He had found his mate. He just prayed his brothers did as well.

PRINCE OF SEDUCTION

Four brothers, a secret kingdom, and an ancient curse.

As one of four Drahcir princes, finding women has always come easily for Elric, and when he finally finds his mate, he intends to convince her to return with him by using his famed seduction. However, she isn't anything like the women he's encountered before, and he realizes it will take more than wiles to win his mate—it will take his heart.

After being left at the altar and devastated, Marin believes Scotland is the answer to healing her broken spirit. But the last thing she expects to find is a man who steals her breath with his kisses and makes her heart skip a beat with his smiles. Even as she tries to keep her distance, Marin realizes she is no match for Elric's seductive charms. And when faced with danger, Marin must choose: Elric and his secret kingdom…

Or life without him.

"Here's your room, ma'am," the bellhop said, with a pleasant smile as he opened Marin's door.

She stepped inside and looked at the brightly painted room and tiled floor. The king size four-poster bed looked so good all she wanted to do was curl up on it and sleep. Instead, she followed the bellhop as he walked about the room, telling her of the mini-fridge and the array of liquors at her disposal.

But when he pulled back the curtains and opened the sliding glass door, Marin sighed as soon as the sea breeze smoothed over her skin. Before her eyes was the magnificent Caribbean Ocean, in all its glory, just a few feet from her room. The white sand glistened in the sunlight and the palm trees swayed in the wind. The smell of salt was heavy, and the heat from the sun made her itch to settle in one of the hammocks strung between the palms and doze.

She inhaled the sea air deeply and instantly felt her muscles relax. Though she might not have wanted to come to Jamaica to get married, there was no doubt she'd been in serious need of some down time.

"Does this meet with your approval?" the bellhop asked.

Marin turned and smiled. "It most definitely does."

"If you need anything, my name is Paul," he said, and started for the door.

She went to reach for her purse to tip him before she remembered she was staying at the Whitehouse, a new Sandals resort where all the taxes and tips were included in the stay.

"By the way," Paul said as he reached the door. "Your fiancé is two floors above you, in the honeymoon suite."

"Thank you."

Marin waited until the door closed behind the bellhop before she allowed her irritation to show. It hadn't been her idea to get married in Jamaica. That had been Johnny's. He wanted something different. And since her parents were dead and she had no other family, she didn't have any argument other than the fact she really wanted to be married in a church.

Whoever said the wedding was really the bride's day had never met Johnny. He'd been adamant about how he saw their wedding, and she had been swayed by the excitement in his hazel eyes.

She really wasn't angry. Perturbed more aptly described her feelings. It just wasn't the wedding she had always dreamed about. Now that she was on the island and feeling the urge to sink her feet into the sand and drift in the turquoise waters, she was glad he had talked her into this destination.

What she was angry about were the accommodations.

Johnny managed to talk her into staying in different rooms until after the ceremony. Marin shook her head and unzipped her luggage. He had some...unique...ideas that sometimes left her shaking her head.

"Sometimes?" she asked herself. "More like most often. For a businessman who is climbing the corporate ladder at the ad agency, his ideas are almost always backwards. Makes no sense to me."

She'd stopped trying to figure Johnny out after their second date. He might be a little odd, but he was always thinking about her. Unless he was thinking about himself first.

Most men would be offended if the woman didn't want to share a room, but Johnny said it was what his parents expected. Never mind that she often stayed at his apartment since he didn't like hers.

He had certain ideas about their relationship, their wedding, and their future. And if she was honest, she'd admit that not all of those ideas were as crazy as wanting separate rooms until after the wedding.

It was just for one night. She had the rest of the day and the night, before the wedding in the morning. And she was going to make full use of the time. A day in the tropics all to herself. It sounded heavenly.

First, she was going to enjoy some of the sun, sand, and water—as well as the steady flow of liquor and food—and then that afternoon she was going to get a massage and facial.

She hurriedly pulled off her clothes, feeling the draining effects of travel leaving her as each piece of clothing hit the floor. Then she slipped on her black bikini, grabbed her black wide-brimmed hat and sunglasses, and headed out her sliding glass door for the beach.

A hammock with her name on it called.

———

Marin stretched before she pushed the covers away from her and rose from the bed. She padded to the window and pulled back the drapes covering the sliding glass door so the morning sun could spill into the room. She unlocked the door and slid it open. As soon as she did, the sound of the surf filled her room.

"I could get used to this."

She stretched her arms over her head to try to work out the kinks from doing too much kayaking, snorkeling, and swimming in one day. She had dozed in the sun, but the call of the waves had been too great for her to ignore.

Her thoughts were interrupted by a knock at the door. After pulling on the plush robe, she opened the door to see a beautiful Jamaican woman holding Marin's wedding gown and veil.

"Good mornin'," the woman said with a cheerful smile as she entered the. "Did you sleep well, ma'am?"

"I did," Marin said, and closed the door. There were no flurries of excitement for the day, only a worry that she hoped everything went according to Johnny's plans, lest he get upset. "I'd heard about Sandals resorts before, and had I known how beautiful and fun they were, I'd have been here sooner."

"I'm glad to hear you're enjoying your time. I'm here to help you get ready for the weddin'."

"Wonderful. I know exactly how I want my hair."

The maid nodded. "Perfect. I'll let you take a quick shower while I get the rest of your things ready. Your bouquet is having the finishing touches put on as we speak. It'll be up here soon."

"I hope the calla lilies turned out okay," Marin said as she grabbed her lingerie out of the drawer.

"Actually, ma'am, the bouquet you ordered was all roses. Red roses."

"What?" Marin asked as she straightened. It didn't take long to realize what had happened. She smoothed the frown from her face. After all, it wasn't the maid's fault. "That's what my fiancé wanted, but I specifically ordered white calla lilies and tulips."

It was the one thing she'd fought for. The calla lilies had been her mother's favorite, and the tulips were her favorite.

"I don't think there's time to change," she said apologetically.

"No, I doubt there is," Marin said as her anger grew, simmering just beneath the surface and threatening to ruin the day. Johnny had known exactly what he was doing. Just another example of how he always got what he wanted.

She was a prime example. From the time she was seventeen she'd been on her own, making her own decisions. Johnny had wanted to run her life, and she'd refused. After a month of dating, she'd broken things off. For the next three weeks he wooed her, promising never to do anything like that again.

For a while he hadn't. It wasn't until now, as she looked back, that she realized he *had* been running her life. It had started as little things she hadn't thought about, like where she bought clothes. Little by little, he took over almost every aspect of her life.

The flowers were important to her. She'd explained all that to him, but he disregarded her wishes. "As he always has," she said.

"Did you say something?" the maid asked.

Marin shook her head and started toward the bathroom. "Nothing. I'll be out in a bit."

But as she stepped into the spray of the hot water, she examined her relationship with Johnny. They rarely fought. He made her laugh and took her to amazing places. She loved him. Didn't she?

"Do I?" she asked herself as she braced her hands on the tile and let her chin hit her chest.

Or was she just used to how things were?

"No. It's just flowers. Johnny loves me."

No matter how she tried, Marin couldn't relax. If Johnny had gone behind her back and changed her bouquet, she was almost positive he'd done the same for the cake. And possibly the decorations, too.

"Is this *his* wedding, or *our* wedding?"

The anger was replaced with sadness.

She kept telling herself that they were little things and she shouldn't be upset. But the truth was, she was extremely troubled. She didn't want to have an argument before the wedding—not that there would be time—but she also didn't want to start their honeymoon off with a fight.

Yet, she couldn't let this go. She had to speak to Johnny. She refused to live her life going on as it was. He had to respect her choices and not continue to change them to suit whatever he wanted.

After turning off the water and climbing out of the tub to dry off, Marin wrapped the towel around her and another around her wet head then opened the door to her room. She turned the corner and saw her gown laid out on the bed with her veil and shoes beside it.

She had splurged on French lace lingerie for the wedding, and she was eager to put on the expensive silk finery. It was a sad state of affairs when a bride was more eager to put on her lingerie than her wedding gown.

Once she had the bra, panties, and garter belt fastened with her hose, she pulled on her robe and waited for the maid to return. As she waited, she gazed at her gown. It was a pretty dress, even though it wasn't the one she had always dreamed of having.

Johnny had spotted the gown while picking out his tux and bought it. He had been right, the gown did look great on. She had never bought a strapless gown before, and wouldn't have this time if he hadn't gone on and on about how it looked on her.

Just one more example of him running her life.

Marin ran her hand down the silk gown. No beads, pearls, or lace adorned the gown. Its simplicity was charming and suited their island wedding.

Laughter wafted through the screen on her sliding glass door, drawing her attention. Marin, curious, walked to the screen and looked outside to see a couple walking down the beach arm in arm. Her white gown and long veil trailed in the breeze. The man had on a tux with his shirt unbuttoned at the collar and his tie hanging open. Suddenly, he lifted the woman in his arms and kissed her.

"Their ceremony just ended," the maid said as she walked up beside Marin.

"They're a lovely couple." Marin couldn't hide the wistfulness in her own voice.

She sat in the chair the maid had set up by the opened window. Reggae music drifted from the speakers hidden throughout the massive resort, over the sounds of the birds and soft wind. She would never be able to listen to Reggae music again without thinking of Jamaica.

Marin closed her eyes as her hair was being dried and

then styled. She tried to quell the uneasy feelings within her, telling herself all brides felt the way she did. She just about convinced herself when the maid announced she was finished.

Eager to see what had been accomplished with her hair, Marin rose and went to look in the full-length mirror. Her dark locks had been swept away from her face and were gathered at the back of her head. Soft wisps of hair hung near her face and neck while the rest of her hair draped down her back in soft waves.

"I love it," she said. "Thank you so very much."

The maid beamed and gathered up her items. "Is there anything else you'd like, ma'am?"

"Just a few minutes alone."

"Of course. I'll be waiting outside when you're ready to go."

When the maid left, Marin looked at herself one last time. "Marin Williams. Mrs. Johnny Williams. Johnny and Marin Williams."

She checked the time and then hurried to apply her makeup. Johnny wanted her to go without, so she had compromised and just put on some bronzing powder, eyeliner, mascara, and lip gloss.

Once that was done, she stepped into her long, A-line shaped strapless wedding dress and zipped it up. She refused to go barefoot as Johnny wanted and bought instead a gorgeous pair of satin stilettos. As she slipped her feet inside the shoes, excitement began to unfurl.

She grabbed the dangle pearl earrings and put them on, then reached for the pearl bracelet, the only two pieces of jewelry she had left of her mother's.

"I sure wish you could be here, Mom," she said softly.

She took one more look in the full-length mirror before

she grabbed the bouquet of red roses, that had been delivered while she was in the shower, and walked to the door. She opened it to find the maid waiting.

"Simply stunning," the maid said with a nod of approval. "Follow me, Ms. Chapel."

With each step toward the wedding gazebo they had set up on the beach, Marin's anxiety and excitement mixed. She couldn't wait to start her life with Johnny, and a family soon after. He might not want kids now, but she was sure he would change his mind.

She spotted the gazebo where the wedding would take place and saw all the red and white decorations that Johnny had wanted. It was a beautiful mix amid the turquoise waters and vivid blue of the sky. All the flowers were in place, as was the cake, the minister, and their witnesses.

The only person missing was Johnny.

Marin laughed as she approached the small group. "He was so worried about me being late that he's late."

Everyone chuckled. Ten minutes later no one was laughing, least of all Marin.

Paul, the bellhop that had seen them to their rooms the night before, had been sent to find Johnny. When Marin spotted Paul walking toward them, his face grim, she knew what he would say before the words ever left his mouth.

"Mr. Williams checked out late last night," he said softly. His dark eyes held pity and remorse, both of which she couldn't handle at the moment.

What? Johnny had left without any word to her? Not even the common decency to tell her that he was calling the wedding off, that he changed his mind, that he needed time? Nothing? What kind of lowlife person did that?

But she had her answer.

Johnny.

Marin didn't bother looking at the others. She knew their gazes would hold the same emotions that Paul's did, and if she was to make it to her room without breaking down, she had to leave immediately.

She took a step and felt her knees begin to give. She stopped and forced herself to breathe and focus. *I'll cry in the privacy of my own room, not so the others can pity me more.*

The resolve gave her the strength she needed to walk to her room. The sidewalk seemed to stretch forever, and at one point, Marin wondered if she would ever find her room again.

Her hands shook so much when she tried to use the card key that it took her three times to get it to work. Once she was finally in the comfort and safety of her room, she fell back against the closed door and slid to the floor as the tears finally came.

2

Highlands of Scotland
1268

Elric sighed into the fading light of day as the sun streaked the sky a mix of vivid purple, pink, and orange. Each hour that passed, each month he counted off, put him that much closer to failing his family and his father's kingdom, Drahcir.

The bloody curse had been with his family for generations, generations that had managed to beat the curse and keep Drahcir and its people alive. But he had a sick feeling in the pit of his stomach that he would fail.

He ran a hand down his face, feeling more weary and exhausted than he had in months. He longed to speak to his family, especially his brothers. Four siblings had never been closer than he and his brothers. They had shared everything growing up, which made it all the harder when it came time for each of them to leave.

How long had he searched for his mate? How many women had he sought, only to realize they weren't for him?

How long had he been alone as he scoured Scotland for the woman who could save his kingdom?

And the answer to all questions was a resounding *too long*.

He was tired of wandering, tired of searching faces, and most importantly, he was tired of fearing that he would fail. As he had often of late, he let out a string of curses that would curl a saint's toes and wished he could see his ancestor that had meddled in the affairs of the Fae and resulted in the curse.

Elric leaned a shoulder against the side of the inn and crossed his arms. Autumn had descended on the Highlands and the cool night air helped to soften his growing ire. He had no wish to go inside the inn, but he must. He had to find his mate and return with her before the fifth moon of the Harvest Year, or the curse would wipe out Drahcir and its people.

All because his ancestor wanted to see if he could make a Fae princess fall in love with him.

Well, his ancestor had succeeded, but the fool hadn't stopped to think what would happen when the princess discovered he didn't love her. What she had done was put the curse not just on Elric's ancestor, but the entire Sinclair family.

He had asked his father once if the curse would ever end. Unfortunately, his father didn't have an answer, and Elric was afraid there wasn't one.

"I don't think you'll find what you seek standing out here."

Elric slowly turned his head to see who had dared to interrupt his private musings. What he saw gave him pause. He straightened from the building and turned to face the man. Long flaxen hair hung down to the middle of the man's back and was held away from his face by several rows of tiny braids. But it was his unusual shimmering blue eyes that alerted Elric he was standing before a Fae.

The Fae smiled. "I'm glad you know what I am. As for the who? You may call me Aimery. I am commander of the Fae army and here to aid you."

"Aid me? I didna think anyone was allowed to help us."

Aimery smiled and crossed his arms over his chest. That's when Elric noticed the Fae's curious clothes. The tunic and pants, though typical of the time, were not made of the coarse wool or even the finer material of the gentry. The fabric was unlike anything Elric had ever seen or would ever see.

"I'm not supposed to help," Aimery said, as though Elric wasn't staring at his clothing. "However, drastic times call for drastic measures."

"I doona understand."

Aimery sighed and let his arms fall to his side. "I know. Elric, you've searched for many years, and your time is running out. You should've found your mate by now."

"I know." Elric knew he should show the Fae more respect, but he wasn't telling Elric anything he didn't already know.

"You haven't found her because she isn't here."

Elric felt as if someone had knocked his feet out from underneath him. "What do you mean she isna here?"

"Exactly that. Your mate is not in this time."

He closed his eyes and leaned back against the inn. Of all the things he thought could go wrong to hinder him, this hadn't been one of them. He had been as certain as the sunrise that their mates were in Scotland, they just had to find them.

"Where in time is she?" Elric managed to croak out as he opened his eyes to gaze at Aimery.

"Many years into the future."

"Then I've failed since I can no' reach her."

Aimery grinned, a twinkle in his eyes. "That's where I come in."

Elric looked sideways at the Fae. "Why are you helping me?"

"Because when someone or something meddles, I like to make sure things are righted as they should be."

"Are you going to bring her here?"

Aimery shook his head, his smile fading quickly. "Nay, Elric. You'll go to her. It will be up to you to convince her to leave behind her world and travel back in time."

Elric swallowed hard, defeat a bitter taste in his mouth. He had known it wouldn't be easy to persuade his mate to return with him to his secret and hidden kingdom, but now he had the added pressure of convincing her to leave her time behind. An impossible task just grew more difficult.

But for his family, for his people, he would do whatever it took to find his mate. He longed to know her, to look into her eyes and know she was the one woman in all the world that was meant only for him.

He looked Aimery in the eye and nodded, determination filling him. "When do I leave?"

"Now. We can't waste any more time," Aimery said as he turned on his heel and began to walk out of the tiny village. "Your mate traveled to Scotland and is only visiting for a short while."

"Do you know anything else of her?" Elric asked. He knew better than to ask Aimery to describe her. It was up to Elric to determine who his soul mate was. He would know it as soon as he saw her, but explaining it would be difficult.

"Aye."

When Aimery didn't say more Elric realized he could ask all the questions he wanted, but the Fae commander wouldn't share any more with him. He was fine with it though, after all, Elric was known for his seduction.

3

Marin clapped along to the bagpipes as a group of local women danced a Highland jig. A smile pulled at her lips as she watched the villagers laughing and dancing.

"Now aren't you glad you came?" Rhonda asked, a knowing smile on her cute heart-shaped face.

Marin laughed as her friend was grabbed by a passing man and pulled into the throng of dancers. Rhonda's short red curls bounced as she followed the movements of the others.

Rhonda had been at the airport waiting as soon as Marin returned to Houston from Jamaica. No words were needed between the two as Marin walked into her friend's arms and let her tears flow. Rhonda had been a rock. Had it not been for her, Marin didn't know how she would have survived the past couple of months.

Though the more time that passed, the more Marin

found herself grateful that she wasn't married to Johnny. It felt good—right even—to make her own decisions again. She'd thrown out all the clothes she hated that Johnny had insisted she wear. Next was buying the makeup she loved to wear, and eating whatever food she wanted to again.

It had been…liberating.

"Good afternoon, lass," a handsome Scot said as he walked by, appreciation in his dark eyes.

Marin let her eyes roam over the tall man. His blonde hair was cut short and spiked on top, and his face was tanned, suggesting he spent a lot of time outdoors. The dark tartan of his kilt complimented his rugged features.

"He's interested," Rhonda said as she returned to Marin's side.

"But I'm not. He's cute, I'll grant you that, but I need some time before I dive back into those waters. Besides, we won't be here long."

Rhonda rolled her eyes and sighed. "At least you aren't pining over Johnny, that shithead."

Marin laughed. Leave it to Rhonda to tell it like it was. "You know I'm not. I was hurt he left me, but I know I'm better off without him."

"Amen!"

"That doesn't mean I'm ready to find another man."

"Sweetie," Rhonda said, as she wrapped her arm around Marin's shoulders. "No one said you had to have a relationship. Have a little fun with the handsome Scot with an accent that makes my knees weak. Besides, I think getting back in the saddle will remind you how fun it is to have a man who treats you right."

"Maybe you should be the one having a little fun with him."

Rhonda squeezed her shoulders. "You're not going to turn into a man-hater, are you?"

This time Marin rolled her eyes as she turned her head to look at her best friend. "Nope. I quite like men. I'm just easing my way into those waters."

"Girl, you're so far away from those waters you can't even see them."

Marin laughed and took a drink of her ale. She was still getting used to drinking it warm, but she liked it.

Rhonda dropped her arm and looked at the ground. "I should've gone with you."

Marin didn't need to ask what she was talking about. They'd had this talk several times, and no matter how many times she told Rhonda it was all right, her friend still felt responsible. It wasn't Rhonda's fault she worked for the largest private investigative company in Houston and landed a huge client two days before Marin left for Jamaica.

But Rhonda's job had allowed her to find Johnny for Marin. The weasel hadn't planned on marrying Marin in Jamaica. It seemed that a week before he accepted a job in St. Louis and boxed everything up and shipped it. As soon as they had arrived in Jamaica, he turned around and went back to the airport to take a return flight to the States.

Rhonda had found Johnny so Marin could confront him. At first, she'd been too numb, and then afterwards she just didn't care. With Johnny out of her life, everything came into focus again. She remembered her dreams, the things she wanted that somehow had been forgotten. In order to get those things, she had to forget the past. She had to forget Johnny.

"I need another ale," she said suddenly. "I didn't expect to like this as much as I do."

"Want me to get it?" Rhonda asked over the music.

Marin noticed her friend and the hunky Scot eyeing each other. "I think I can handle it," she said, then laughed when she realized Rhonda wasn't even listening.

She walked to the "bar" they had set up outside. Though the festival was outside and most of the natives had on just a thin long sleeve shirt and pants or kilt, Marin had a thick wool sweater she had bought the day before, and a coat. And she was still cold.

"Wish I'd have bought the gloves and scarf as well," she said as she blew into her hands.

The temperature was quite different from the hot, humid weather of southeast Texas. With a smile, she paid the bartender for the ale, then turned around to look for Rhonda. She wasn't surprised to see her friend talking to the handsome Scot. Marin looked around the quaint little town and the ruins of a great castle high up on the hill.

History had never been a subject she enjoyed, but she found herself intrigued with the ruins and the ancient people of Scotland. The more she stared at the ruins, the more she found herself drawn to them.

"A new day, a new life," she said as she started walking to the ruins for a closer inspection.

***

Elric didn't know what to expect when Aimery said they would travel through time, but he wasn't prepared to be hurled through a dark space with sound so loud he thought he might never hear again. He didn't question Aimery when the Fae told him to keep his eyes closed.

And as soon as it began, it stopped.

"Open your eyes," he heard Aimery say from beside him.

Elric slowly cracked his eyes open, expecting to still be

tumbling head over heels as he was sure he had been just moments ago, yet he stood still and straight.

"Look through the doorway."

Still a little disoriented, Elric did as Aimery commanded and found himself looking through what seemed to be an oval entry way that shimmered like the waters of a loch. Except these waters were clear, and as he gazed through it, he found himself watching several groups of people celebrating.

"You're in the year 2013," Aimery explained. "The Scots of this time still celebrate the Scottish heritage. They love to wear their kilts, which I've made sure you have to fit in."

Elric swallowed and glanced down to find his tunic and trews gone, replaced by a kilt. "It's rather…freeing. When do my countrymen begin to wear these?"

"Around the seventeenth century. You'll get used to it."

"Already have." He grasped his sword. "They doona wear weapons."

"Many things have changed. You should leave your sword with me, but I'm afraid you might need it."

It was something in Aimery's voice that caught his attention. He tore his gaze from the oval to the Fae. "Need it for what?"

"The Tnargs."

Elric's entire body shuddered. "They're real?"

"Very much so. One attacked Lucian when he returned to Drahcir."

"You spoke to Lucian? Why didna you say so? Is he all right? Did he make it?"

"Yes. You didn't ask, and yes and yes," Aimery said, with a small smile. The smile dropped suddenly. "Be vigilant. If I knew your mate was in another time, chances are, the Tnargs do as well."

Elric nodded and stepped toward the shimmering wall of water, only to have Aimery stop him with a hand on his shoulder. "When you and your mate are ready to leave, return to this spot. The doorway will be hidden, but if you know what you're looking for, you'll be able to use it. Don't step through unless you have your mate, for I cannot take you back to her time again."

With a deep breath, Elric regarded Aimery for a moment. "Thank you for helping me."

"Just return with your mate," Aimery said.

Without another word, Elric stepped through the doorway. He anticipated being drenched, but it was as if the water wasn't there, only a mirage. He scanned the crowded valley below as he tried to get a feel for the time.

Bagpipes sounded around him as a group of people danced and sang. Another group was crowded around different makeshift shops as they hawked their wares. The last group was near a structure that sold only liquids, and if Elric knew anything about his countrymen, he knew they were drinking ale.

A smile pulled at his lips. A large tankard of ale sounded delicious, but he wanted to look around the area first. No one seemed to have noticed that he appeared out of nowhere, and he wanted it kept that way.

Aimery had been right. Most of the men wore kilts, but it was the women who surprised him. Gone were the gowns that molded to their curves, and in their place were thick shirts that hung limply on their forms and tight pants that gave a hint to their backsides.

Elric had always been kidded by his brothers that he was a traditionalist, and in this case, he was. He didn't like the clothes worn by the women and hoped his mate wore something less...distasteful.

People nodded and smiled as he passed them. He hoped Aimery brought him to the town where his mate was so that he didn't have to travel this Scotland in search of her. But he wasn't taking any chances. He would search the festival first, and then if he didn't find her, he would search the surrounding villages.

As he passed a tall Scotsman with blond hair—that he had cut too short on top—and a woman with short red curls, he noticed how both stared at him. He gave a nod of hello and continued on, but felt their stares long after he had passed.

It didn't take long to walk the festival and search the women. None were his mate. The disappointment that welled up inside threatened to choke him. He breathed in the Highland air and lifted his face to the sky. The sun broke through the thick clouds and gave some warmth to the ever-increasing chill.

Elric found his gaze drawn to the old ruins of a castle. "What has this time come to if they let a castle fall?" he murmured to himself.

It took men scores of years to build the mammoth structures, and it was a sad sight to see it destroyed. Just as he was about to turn away, he spotted a lone figure atop the hill gazing at the castle. The sun was behind her, silhouetting her as her long dark hair lifted in the wind.

A fission of awareness snaked down Elric's spine. His blood quickened as he gazed at the woman. He began to move toward her. The closer he got, the faster his heart beat. Could it be, after all these years, he had finally found his mate? Could it really be that easy?

He walked up from behind. He wanted more time to study her, to gather his thoughts on what he would say. At one time he had planned everything out, down to the last sentence of what he would say to his mate. Yet now as he approached her, he couldn't recall anything of his speech.

A gust of wind whipped around him as he reached the top of the hill. He watched as she wrapped her arms around herself in a bid for warmth. Her wavy auburn hair danced about her head as she stared at the castle. He couldn't tell much about her figure through the thick, bulky clothes she wore, much to his disappointment.

Just as Elric was about to approach, another man walked up and tried to talk to her. It was obvious from the man's staggering and slurred speech that he had imbibed too much.

"A pretty lass such as yerself doesna need to be alone," he said.

She turned her head toward the man and Elric got a better view of her profile. "Thank you for the offer of company, but I'm fine."

Her accent intrigued him. Aimery had said she was visiting Scotland, but from where, Elric had no idea.

"Ah, an American," the man said, and moved closer.

Elric didn't know what an 'American' was, but he didn't like how close the man was to her. He walked closer in case he needed to protect her.

"Please," she said, and turned her face from him. "I thank you for the hospitality, but I just want to be alone."

"I can no' do that."

Elric had had enough. With his tone soft and unthreatening he said, "Listen to the woman and leave her alone."

His gaze was drawn to the woman when she faced him. With his breath locked in his lungs, he stared into her oval face, memorizing every detail from her high cheek bones, small chin, and plump kissable lips. Her skin was the color of cream, her eyes a beautiful hazel mix of soft brown and dark green.

He was entranced, captivated.

Fascinated.

Marin heard the second male voice behind her and turned to face the newcomer. By his easy tone she wasn't expecting the very virile, very handsome man before her. If there was ever a picture in the dictionary beside the word warrior, it would be this man.

He was the definition of rugged Highlander. Though he sported a kilt, it was a little different from the rest of the Scots at the festival. And the white shirt beneath it certainly wasn't the polyester blend the others wore. In fact, it looked rather…authentic. Marin swallowed when she noticed the sword at his hip. By the way his hand casually rested on the hilt, it wasn't there for show.

Her gaze jerked back to his face, and her mouth went dry. She'd heard about instant lust before, but until that moment had no idea what it was. One look at the Scot and she couldn't catch her breath.

His mahogany locks hung well past his shoulders, making him even more striking. She'd always had a thing for men with long hair, and this Highlander pulled it off to perfection.

Her eyes roamed over his face to find a high forehead along with a small dent in his nose that suggested it had been broken. His cheeks were hollow, his mouth sinfully wide with the bottom lip fuller than the top. Dark brows slashed over his green eyes, the same vibrant green as the grass and trees.

Marin tried to swallow as she noted his wide shoulders and the thick sinew she glimpsed as he turned to her unwanted visitor.

"You've had too much to drink this day, my friend," the man said to the drunk. "There are plenty of women below who need your attention."

The drunk looked from the warrior to the festival. "Aye. Ye're right," he said, and walked away.

For several minutes Marin watched the drunk stumble his way down the steep slope to the crowd in the valley. She had wanted to be alone with the castle ruins, and was about to ask the warrior if he could leave, when she raised her eyes and found him staring at her intently.

There was something in his gaze that made her very… aware…of him. The very air sizzled with a current of lust she couldn't dispel, and wasn't sure she even wanted to. Did he feel it too? Is that why he looked at her with such a smoldering stare?

"My name is Elric Sinclair."

His voice was as smooth as velvet, as dark as sin. It sent her blood rushing through her, warming her as nothing else had been able to. No longer did she feel the cold, not with his beautiful green eyes watching her. "Thank you for your aid."

"I'm no' one to leave a damsel in distress."

Marin found herself smiling. "Now that is something I've never been called."

His dark brows rose as he crossed his arms over his thick chest, his arms bulging with muscles. Her gaze raked over his thick legs, narrow waist, and wide chest to his face. His green eyes studied her silently.

"I see you like our history," he said after a moment.

Marin glanced over her shoulder at the ruins. "I think it

sad that such a significant part of Britain's history is left to this."

"Britain, aye?" he said with a frown. "But no' all castles are torn down?"

Was it her imagination or had he asked that as a question? "No," she said and turned to the castle. She felt Elric move beside her, but he didn't get too close. She realized she had never given him her name. "By the way, I'm Marin. Marin Chapel."

He smiled and bowed slightly. "Nice to meet you, Marin. An unusual name you have."

"My parents liked the unusual."

"That isna always bad."

Marin tried to ignore the pull of Elric's body and the way his brogue made her knees weak. It was like he had some kind of magic power over her that she wasn't able to deflect. She could hear every breath he took, sense every glance of his eyes.

"You feel it, do you no'?" he asked softly.

She jumped and looked at him. Her lips parted, but she didn't know how to answer.

"You feel the draw of Scotland's history," he said, with a slight pull of his lips. "They say that if you can feel the draw that you were Scottish in another life."

Marin closed her lips and licked them as she tried to pull herself together. There was definitely something about Scotland that put her off kilter. Or it had as soon as Elric showed up. "I've never heard that saying, but I suppose it could be true."

"So you believe in past lives?"

She shrugged and tried not to notice how intense he had suddenly become. "I don't disbelieve or believe it. I've seen no proof either way to show me that it is or isn't true."

The intense light of his green eyes dimmed. "Ah," he said sadly.

"Do you believe in past lives?" Marin found herself asking.

"I most certainly do. When two people meet and feel a connection that goes deeper than anything they can explain, a love so strong, so true that it could only be they are soul mates…then it proves past lives."

"How?"

He turned to face her, moving closer as he did. Marin didn't back away. She was captivated by the Scot, and wanted to know more about him, about Scotland, about anything he wanted to tell her.

"When two souls find each other again and again in different lifetimes, their love grows stronger, allowing them to find the other quicker each lifetime. 'Tis magic."

She had never thought of anything like that before, and it gave her pause. "How do you know this?"

"I've seen it," he simply said.

She glanced at the crumbling ruins of the castle and the weeds and ivy that covered the few stones that stood upright. "What happens if the souls don't find each other?"

"They continue looking in the next lifetime."

"You sound so certain."

He smiled seductively. "That's because I am. Do you no' believe in love?"

"Oh, I believe," she said. "My parents were madly in love with each other. It used to embarrass me as a kid, but as I grew older I realized what a precious thing my parents had."

"Are they still alive?"

Marin shook her head. "They were rarely apart, and that was true even in death. They died within weeks of each other. It was as if Dad couldn't live without Mom."

"I'm sorry."

There was only kindness in his eyes, and Marin realized it felt good to talk about her parents and the love they had, a love she doubted she would ever find. "Do you believe in love?"

"Most certainly."

He said it with such conviction that it left her speechless for a minute. "Have you found your soul mate?"

He nodded.

Marin sighed and wrapped her arms around herself. "You're very lucky then. Not many people are so sure of such things."

"Come with me," Elric said, and held out his hand to her.

For a man who had found his soul mate, he was spending a lot of time with her. She wanted to tell him to go back to his woman, but she couldn't. She wanted him to herself. "Where?"

"Into the ruins," he said and took her hand when she didn't offer it. "Let me show you what it was like inside a castle."

Marin let her cares go as she laughed while Elric pulled her after him. And once she entered the ruins, it was like she had walked through an invisible doorway that brought her senses to life.

She took a deep breath and smelled the earthy scent of Scotland and the history of the castle. Her gaze wandered over the weathered gray stones as she imagined what the castle had been like before it had been destroyed.

"Close your eyes," Elric whispered into her ear as he came up behind her.

Chills raced down Marin's spine and across her skin. It never entered her thoughts not to do as he asked. She could feel the length of him against her, his heat surrounding her, and his warm breath fanning her neck. She had the sudden and nearly uncontrollable urge to lean into him.

"Listen close and you can hear Scotland opening her past up to you," his deep, velvety voice spoke softly. "The castle is alive with activity. A fire roars in the great hall, servants scold children as they race through the hall and try to get sweetmeats, and the mistress of the castle readies everything for the evening meal. Her husband walks through the door, searching for her. He spots her near the dais where they would sup and hurries to her."

Marin could feel, hear, and see all that Elric whispered in her ear. It was as he had said, Scotland opened her history for her to glimpse inside.

"The lord stops in front of his lady wife," Elric continued as he slowly walked around her.

Marin desperately wanted to open her eyes, to look at Elric. But at the same time, she wanted to see what the past held. She reached out with her hands and touched Elric's abdomen. His stomach clenched, but he didn't push her away. Instead, he walked closer so that her arms were nearly around his waist.

"His lady gives him a welcoming smile, seeing the desire and heat in her husband's eyes. He doesna take her upstairs as she wishes. Instead, he teases her."

Marin opened her mouth to ask how the lord teased his wife when Elric's hand came to rest on her back and gently pulled her toward him.

4

*E*lric was nearly undone with desire. He stared at Marin's elegant beauty. Her wavy auburn hair hung just past her shoulders, and he wanted nothing more than to bury his hands in her hair and pull her against him for a searing kiss.

Somehow he held himself in check. He couldn't ravish his mate upon first meeting her. She was already skittish. If he didn't tread carefully, all would be for naught.

He gazed down at her full, wide lips and lifted his hand. "The lord teases his wife with his finger," he said, and traced Marin's dark pink lips. He saw her tremble and lean toward him. "The lord sees his wife's desire flare in her eyes, yet still doesn't take her to their chamber."

Elric had always been a master of seduction, but it had never backfired on him so thoroughly before. He wanted Marin with a ferocity that frightened him. His cock throbbed with need, and the urge to back her against the wall and bury himself inside of her was strong—nearly too strong to ignore.

He knew she felt something by the way her body

quivered, and it wasn't because of the chill. She might not realize they were soul mates, but given a little time she would understand what bonded them.

As much as he wanted her right then, the first time with his mate would be somewhere warm and seductive, not in the middle of the castle ruins where someone could walk upon them.

Suddenly, Marin's eyes flew open. She searched his face and backed away a step as she slowly shook her head.

"It's useless to fight the pull of Scotland, Marin," he said softly. "Once she has touched your soul, she'll always be a part of you."

"It isn't Scotland I'm worried about."

Elric knew he had frightened her, but it wasn't him exactly as much as it was what connected them. She had a lost look about her, a fragility that made him want to take her in his arms and protect her from the world. Yet, he sensed great strength in her as well. "You've been hurt by someone," he said as it suddenly dawned on him.

She shrugged, a defensive look coming over her lovely face. "Hasn't everyone been hurt at one time or another?"

"What did the bastard do?"

She turned her back to him. Elric leaned against the stones and waited with a casual stance that belied the fury within him. The wind whipped through the ruins, whistling softly as it brushed past them. It was almost as if they were the only two people in the world, and only the laughter and music from the valley below reminded him differently.

"He left me," Marin said so softly Elric didn't think he had heard her correctly. "On the day of our wedding. He left me."

Elric clenched his jaw and fought the anger that swept over him. "Did he at least tell you why?"

Her auburn hair swung side to side as she shook her head.

"He's a cowardly bastard that doesna deserve you then."

She turned toward him, a small smile on her face. "Most people just tell me how sorry they are, they never say anything about Johnny. But I know now that it all worked out for the best."

"Is that his name? Johnny?" Elric asked, distaste curling his lip.

"Yes."

"I could've told you just by his name, lass, that he wasna the man for you."

Her smile widened. "Is that so? Well, I'm not in the market for a man at the moment, but I'll be sure to seek you out when I am."

He wasn't deterred by her lack of wanting male attention. "Are you no' the least bit curious what name I would say?"

"A little." She cocked her head to the side and regarded him a moment. "All right, what name would you say?"

Elric pushed off the stones and walked toward her. "You need a man who will be strong for you. A man who will support you in all you do and be there for you when you need him." He walked around her, breathing in her fresh, clean scent. "You need a man who will protect you from the evils of the world, a man who would cherish you and love you all the days of his life." He stopped in front of her and stared into her hazel eyes. "You need a man who you could trust unequivocally."

"There isn't such a man that I've found."

"You have no' looked in the right places." He stepped closer and tugged a strand of hair caught in her long eyelashes.

"I'm not looking at all right now."

"Ah, did you no' know that's when fate seeks you out?" he asked, and leaned close until his mouth was inches from hers.

He stopped just short of kissing her. With a wink, he turned and walked away.

Marin blinked into the mirror, her thoughts on Elric as it had been most of the day. For long moments after he had nearly kissed her, she stayed and watched as he returned to the festival and disappeared into the crowd. Only then did she drag in a ragged breath. She had looked at the ruins and was able to continue to feel Elric beside her, his warmth calming her.

All she had thought about after that had been Elric. And no matter how many times she glanced up seeking him out in the crowd, he wasn't to be found. It was like he just disappeared. He was intense and seductive and entirely too charming for his own good. And damned handsome as well. It was a lethal combination.

And by the time she dressed for dinner, she convinced herself that Elric had just been a figment of her imagination.

"I've lost my mind," she said aloud. It must be Scotland and her history that made her feels things that weren't normal. At least, that was the only explanation she could come up with.

She looked at her reflection in the mirror and gazed at the long, full black and silver skirt and a form-fitting black sweater, one of the nicest outfits she had packed. She wasn't sure why she decided to wear it since she was just having dinner with Rhonda, but it had felt right. She had even put on the black and silver chandelier earrings and necklace.

Marin had never been one to lie to herself, and the poor attempt to tell herself that she was dressing this nice to impress Rhonda was a bad lie. She was dressing in the hopes of seeing Elric.

It was silly and stupid, but the idea that he could be there sent a spike of lust so hot, so fierce through her that she had to hold onto the wall to keep herself upright.

There was a quick knock on the door adjoining her's and Rhonda's rooms before it opened and Rhonda stepped in. She whistled and came to stand beside Marin. "So you did meet a man today."

Marin frowned. "Why do you say that?"

"A woman doesn't dress like that unless she has a date. You look fabulous, sweetie. Who is the man? Was he at the festival?"

Marin turned away from the mirror and went to the closet to find her shoes. She tugged on the tall, high-heeled boots and zipped them. "I'm an idiot. I'm not ready to date, to have dinner, to have sex. I'm not ready for anything."

"Is that why you're dressed in a killer outfit that would make a saint drool?" Rhonda asked, her arms crossed over her chest and her brows raised.

Marin sighed loudly. "I don't really know. I did meet someone. He's very different, Rhonda. He's handsome, intense, seductive, and oh so sexy. It was like no matter how hard I tried to pull away from him, there was an invisible rubber band that snapped me back."

"Then stop fighting it," her friend said as she sat beside her on the small couch. "You deserve some happiness, and if a kilt-wearing, handsome Scotsman is interested, then run, don't walk, to him."

She laughed at Rhonda's words and gave her friend a hug. "Thank you."

"You're welcome."

"No," Marin said and took her hands. "Thank you for everything. For not telling me how stupid I was not to see the asswipe Johnny really was, for not telling me 'I told you so', and for not letting me wallow in my self-pity."

Rhonda shrugged and blinked away tears. "What are friends for? Besides, we always said we'd visit Britain together."

"You're the best. The sister I never had."

"Ditto. Now," Rhonda said, and stood up. "Stop this now or we'll both be blubbering idiots, and you'll have to redo your makeup."

Marin quickly applied her lipstick as she covertly watched Rhonda checking her watch. "You're not coming to dinner with me, are you?"

"No," Rhonda said, her face scrunched in her 'I'm sorry' mode. "I've got a date. With Lachlan, the handsome Scot."

"Good," Marin said as she replaced the lipstick in her bag. "Have fun and be careful."

"Oh, I will." Rhonda drew on her coat. "Don't do anything I wouldn't do," she called as she walked back into her room.

Marin took a deep breath before she exited her room. It was too bad the small inn didn't have room service. She didn't relish eating alone, but she had to eat. It was just after seven as she slowly made her way down the stairs. She let her eyes scan the dining room/bar as she reached the bottom step.

The room was crowded, but not too loud. She found an empty table near the large fireplace and walked to it. She sat, and instantly a young waitress was there to take her order.

Marin ordered a glass of wine and the special of the night, which was some kind of grilled fish.

Marin didn't have long to wait before the wine was placed in front of her. She sipped her drink and stared into the fire as she recalled her conversation with Elric. Word for word. The fact she had wanted his kiss, had felt bereft when he left her, made her take stock of herself.

No man had left her feeling so…off kilter. She wanted Elric's company now, to listen to his lilting accent and feel his heat. The current was charged when he was near, making her nervous and excited all at the same time.

She leaned back in her chair and suddenly felt that current. He was watching her. Slowly, Marin let her gaze wander the room until she saw him in the corner alone. Elric gave her a smile and slightly nodded his head in her direction.

There was something about the feral look in his eyes that made her heart pound and her stomach flip. When he suddenly stood and walked to her, Marin's stomach dropped to her feet as she grew more and more nervous.

"Eating by yourself?" Elric asked as he reached her.

She nodded and glanced at the chair opposite her. "Would you like to join me?"

"Aye, I would. Thank you." He pulled out the chair and sank into it. "Do I frighten you?"

Marin gazed at the man before her. He wasn't the typical twenty-first century man. While most had changed from their kilts to jeans and a sweater, Elric still wore his kilt.

She licked her lips and tried to form a response to his question. "You do, and I'm not sure why. It's not just because I've been hurt. I feel different when I'm around you."

"Different how?"

"I can't explain it."

He smiled and leaned back in his chair. "Are you hungry?"

She was, but not for food. Marin nearly fell out of her chair at her thought. She looked away from Elric's knowing green gaze to her hands. "Not really."

"Good," he said and suddenly rose. He took her hand and tugged her to her feet. "Come with me."

"Where are we going this time?" she asked, a little frightened, yet thrilled. She had never been so impulsive or adventurous.

The enthusiasm waned as they left the small hotel. The chill of the day was gone, and in its place a damp, cold night had descended. Marin shivered and wrapped her arms around herself. She needed her jacket.

"Do you ride?"

She turned and looked at Elric. "Ride? Ride what?"

He chuckled and grabbed her hand again as he walked around the hotel. "Horses, Marin. Horses."

"I'm from Texas, of course I ride horses."

"Good," was all he said as he continued.

They didn't stop until they came to the barn at the back of the hotel. Elric released her hand long enough to open the stable door, then shut it after her. Marin inhaled the smell of horses and smiled. She had always loved horses.

She slowly followed Elric as he walked through the stables until he came to the back. There, a young man stood holding a horse. One horse. Did Elric expect her to ride alone? If he did, he was in for a rude awakening.

He patted the young man on the shoulder and took the reins from him, then turned to Marin. "Are you ready?"

"Who is going to ride?"

That sexy, secretive smile of Elric's returned. "Why, both of us."

Marin's breath lodged in her throat. No one had ever done anything so romantic, so seductive, so…thoughtful for her. She took Elric's hand and let him lift her onto the horse before he mounted behind her. His thick arms came around her and held the reins.

"Do you trust me?" he asked into her ear.

To her surprise she said, "Yes."

With that, he nudged the horse and they cantered out of the stables into the cool night air. She let herself lean back against his wide chest as he maneuvered the horse. With every step of the horse, she became more and more aware of Elric and his body surrounding hers. His long legs molded to her, easily guiding the horse.

Her bottom rubbed against his groin, and there was no mistaking the hard bulge that she felt. Just knowing he wanted her made her nipples harden and moisture gather between her legs. His warm breath fanned her neck and cheek as he wrapped an arm about her waist to hold her close. His arm, nestled just under her breasts, was nearly too much to bear.

She wanted him, wanted to feel his hands on her breasts. Her body was a mass of quivering nerves by the time he stopped the horse. For a long moment they sat in silence, and that's when she finally noticed where they were—the ruins of the castle.

When Elric slid off the horse, Marin instantly missed his warmth. She hadn't noticed the cold when his body surrounded hers, but now it was quickly seeping into her bones. He held out his arms, and she moved into them. Slowly, he slid her down his body, his eyes boring into hers.

But she couldn't look away. She was drowning in his green depths and the desire she saw there.

His fingers intertwined with hers as he quietly led her into the ruins. She hadn't noticed the back part of the castle before, the part that hadn't been torn down. It wasn't until Elric led her to the stairs that she saw part of the castle could still be inhabitable.

A torch was mounted at the base of the stairs, and Elric grabbed it as they started up. Through the narrow climb, Marin couldn't help but feel as if she were going back in time. The light from the torch cast shadows on the wall, but she wasn't scared. She knew Elric would protect her. He was her warrior.

And when he stopped in front of a door and faced her, the torch held high to shed light, she knew what was inside.

"You know why I brought you here?" he asked.

"Yes."

"If you want to leave, tell me now, and I'll return you to the inn."

She'd never been so sure of anything in her life. Elric, their meeting, her dining alone. It had all led to this, to him. But words would never be able to give him an explanation.

To answer him, she opened the door and stepped inside. Her heart skidded in her chest when she saw the multitude of candles and the pile of blankets on the floor. Her body quivered with a desire so deep and strong that she wondered if she would ever be the same after this night.

Elric shut the door and put the torch in its holder, then turned to face Marin. She looked like a goddess in the light of the many candles. She was magnificent with desire glazing her eyes.

He took a step toward her and wondered if he should tell her everything before he made love to her, or wait until after her body was sated. She answered his silent question when she held out her hands to him.

Making love to women had always been second nature to Elric, but this time…this time was different. Marin was different. She was his mate, and he wanted their first time to be something they always remembered and cherished.

When his hand took hers, he found his shook slightly. His blood pounded loudly in his ears, and his heart thumped wildly in his chest as his thickening cock begged for release. He gently pulled her to him until their bodies touched. His eyes moved across her lovely face and stopped at her mouth.

Her lips were parted and her chest rose and fell swiftly,

as if she too anticipated what was between them. In the distance the soft sounds of a lute and violin filled the air.

Elric laced his fingers with hers and began to move with the music. His eyes never left her face, not even when she closed hers and swayed with him. Elric didn't know how long they moved with the music as it wove its spell around them. All he knew was that he was alone with Marin, his mate, and he was going to claim her and her body as his.

Slowly, he ran his hands up her arms, over her shoulders to her slender neck. He cupped her face with his hands and gently traced her lips with his thumb. Her warm breath skidded over his skin, heating his already hot blood.

He wanted to strip off her clothes, lay her down on the blankets and plunge into her. His need for her had grown until it was drowning him. He lowered his head until his lips brushed hers. A smile pulled at his mouth when he heard her sharp intake of breath.

Her hands gently came to rest on his waist as she leaned into him. The feel of her full breasts pressed against his chest caused his balls to tighten with anticipation. Yet, somehow, he held back.

He let his tongue trace where his thumbs had been before he gently nipped at the corners of her mouth.

"Elric...please," Marin murmured.

He shifted his arms until one cradled her head and the other moved to her back as he pressed her tightly against him. Then, he took her in a kiss that held all his hopes, desires, and needs.

Her arms snaked around his back as her nails raked across him. A sigh escaped her as she leaned her head to the side and thrust her tongue against his. Elric broke the kiss and looked deep within her hazel eyes. He smoothed back tendrils of hair from her face and found that he wanted to tell her everything about the curse, his kingdom, and her role in it. It suddenly became very important to him that she know everything before he took her body, because once they were joined, there was no turning back.

"Marin, I must tell you something," he began, but she put her finger on his lips to stay him.

"Not now," she said softly. "I don't know if it's this land, the history, you, or the magic of this night, but I don't want to talk. I want to feel. Make me forget the outside world, Elric, even if it's only for a few hours."

Elric wasn't about to deny her, not when he saw the look of need in her hazel eyes. He took her hand and led her to the pile of blankets he had readied for them. Once she sat, he kneeled in front of her and reached for a foot. He tried to tug off the shoe, but it wouldn't budge. It wasn't until she reached for a little contraption on the side of the boot and pulled it down that he was able to pull off the boot. He found the little contraption on the other shoe and pulled it down, hearing a soft zipping sound as he did.

Once both boots were off, he looked down to find her legs encased in wool stockings. He raised his brows at her. "The air doesna hold that great of a chill."

"It does for me. I'm not used to his cold."

He forgot about the wool stockings as he leaned forward for another kiss. Her lips were like nectar from the Fae. He couldn't get enough of her sweet taste. Gently, he leaned into her until she lay back on the blankets, and though he wanted to cover her body with his, he didn't. He supported himself with his arms, hovering just over her as he took her lips again and again.

He shifted to her side as he kissed along her neck and nipped at her ears. His hand reached to the buttons on her sweater. When he had them all opened, he lifted his head and gazed down at her body. A black and silver flimsy garment held her breasts. He found himself intrigued and traced the top of the lace.

A soft sigh passed through her lips. Elric glanced at her and smiled. "What is this?"

"A bra," she said, and licked her lips. "It helps to hold me."

"Hmmm," he murmured as he bent down and kissed the top of each breast. The bra was not only beautiful, but Elric found it quite…erotic. The women of his time wore nothing like it, and though he wanted to inspect it, he wanted to taste her breasts more.

He pushed her shirt off her shoulders, then sat her up to pull it completely off. To his surprise, Marin reached around her back and unfastened the bra. His breath locked in his chest as the lace fell away. The light from the candles set a soft glow to her skin, and as he watched, her nipples hardened before his eyes.

Yet, when he reached for her, she hurried to stand. He turned to see what she was about and found her reaching underneath her skirts. Curiosity held him still, and it wasn't long before he saw her tug off her wool stockings. She gave him a shy smile. In return, he leaned back on his hands and let his eyes roam over her.

"Take the skirt off," he said.

No woman had ever taken her clothes off for him, and he found he quite liked it. As Marin unfastened her skirt and let it drop to her feet, he dug his fingers into the blankets to keep him still.

More black and silver lace hid her sex from him, and just as with the bra, he found the hint of her woman's hair barely visible through the lace almost more than he could bear.

He sat forward and grabbed her hand to tug her to him.

Elric ran his hands over the lace and looked up at her. "Do you know what this does to me?"

She shook her head as she licked her lips. Her auburn curls danced around her face as she gazed down at him.

"The sight of this barely hiding your sex from me drives me wild. I want to lay you down and bury myself inside of you."

"They're panties," she said, her voice shaky.

"They're coming off."

Elric caught the waist of her panties and pulled them over her hips and down her legs until she stepped out of them. And then she stood before him in all her glory. With her full breasts, trim waist, flared hips, and lean legs, Marin was perfect in his eyes.

"You're magnificent," he said as he tried to pull her down to him.

She shook her head and smiled as she squatted in front of him and began to tug off his boots. Elric watched as her hands gently pried off his boots, then reached for his tunic.

He unfastened the pin that held his tartan in place over his heart and set it aside. He sucked in a breath when her soft hands met his flesh as she pulled his shirt over his head. For a long moment, they simply stared at each other, then Elric rose to his feet.

With Marin kneeling in front of him, she unfastened his sporran and gently set it down. Her gaze moved briefly to him before she reached for his kilt. After a few moments, he realized she didn't know what she was doing, and with just a flick of his wrist, the kilt dropped to the ground. He smiled as her eyes grew round.

"You really don't wear anything under the kilt."

"Nay," he said, and sat beside her. He lifted her chin until her eyes met his. "I want you, Marin. I willna lie about it, but I'll give you one more chance to change your mind and leave."

"I want to stay. I like how I feel when I'm with you."

With her words, the dam broke on his control. He cupped the back of her head and pulled her against him for a fiery kiss that soon turned frantic with need. His cock begged for release, but he held tight his restraint and learned Marin's body.

Her skin was soft as lamb's wool and her body as responsive as only a mate's could be.

Marin closed her eyes and gave up to the delicious feel of Elric's hands and mouth on her body as she fell back and he moved over her. He knew just how to touch her and just where to touch her. It was as if he had delved into her deepest fantasies and given them all to her in one night.

She was adrift in a sea of lust so deep she might never find the shore. And she wasn't sure she wanted to.

Her breasts grew heavy as his fingers grazed the undersides and his mouth kissed her neck. The heat of his body surrounded her and drove her wild for his touch. He teased, he kissed, and he licked her neck and all around her breasts. Everything but her nipples.

She was going crazy with need. Her hands ran over his thick shoulders and neck as his muscles moved beneath her hands. She arched her back as his finger came close to her nipple, and just as she thought he would finally give her some release, he moved away.

Marin bit her lip and sighed as his warm mouth kissed between the valley of her breasts. Finally, he cupped her breasts, sending tiny spasms of pleasure through her. And just when she thought she would die from need, he gently ran his fingers across her nipple.

A soft cry tore from her throat as desire shot through her. As if to torment her, he ran his finger all around her nipple, sometimes touching, sometimes not. He tormented first one breast, then the other, until her breasts were aching and full. Only then did he take a nipple in his mouth and suck.

The feel of his warm mouth on her nipple sent liquid heat through her. Her sex clenched with need, and she rubbed her hips against him, seeking the release she knew he could give.

But the torment to her breasts was far from over. He flicked his tongue over one nipple as his fingers squeezed and plucked at the other. Her fingers plunged into his thick, dark hair as her body melted against him.

When he sat up and trailed a hand over her breasts and down her stomach, Marin opened her eyes to watch him. The way he gazed at her body made her feel beautiful and loved, something she had never experienced before.

Marin didn't know whether to be shocked or excited at the ease in which her body responded to Elric and how much she trusted him. When he parted her legs, she didn't hesitate or refuse. She opened them, letting his gaze linger on her sex. The sight of his eyes feasting on her hungry sex made her blood heat with longing. She wanted to be everything Elric thought she was and more. And the one thing she feared above all was disappointing him.

She forgot all about her fears when his hands moved over her thighs. And just as he had with her breasts, he teased her again. His hands touched her thighs, her stomach and her hips, but never the place that sought him the most.

Her hands clenched the blankets as she fought to keep her body still.

Her senses were in a riot. She could hear her blood pound in her veins, her breath leave her lungs, and her heart beat wildly in her chest. She could feel the heat from Elric's body, his hard muscles and his gentle caresses over her skin. She could still taste the seduction and need in Elric's kiss.

So when his finger finally delved in her moist folds, she didn't hold back her cry of pleasure. His finger moved over her tiny bud, bringing ripples of bliss shooting through her. And when he pushed a finger inside of her, Marin sighed.

He settled between her legs, his breath fanning her hot, moist center and driving her wild. Marin could feel the pleasure building with each stroke of his finger inside of her, bringing her higher and higher. And when his tongue touched her tiny bud, she shattered into a million pieces as her orgasm claimed her.

Before the last of the tremors left her body, Marin opened her eyes to see Elric rise over her, the blunt head of his thick arousal poised to enter her. She smiled and reached for him. He entered her in one fluid motion, burying himself to the hilt. She wrapped her legs around his waist and waited for him to reach his own climax.

But when he began to move within her, Marin felt herself building toward another orgasm. His thrusts went deeper, faster, and harder. She clung to him as her world began to spin out of control. Her body erupted in a tidal wave of intense pleasure.

Elric plunged deep inside of her before stiffening and crying out his pleasure.

6

*M*arin's eyes grew heavy as she lay on Elric's chest, his arm idly caressing her back. She smiled at the exquisite lovemaking they had shared. It had been…soul-stirring, shattering whatever shell she'd put herself in after the disaster in Jamaica. She wasn't naïve enough to think this happened every day. She knew first-hand how fortunate she was to have found Elric, but she also didn't expect him to stay.

She had to return to the US in just a few days. But until then, she was going to spend as much of it with him as he wanted. Just thinking of leaving Scotland and Elric seemed…wrong.

"What is on your toes?" Elric suddenly asked.

Marin leaned up and lifted her foot. "Nothing."

"You have colored your toes."

She giggled and lay back on his chest. "I painted my toenails, if that's what you mean."

"Do you do that often?"

She found his question puzzling, and as she thought of the night and his not knowing what a bra and panties were, she knew something wasn't right. "How do you not know about nail polish? And for that matter, did you really not know what my bra and panties were?"

"Nay," he answered without hesitation. "I didna know what you wore, nor do I know about this polish you speak of that you put on your toes."

Marin sat up and looked at him. At one time in her life she would have pulled the blanket up to cover her nakedness, but she felt at ease with her body around him. She'd think about that later. Right now she was focused on learning why he didn't know such basic things. "How is it you don't know?"

He took a deep breath and ran a hand down his face before he sat up. "Our meeting wasna an accident, lass."

"What do you mean? Have you been stalking me?"

Elric's brow furrowed. "I doona know what you mean. I've been searching for you, aye."

"Why me? I'm not anyone special."

"You're verra special to me and my kingdom."

Marin blinked, her heart missing a beat. "Did you say kingdom?"

"Aye. I am from Scotland, Marin, but no' the Scotland you know."

Her skin went cold as his words penetrated her mind. "You're scaring me."

Elric rose to his feet and reached for his kilt. "That isna my intent. There is so much to tell you, but I doona know where to begin. I had thought this would be easier."

"Just tell me. Please." Since he was getting dressed, Marin reached for her bra and panties and slipped them on, then hurried to finish dressing. She was zipping her boots when she looked up to find him braced against one of the windows as he gazed outside, a longing on his face that made her take a step toward him.

"My family is cursed, Marin. It's a curse we are likely to never break."

She considered herself a realist, but something in his tone made her believe him. So many questions rushed through her head, but she settled on one for the moment. "Why were you cursed?"

"My ancestor dabbled where he shouldna have."

Now her curiosity was near to bursting. "Dabbled with who or what?"

Slowly, Elric turned from the window to face her. "The Fae."

"The Fae." Marin wasn't sure what she had expected him to say, but it wasn't that. When he didn't smile or laugh, she took a deep breath. "As in faeries?"

"Aye."

She had two options. She could either believe Elric had escaped from some mental institution or there really were Fae. Since she didn't want to think she had experienced the best sex of her life with a crazy person, she opted to believe him. For the moment. "Can you prove it?"

Elric chuckled. "Aye. I know it sounds as if I'm daft, but I'm no'."

"All right. So, there's Fae and your family was cursed. Tell me how you were cursed."

He leaned back against the stones and crossed his arms over his chest. "You're taking this all very well. Too well actually. I expected many things, but no' the calm way you're standing there."

"Right now I'm listening. I'll form an opinion later."

"It's only going to get worse, but I'll tell you everything."

She gave him an encouraging smile. *Worse? Oh, God.* "Good."

"In order for my kingdom, Drahcir, and its people to survive, each generation must leave the kingdom in search of their mates. We are given a certain amount of time in which to find, and convince, our mates to return with us to Drahcir. The mates must return willingly."

Marin swallowed as chills raced over her spine. "Mates? As in soul mates?"

"Aye."

"You've been searching for your mate?"

He nodded and let his arms drop. "I was searching. I found my mate, Marin. It's you."

Words eluded Marin. She could only stare at him, now wondering if she was mental since she actually believed him. Or was it that she just wanted to believe him? It was too confusing, her mind jumbled with emotions she couldn't even begin to sort through there were so many.

"Oh, God," she whispered, and put her hand to her head. "Let me get this straight, because I must have misunderstood somewhere."

She licked her lips and clasped her hands in front of her as she began to pace. "Your family has been cursed. By a Fae. Because...."

"Because the fool wanted to see if he could make a Fae princess fall in love with him."

"I gather she did or there wouldn't be a curse," Marin said as she glanced at him.

He simply raised a dark brow in response.

"You must return to your kingdom, Drahcir, with your mate before a certain time?"

"Correct."

Marin stopped pacing. "Did I leave anything out?"

"Nay. But there's more."

She didn't know how much more she could take. She closed the short distance between them until she stood before him. "What's the rest?"

"Marin, you asked me if I was from Scotland, which I am, but you didna ask me from when do I come?"

"When?" The world began to tilt. She took hold of the wall, the stones both cool and smooth beneath her palm. It helped to right her once more. "I guess that would explain the bra and panties and the toenail polish."

"What would?" he asked.

She shook her head. "Sorry. I talk to myself sometimes. It's a bad habit."

"There's worse," he said with a grin.

She tried to return the smile, but she was too busy trying to take all the information in. "So, *when* do you come from?"

"It's a wee bit harder to answer than that. Drahcir was not only cursed, but it was also hidden from the known world."

"When, Elric? I must know when."

"Time goes differently in my kingdom. I've been gone nearly three years, yet by the time I return it will have only been months."

Marin sank onto the blankets as her knees gave out. "The only explanation is that you time traveled here."

"I did, aye," he answered. "A Fae helped me since someone made sure my mate wasna in my time."

She rubbed her forehead as a headache began to develop. "I'm confused."

"I know," Elric said with a deep sigh as he squatted down. "I'm making a bloody muck of it."

"No. It's just a lot for me to take in. Try to explain the time travel part again."

Elric moved until he sat opposite her on the blankets. "Drahcir is hidden deep in the Ben Nevis Mountains."

"That's the tallest mountain range in Scotland."

"Aye, and near frozen as well. When we were cursed, the Fae also hid our kingdom. With it being so deep in the mountains, no' many dare to venture into them. We may come and go as we please, but we can never share the location of the kingdom. If any outsiders ever discovered it…"

"Your kingdom would no longer be yours."

"Aye," he said with a nod. "Through the generations, we've been able to venture out of our kingdom, unaware of the year we were stepping into, but it has always been that our mates would be in that time. We just had to find them."

"And they were always in Scotland?"

He nodded.

Marin leaned to the side and braced herself on her elbow. "Now, the twenty-first century woman in me says that's a crock."

"A what?" he asked, his forehead creasing in a frown.

"Not believable," she answered. "If you and your kingdom were cursed, don't you think it's a little convenient that you can venture out at any given time and your mates will be waiting for you? And in Scotland as well?"

"You make it sound easy, but in truth, it is anything but. In the three years I've searched, I didna find you. It took a Fae to discover that someone had moved you to this time. The Fae are no' supposed to interfere, yet Aimery did."

"Why did he? What happens if another Fae finds out he helped you?"

"Aimery is the commander of the Fae army and a verra

powerful Fae. He answers only to the king and queen as commander."

Marin nearly rolled her eyes. "Then, if he can shift you through time, why can't he erase the curse?"

"No one can. Once a Fae curses you, it lasts until they say otherwise."

"Can't you and your family talk to this Fae princess and right the wrong that your ancestor did?"

Elric chuckled. "If only it were that easy. That Fae princess disappeared after she set the curse, never to be seen or heard from again. Some say she turned into a dark Fae, others that she died. We've asked the Fae many times, yet no one can give us an answer."

"Wow." Marin fell back on the blankets and looked at the ceiling of the castle. "What a mess."

"That's one way of putting it. Do you have any more questions?"

She had several, but none that she was ready to ask. She was still reeling from the 'mate must return' part. And though she had greatly enjoyed their lovemaking and conversation, it didn't mean she was ready to go anywhere other than out to dinner with him.

Marin sat up and gave him a bright smile. "I've had a lovely night. Thank you. But I think I'm ready to return to my hotel."

He sat up with her, and the regret in his green eyes sent warning signals off in her head. "You can no' do that, lass."

7

Elric saw the fear enter Marin's hazel eyes and regretted it instantly. "There is much we still need to discuss," he said quickly. "If I let you return now, you may leave, and if you leave and I return without a mate, my city and all its people disappear."

"What?" she cried as she scrambled to her feet. "Why are you lying? I liked you, Elric. I had even hoped to see you again, but your stories are scaring the shit out of me."

He knew he was making a muck of things and wished he had Sorin's smooth tongue to aid him now, but his gift had been seduction, not talking. He stood and walked back to the window where he looked out over the village. He didn't like this future time he was in. Things were too different, foreign. He saw signs of his Scotland, but it wasn't the same. If only he could return to Drahcir.

"I'm no' lying. Nothing I've said tonight has been fabricated."

"Then let me leave."

He dropped his head against the cool stones. How he

wished he could ask his father for advice. "I can no'. All of my people are counting on me."

"Please," she cried, and moved toward the door.

Elric wanted to let her leave, to see the trust once more in her eyes. He couldn't take her back to Drahcir unless she was willing, and she was certainly anything but willing. He couldn't make her stay here either. If he wanted her to trust him, he was going to have to trust her as well.

"Before I take you back, I must tell you the rest," he said as he faced her.

"There's more?" she asked, her eyes wide.

He nodded. "If I had never found you, you would've been able to go about your life as normal. I'd have had to return to my kingdom and watch it and all its people disappear forever."

"But you did find me," she said softly.

"Aye. And now that we've shared our bodies, things have…changed."

Her tongue peeked out to wet her lips. "How exactly?"

"We were given special ways to be able to detect our mates."

"What was yours?"

"Just a sense," he said. "A rightness about you that was lacking in all the others."

She smiled and leaned against the door. "Go on."

"Even though we were given the special ways to help ensure that we didna make a mistake, the Fae gave us another way of seeing we made the right choice."

"And what would that be?"

Elric sighed, knowing this might be the one thing that sent her screaming from him. He quickly removed his tunic and held out his left arm. Even in the dim candlelight, the markings were beginning to darken.

"A tattoo?" Marin asked.

"In a manner," he answered. "It has always been on our skin, but when we find our mates and share our bodies, it brings out the markings."

"It's beautiful," she said and ran her hand over the intricate knotwork that ran from his shoulder to his elbow.

"You'll have one as well."

Her gaze snapped to his. Then, slowly she began to pull off her sweater. Elric kept his breathing calm, but inside his heart raced. She peeled back her shirt and he spotted the markings.

"Oh my God," she murmured. "This can't be happening to me. Nothing out of the ordinary has ever happened like this."

Elric clenched his fists as he fought the urge to take her in his arms, yet he sensed that she needed to gather her thoughts and sort through everything first.

"Is there anything else?" she asked as she jerked her sweater back on.

"Actually," he said hesitantly, "there is. When I said things had changed, I wasna lying. Now, if you decide against returning with me, you'll never find happiness. Neither of us will. We'll only be happy with each other."

Marin sighed and briefly squeezed her eyes shut. "Unbelievable. Take me back," she said, her voice shaking. "Now."

Elric went around the room and doused the candles before he reached for the torch. He led the way down the stairs where he once again set the torch in its holder and walked Marin to the horse. Just as he was about to lift her onto the horse, he stopped and listened.

"What is it?" she whispered.

Though she might be distraught over everything she had

learned, her fingers dug into his arm and she moved closer to him. She instinctively knew he'd protect her, and that was a good start to his way of thinking.

"We're being watched." He looked down into her hazel eyes and tucked a lock of auburn hair behind her ear that had gotten caught in the wind.

"Do they mean us harm?"

He shrugged. "I doona know."

"It's probably just some drunken men from the festival."

He wasn't about to tell her that he thought it might be a Tnarg and he needed to get her to safety fast. "Stay here," he said, and turned to a pile of rocks several paces behind him.

Since the men of the time didn't walk around with weapons, Elric had buried his sword. He shifted aside some of the old, crumbling stones and pulled out his weapon. After he fastened it around his waist, he walked back to Marin.

"That's real, isn't it?" she asked.

"Verra." He grabbed the horse's mane and vaulted onto his back, then held out his arm for Marin. He easily swung her up behind him, and when her arms wrapped around his torso, the desire that flared within him had him shaking.

With a quick tap on the horse's flanks, they set off. The horse must have felt his agitation and worry because he snorted and jerked his head up and down several times before he settled into a comfortable canter. Elric was vigilant of his surroundings at all times. The noise of this time made it difficult for him to discern where the threat to them was, but he caught a glimpse of a dark-haired beast just before they reached the village.

It was a Tnarg.

Elric cursed under his breath and knew he would have to stay with Marin at all times until she made her decision. He maneuvered the horse to the inn's stable and dismounted. When he reached for her, she easily slid into his arms.

"Are you still angry with me?" he asked, and ran a hand down the side of her face.

She shook her head. "It's hard to take it all in at once, and based on the tattoo on my left arm, I know you aren't lying. But, you're asking me to leave all that I know, my time, my friends…my life…to go to an unknown place that is stuck in some kind of time warp. How do I know I'll be happy?"

"How do you know that you willna? Are you so happy here that you are willing to risk your future and my kingdom?"

"Don't," she said, and backed away. "I have enough to think about without the added stress of thinking of killing all the innocents of your kingdom. Just let me think on this for a while."

Elric was just glad to hear she wanted to think on it and hadn't run away from him. "How long do you need?"

"I don't know," she said with a shrug. "Give me a few days."

He didn't like it, but he would do it. He gave her a curt nod and dragged her against him for a long, slow kiss. He wanted her to remember his taste as she fell asleep, he wanted her to dream of him and his touch.

When he finally lifted his head, her lips were swollen and desire blazed in her eyes. "You can no' deny the attraction between us."

"No, I can't," she said and took a step back. "And I won't."

"Doona go out alone at night," he called as she reached the stable door.

She stopped and turned to him. "You're keeping

something from me."

Elric offered her his arm. "I just worry. Let me walk you back inside."

She hesitated only a moment before she took his arm.

Marin shut the door to her room and leaned back against it. Her mind reeled with everything Elric had told her. It was hard to discount any of it though, especially with the mark on her arm.

She walked to the bathroom and took off her sweater. For long minutes she stared at the elaborate knotwork and Celtic influence of the marking. It had darkened since she had first looked at it, making it nearly black now.

"The proof I've asked for is before my eyes," she said to her reflection.

She wouldn't call what she felt for Elric love, since she had just meet him earlier that day, but there was most definitely something that connected them, something that drew her to him like a moth to a flame. But could she leave everything she knew? All her family was gone, so the only person she would leave behind was Rhonda.

Marin took a deep breath and pulled off the rest of her clothes to get ready for bed. As she snuggled in her flannel pj's and buried herself beneath layers of blankets on the bed, she couldn't stop thinking of Elric. She missed his warmth, the way his green eyes sparkled when he teased her, and his gentle touch.

Most of all, she missed his presence and the way he made her feel.

She closed her eyes and recalled the promise in Elric's eyes. A promise for a new life perhaps?

8

Elric waited until he saw Marin shut her door before he hurried back to the stable. He jumped onto the horse's back and nudged him into a run. If the Tnarg was out there waiting, he had to find the creature before it got to Marin.

The Tnarg left an easy trail to follow. Its long, wide prints were unlike anything Elric had ever seen. If it hadn't been for his brother, Lucian, discovering the ancient text in their library that detailed the Tnarg, Elric wouldn't know what it looked like or its hunting habits.

The ancient text had described in detail what the Tnarg would do once it found Marin, and Elric would die before he allowed it to come near her. He had expected to find the desire he felt for Marin, but he hadn't anticipated the deep feelings so soon. It surprised—and pleased—him.

He focused back on the Tnarg and stopped his mount. Next, Elric closed his eyes and opened his senses. If he was right, the Tnarg would try and attack by tomorrow. Elric wanted the beast dead. Tonight.

The crack of a small twig behind Elric caught his

attention. Slowly, he reached down and grasped the hilt of his sword as he silently drew it from its scabbard. The Tnarg was behind him in the forest. One of them would die this night, and it wasn't going to be Elric.

Marin hadn't left her room all day. Rhonda tried repeatedly to draw her out, but not even the revelry from the festival could drag Marin from the safety of the inn. She knew she was being a coward, but she needed time to think without Elric's seductive persona clouding her judgment.

She had tried to think of what it would be like to say goodbye to Elric, and then had tried a scenario where she agreed to go with him. Her head began to ache with the choices swirling through her mind. And, to make matters worse, storm clouds had rolled in, bringing rain and a ferocious lightning storm.

A crack of thunder drew her attention to the window. It had begun to grow dark, but because of the time of day or the storm, Marin didn't know. She couldn't believe she had been so lost in thought that she hadn't noticed the passing of time, but by the grumbling of her stomach, it was a distinct possibility.

She stood and walked to the window. People from the festival were running to get out of the downpour, and that's when she spotted Rhonda with Lachlan. Marin smiled as she watched her friend with the Scotsman. Rhonda deserved some happiness, and she sincerely hoped Lachlan gave it to her. She was about to turn to get find boots to go downstairs and get food when her door was suddenly thrown open.

In the doorway stood the most fearsome creature Marin had ever laid eyes on.

She tried to swallow as her stomach plummeted to her feet like lead. The creature's red eyes blazed with fury as it stared at her. It stood at least six feet tall, with a brownish mass of matted hair covering its body, and long talons on its hands and feet.

Marin might have taken some self-defense classes, but nothing had prepared her for an attack from a creature like this. Give her a drunk, randy man and she could bring him to his knees with one punch. Now, all she wanted to do was run to Elric.

Elric.

She wished she hadn't been hiding from him all day. Maybe if she had been with him, the creature wouldn't be in her room now. Marin made to move toward the door connecting her room to Rhonda's, and the creature snarled and hissed as it stepped farther into the room.

With no weapon and the thunder drowning out any noise she might make, Marin knew her situation was hopeless. Before she could blink, the creature suddenly flew toward her. Marin fell to her side and rolled away as something crashed behind her.

She didn't look over her shoulder as she scrambled to her feet and made a run for the door to Rhonda's room. She was just feet from the door when something latched onto her foot. The sensation of several blades cutting through her jeans and into her skin let her know the creature had gotten a hold of her.

Marin kicked out and felt her foot connect with something. She looked over her shoulder and saw the beast holding onto her foot and growling, showing its huge fangs. It began to pull her backward. She clawed at the rug and screamed.

"What the bloody hell?" came a male voice from the doorway. She looked over to see Rhonda and Lachlan.

The creature let out a loud growl and turned back to Marin. As she was being yanked backward, she reached for anything she could get her hands on. Something touched her hand, and she immediately grabbed hold of it, then launched it at the creature. One of her heavy hiking boots landed squarely on the beast's head.

It howled its fury and tugged even harder. Out of the corner of her eye she saw Lachlan and Rhonda beating at the creature with shoes and even a hair dryer that Lachlan swung by the cord.

Suddenly a loud, booming war cry filled the room. Marin turned to find Elric running at them with his sword swinging over his head. Luckily, Lachlan stepped aside as Elric brought his sword down and embedded it in the creature's chest.

"Are you hurt?" Elric asked as he reached for her.

Marin's eyes were fixed on the creature with Elric's sword sunk into its chest as it tried to pull the weapon out with one hand. It was still breathing, its red eyes filled with hatred, and no matter how hard she yanked on her foot, it wouldn't release it.

"It has my foot," she finally said.

She watched as Elric pried open the beast's long fingers and freed her while it growled at him and tried to bite him.

Marin scrambled to her feet. "It isn't dead."

"Nay," Elric said as he looked her over. "We doona have much time."

"What the bloody hell is that?" Lachlan demanded, his brogue thick with surprise.

Elric looked over his shoulder at Lachlan and Rhonda.

"Something you want no part of. You need to get out of here. Now."

"I'm not going anywhere without Marin," Rhonda said, though her voice shook with fear.

Marin licked her lips and moved away from the creature. "We can talk once we get out of here."

"Good idea," Lachlan said.

The words had no sooner left his mouth than the long, low growl of the creature filled the room. As one, all four turned to stare at it. Marin's mouth fell open as she watched it pull the sword from its chest and stand. There was no gaping wound or blood. It was as if it had healed itself. Its gaze turned to her, and her blood turned to ice.

She saw the creature and Elric move at the same time. The beast reached out toward her, and she felt its long talons slice through her sweater and into her skin. Everything seemed to move in slow motion as Elric bellowed and pushed the creature toward the window. Glass shattered as it plummeted to the ground.

Marin looked down when she felt something soaking her jeans. It took her a moment to register that it was blood. Her blood.

* * *

"Marin!"

Elric jerked at the woman's scream. He moved to catch Marin as she began to crumple. After one look at the blood, he lifted her thick tunic and spotted the four long gnashes in her side. He quickly rose to his feet and pulled back the bedding until he found the linens. With one jerk, he pulled the linen free and began to wrap it around Marin.

"Help me," he bellowed to the man as he tried to sit Marin up.

The man swallowed, visibly shaken. "Thank God for you. That…thing…would've killed us for sure."

"Aye," Elric said. "It would have."

"I'm Lachlan."

Elric glanced at the man and nodded as he finished bandaging Marin. "Elric. We need to get out of here fast. The Tnarg will return soon."

"The what?" the woman asked.

"It's all right, Rhonda," Lachlan said and moved to her. "We'll go with Elric and Marin."

Elric didn't wait around to see what the couple did. He had to get Marin away from the Tnarg immediately, before it killed her. And there was only one place he knew he could go.

"You can't take her in the rain," Rhonda shouted as they caught up with him.

Elric didn't spare her a glance as he walked down the back stairs. "I doona have a choice. It's either the rain or the Tnarg."

To his surprise, Lachlan held open the door for him. The rain was coming down in sheets, making it near impossible to see but a few feet in front of his face. The Tnarg could be anywhere, and it sent chills of dread racing across his skin.

"Where are you going?" Lachlan yelled over the rain.

Elric ran into the stables. "Bolt the doors behind us!"

Once they were locked inside, he set Marin down and checked her bandage. The blood hadn't slowed. "I must get Marin to safety. I doona have time to tell you everything. I'm leaving and taking Marin with me. It's the only thing that will keep her alive."

"I'm not letting you take her without me," Rhonda said, her arms crossed over her chest, her red hair plastered to her face as she stared at him with amber eyes filled with determination.

Elric slowly rose to his feet. "Know this, if you follow me, you'll never be able to return."

"Just where are you going?" Lachlan asked.

"To another time."

Rhonda put a hand on his arm when he went to reach for Marin. "Did Marin know of this creature?"

"I went searching for the Tnarg last night to kill it, but never found it. I was keeping a watch over Marin," Elric answered. It irritated him to be taking time to explain to Marin's friends, but he knew he didn't have a choice. "She was making a decision on whether to return with me and save my people or not."

Just as Elric expected, Rhonda opened her mouth to ask another question, but a loud banging on one of the stable doors stopped her.

"The Tnarg," he said, and scooped up Marin in his arms. "Thank you for your help," he said to them, before he raced to the other end of the stable.

As he reached for the bolt, Lachlan's hand freed it. Elric raced into the rain and to the spot where Aimery had opened the doorway. Behind him, he heard the screams as the Tnarg chased them.

Elric saw the doorway open as he approached. He stopped and looked at Lachlan and Rhonda. "Thank you for everything. Now, you must run and hide. The Tnarg wants me and Marin, but it might attack either of you."

He stepped through the doorway and sighed. The consequences of bringing Marin through time without her consent could be severe, but he would do it again if it meant saving her life. Whether she returned with him to Drahcir was another matter entirely.

"Oh. My. God," he heard from behind him.

He turned and found Lachlan and Rhonda. "What are you two doing?"

"I don't know you," Rhonda said and put her hand on Marin's forehead. "She's my best friend, my only family, and I'm not about to let you take her away until I hear what she wants you to do."

He moved his gaze to Lachlan.

Lachlan shrugged and grinned. "I always loved adventure."

Elric silently groaned and turned toward the small village. He wasn't surprised to find they weren't far from the base of the Ben Nevis Mountains. He was almost home.

"We need to find clothes so you can blend in, and I need to tend to Marin."

Relief went through him when he saw the small cottage at the edge of the village. He hurried to it and knocked. It opened to show an old woman with kind brown eyes and white hair pulled away from her face.

"I knew you would return," his aunt said with a warm smile. "Come in, come in, lad."

Elric hurried to the bed and placed Marin on it. He moved to see about her bandage, but his Aunt Ivy pushed him aside. "Let me, lad. She and her friends are going to need clothes. See what you can find while I'll tend to her."

He didn't want to leave Marin, but he knew Ivy was right. Rhonda stayed with Marin while he and Lachlan found clothes for all of them in a chest in a back room. By the time they returned, Marin was out of her wet clothes and sitting up in bed.

"Hello," he said. He'd never known such fear as he'd felt

when the Tnarg had attacked her. To see her sitting up with her color returning helped to calm his racing heart.

She smiled tiredly. "Hello. I hear we've time traveled."

"It was either that or let the Tnarg kill you."

Her smile grew. "Then I'm grateful you chose to bring me here."

He was so relieved she wasn't angry that he wanted to kiss her. "How are you feeling?"

"So-so. I must have lost a lot of blood."

He nodded and handed the clothes to Rhonda. "I hate to do this, Marin, but you must make a decision now. The Tnarg will return here, if it hasna already."

"My decision was already made," she said as she lowered her eyes.

Elric didn't like the taste of failure, and the thought of his people and kingdom disappearing into nothing turned his stomach. "I understand. Dress," he said as he turned on his heel and left the cottage.

He stared up at the mountains with the moon slowly ascending. It was a clear night, so different from the storm they'd left behind when they crossed through the doorway. If he closed his eyes he could see the beauty that was Drahcir and the love and laughter of his family. He would return to them soon though. He would not send them into death alone.

Something touched his hand, and he looked down to find Marin beside him. "You shouldn't be standing."

"You certainly can't carry me everywhere," she said. "Besides, Aunt Ivy was most determined to get some vile liquid down me that seems to be doing the trick."

Elric chuckled. "Ivy is a descendent of my mother's family. Someone has always remained in this cottage to help us. I made my way to Ivy the moment I left Drahcir."

"That was a good idea."

"I've been thinking. I might be able to convince Aimery to return you and your friends back to your own time."

"Why?" she asked. "I thought you wanted me."

Elric turned to face her. "I do want you, Marin. I want you more than anything, and not just to save my kingdom. I want you because you're the other half of me, the part that's been missing from my life. But inside you said—"

"That I had already made my decision," she interrupted him. "I don't think I could live without you, and frankly, I don't want to try. It scares me that I feel this way after only just meeting you, but the idea of living my life without you seems wrong in so many ways. The only thing that feels right is being with you. Wherever and whenever that is."

He gently drew her into his arms, careful of her injured side. "If I'd have had more time, I'd have wooed you properly. I really did make a muck of things."

"You did, but then again, I have to work things out on my own sometimes. I can be stubborn that way. I just want you to know what you're getting into."

"We'll take the time to get to know each other properly once we're in my kingdom."

She grinned up at him and ran a finger over his lips. "Only if we're in the same bed every night."

"I can make that happen." His green eyes twinkled. "You've made me the happiest man in this realm."

"I'll be even happier once we're away from the Tnarg."

"Only the gates of my city will ensure that."

"Then what are we waiting for?"

He stopped her as she started to walk away. "Marin, your wound is severe and you've lost a lot of blood. The trek to Drahcir is not an easy one. The cold alone does some people in."

She gently touched his face. "I trust you."

At that moment, Elric would have moved the mountains for her. He turned toward the cottage to ask Ivy to borrow her horses only to find her behind him.

"Already done, lad. I sent young Lachlan to saddle the horses. He cuts a fine image in a kilt, just as you do."

Elric leaned down and gave her a kiss on her cheek. "Thank you, Aunt Ivy."

"Just keep her safe and tell your mother I said hello."

He gave her a nod as Lachlan walked up with the horses. Across all four saddles were thick, fur-lined cloaks. He watched as Lachlan lifted Rhonda's cloak and wrapped it tenderly around her shoulders. The clothes they had found fit her well, and the smile she gave Lachlan bespoke deep feelings.

"They look good together," Marin said.

Elric nodded. "Aye, they do. How do the clothes fit?"

"You did a good job. The dress is only a little tight across my breasts."

He reached for her cloak and helped to fasten it around her. "This will keep you warmer than you realize, as will the thick wool stockings. If I know Ivy, she packed extra blankets and anything else we might need in the bags."

"Then we're set?"

"Aye," Ivy said as she slowly walked up, using a cane to balance herself in the thick snow. "Take care of your injuries, lass. I worked my magic on them, but the wounds came from a Tnarg and could easily get infected if you're not careful."

"I will. Thank you again."

"One more thing," Ivy said. "Once you get into the mountains, you might think your bones will freeze into place, but keep the faith in Elric. When he brings you through the gates of Drahcir, it'll all be worth it."

Elric knew Marin wanted to talk more to Ivy, but there wasn't time. He helped Marin mount her horse, then swung up onto the back of his mount. With one last wave to Ivy, he nudged his horse into a walk.

His senses were on full alert. He couldn't allow the Tnarg to sneak up on him again. If only he'd been able to kill it in the forest, but it was a sneaky creature and managed to outmaneuver him. Elric sighed. This should be a happy moment in his life.

He had succeeded in finding his mate and convincing her to return with him to Drahcir to save his people and the kingdom. Instead, he worried that they might never make it.

A loud roar in the distance had Elric gripping his sword.

The Tnarg had found them.

Marin shivered as they rode deeper into the mountains, the light from the full moon lighting their way. Ever since the Tnarg had roared, Elric had been like a man possessed. She feared if he had been able to, he would have run the horses instead of walking them, but the steep climb and thick snow prevented it.

She was as fearful of the Tnarg as Elric, especially after feeling its talons on her skin, but the frigid temperatures kept her from thinking of anything other than warmth. Her teeth wouldn't stop chattering, and she had no idea how the horse managed to keep plodding through the falling snow.

"We can no' make it to Drahcir tonight," Elric said as he pulled up beside her. "We'll have to stop."

Marin nodded, unable to talk though the chattering of her teeth. She had no idea how much longer they trudged along before Elric suddenly veered off their path. She wearily followed him as she willed herself to stay in the saddle. All of a sudden, she felt hands on her and looked down to find Elric lifting her off the horse.

"You're near frozen," he said as they walked into a cave. "I'll build a fire to warm you."

She snuggled against his warmth, eager to feel her own hands again. The cloak, wool stockings, and thick skirts had indeed kept her warmer than she would have thought, but she wasn't used to this kind of weather.

"Lachlan, take care of the horses," Elric called as he sat her down and hurried from the cave.

Rhonda came to sit beside her and sighed. "I'm freezing, and I'm in a cave. A cave, Marin. You know how I hate to rough it."

Marin laughed. "I'm just glad to be out of the snow."

"Ugh. I do agree. I'm starving, too."

"There might be something in here," Lachlan said as he tossed two bags at their feet.

Marin tried to open a bag, but her fingers were too stiff.

"Here, let me," Rhonda said, and took the bag from her hands. She opened it and peered inside. "It's food."

Marin smiled as Rhonda rummaged in first one bag, then the next. It wasn't long before Elric returned with a few sticks in his arms.

"The wood is wet, but we can no' make a large fire anyway. I tried to bring us as far back into the cave as we could go, and with the horses in here with us, the Tnarg might pass us by."

"Won't it know where we're headed?" Marin asked.

Elric stopped piling the sticks and raised his gaze. "Aye, it knows. It'll be waiting for us."

Marin shuddered, but this time not from the cold.

———

A few hours of sleep and a little warmth did wonders for Marin. Her wounds pained her only a little, and just as Ivy had instructed, she checked the wounds as often as she could.

"We should reach the gates of Drahcir before nightfall," Elric said as he clasped his cloak around his wide shoulders and glanced at the entrance of the cave where the sun shone.

Marin never tired of looking at him. He was everything she had ever thought a Highland warrior would be: tall, ruggedly handsome, and fiercely loyal to the ones he cared about. That pretty much summed Elric up in her opinion.

Lachlan had saddled the horses and Elric stood looking at her, waiting. It was time for them to leave, but she wasn't ready. The few hours in the cave had been pleasant. Though, with Lachlan and Rhonda with them, Marin hadn't been able to do more than snuggle against Elric.

"Have you changed your mind?" Elric asked, his voice heavy with doubt.

She walked to him and traced his lips with her finger. "Never. We're safe here. Out there..." She let her voice trail off because she couldn't find it within herself to finish it.

"I'll protect you," he vowed.

It still amazed her that this man she had just met was willing to lay down his life for her, and she had no doubt he would do just that if it meant she would live. If there hadn't been proof on her arm and his, she might still be wondering at his sanity.

But once she had accepted what was before her, she found it easy to open her heart and soul to him. He offered her something no one ever had—love.

She rose up on tiptoe and kissed him. A moan rumbled through his chest as he molded her body to his.

"I want you," he whispered in her ear, and moved her

hand to cover his hard rod.

With a smile she stepped away from him. "Then get me to Drahcir, and you can have me any way you want me."

The words had no sooner left her mouth than he took her hand and pulled her out of the cave. The cold air hit her like a freight train as Elric lifted her atop her mare. With a small pat on her leg, he turned away and mounted his horse.

"Everyone, keep your eyes and ears open. The Tnarg is powerful and deadly. It willna be able to touch us once we reach the gates of Drahcir."

"Our haven," Marin whispered.

Rhonda clicked to her horse. "Then let's get moving please."

Hours passed with no Tnarg sightings as they traveled by horseback. But Elric wasn't fool enough to believe it would leave them alone. It had proven its tenacity in Marin's time, and if he had learned anything of the beast, it was that it was very intelligent. It was most likely waiting for them.

And he knew where.

The pass was just up ahead. A narrow slit between the walls of the mountains that was treacherous on any given day, but deadly if something was waiting for you. There was very little room in which to maneuver a horse, and even less in which to try and defend oneself.

Elric looked over his shoulder to see Marin riding close behind him, then Rhonda and Lachlan bringing up the rear of their small party. At first, he hadn't been too sure of Rhonda and Lachlan coming, but now he was grateful for an extra body to help ward off the Tnarg.

When they reached the entrance to the pass, Elric pulled

his mount to a stop and dismounted. He walked to Marin and motioned Lachlan and Rhonda over. "Listen carefully. The pass is narrow and a perfect place for the Tnarg to attack."

Marin visibly swallowed. "How much farther to Drahcir?"

"Once we get through the pass, you'll be able to see the gates."

"All right," she said slowly, and glanced through the pass. "Do we continue on as we have?"

Elric shook his head and helped her off the mare. Then he unbuckled the long dagger at his waist. "I want you to keep this with you," he said, and helped her strap it on under her cloak. "I'll go first. Once I reach the other side, I'll whistle three times. That's when you ride through."

"What about us?" Lachlan asked.

"Since the Tnarg is after Marin, once she's with me, I think it'll be safe for both of you to ride through together. I'll issue another three whistles when Marin has reached me."

"And if we don't hear the whistles?" Marin asked.

He looked into her troubled hazel eyes. "I'll get through," he promised. He wasn't about to tell her he was terrified of her riding alone through the pass, but it was the only solution he could come up with.

If he was with her and the Tnarg attacked her from behind, by the time Elric dismounted she would be dead. With him going ahead, he would have ample time to try to find and kill the Tnarg before Marin rode through. But, just in case he didn't, she had a weapon.

"I'm scared," she whispered.

Elric pulled her into his arms and rested his chin atop her head. "I know."

For a long moment they remained as they were, oblivious to the bitter cold, or the stares from Lachlan and Rhonda. There was so much Elric wanted to say to her, and though he had planned to save it until their wedding, he felt the need to say some now.

"Marin," he said, and leaned back. "Thank you for trusting me and coming with me."

She smiled up at him. "How could I refuse a man with seduction skills as good as yours?"

Elric grinned and glanced away. "I wasna given the fine tongue of my youngest brother, Sorin, the insight of my elder brother, Lucian, or the wisdom of my eldest brother, Keiran. However, I do know that I feel whole now, with you at my side. You are a part of me, my soul."

For several moments she simply stared at him as she rapidly blinked. "I don't know your other brothers, but I know what I see before me, and there is no man more handsome, well spoken, wise, or insightful than you. I never believed people who said that they had fallen in love at first sight…until now. You say that I am a part of you, but I believe that you have always been a part of me. I want to walk beside you through the gates of Drahcir, and I refuse to allow one hideously ugly beast to threaten that."

Elric smiled as he kissed her. What was supposed to be a simple kiss turned into a raging fire. His body wanted her, needed her with an intensity that frightened him. He pulled away before he lifted her skirts right then and buried his cock deep inside her.

He stared at her a heartbeat longer, etching her face into his memory and the feel and taste of her into his senses. Then he leapt atop his horse and grabbed the reins.

"I'll see you soon," he said, before he disappeared into the pass.

$\mathcal{M}$arin fingered the long dagger Elric had given her and waited. It had seemed as if ages had passed since she had watched her mate disappear into the narrow pass, a pass in which Elric was sure the Tnarg laid in wait for her.

"How long do we wait?" Rhonda asked.

"Until we hear Elric's whistles," Lachlan said. "Elric is checking the pass as he goes. If there's a chance he could kill the Tnarg before Marin rides through, then he'll do it."

Marin shuddered and wrapped her cloak tighter about her. "I don't like that he went alone. The Tnarg is very powerful."

"He'll be fine," Lachlan said.

Marin gazed at the snow at her feet. Her toes had begun to grow numb about a half hour before, but she refused to move from the spot she had last seen Elric. It boggled her mind that he had somehow managed to become so important to her in such a short amount of time. Her feelings for him ran deep, as deep as feelings could go. And though they hadn't spoken of love, it was there.

Suddenly, she heard the three whistles.

"He made it," she said as she lifted her skirts and made her way to her horse. "Lachlan, please help me."

In the next instant, he had lifted her atop the mare. "Be careful, Marin. Keep your eyes open and your weapon ready at all times."

She swallowed and nodded, then looked at Rhonda. She gave her friend a big smile. "I won't keep you waiting as long."

Rhonda's laughter followed her into the pass. She looked over her shoulder for one last look at her best friend and Lachlan, but they were already out of sight. With a deep breath, she turned back and stared down the long pass.

The silence was deafening. Chills raced along her skin. The place was eerie, and made more so by the fact the Tnarg could be waiting for her.

Marin pulled the dagger from its scabbard and gripped it in her right hand. She wrapped the horse's reins around her left hand and kept her eyes moving as Lachlan had advised. All she saw were snow and ice. The walls of the pass looked to be several feet thick and as high up as fifty feet, from her estimate. Though there were a few places something or someone might be able to hide, those places were few and far between.

With each step of the mare's sturdy legs, Marin became more confident. She nudged the mare into a slow canter and let her mind wander to the memories of the night she and Elric had first made love.

Elric jerked his horse to a stop when he heard the whistle. His heart lodged in his throat as he desperately tried to turn his horse around. He was at one of the narrowest parts of the pass. Another hundred strides or so and he would have made it through.

Once he had gotten his horse backed up, then turned around, he leaned low over his mount's neck and urged him into a run. He had to reach Marin before the Tnarg did. The Tnarg was smart, but Elric never imagined it would have known about his whistle.

With his blood thundering through his ears, he pushed the horse faster. He had to reach Marin before the creature did. Marin came into view, and he knew the instant she realized something was wrong. She jerked slightly on her reins, but when she looked over her shoulder and let out a scream, Elric knew real, terrifying fear.

"Marin!" he bellowed as he drew his sword and squeezed the horse with his knees to urge him faster.

He spotted the Tnarg as it yanked Marin from her mount. Rage erupted inside Elric as the beast slashed at Marin again and again as it straddled her. The Tnarg blocked Marin from Elric's view, and he worried that he might be too late to save her, but he would avenge her.

As he approached, he kicked free of the stirrups and launched himself at the Tnarg. Elric grabbed hold of the creature around its neck and rolled it off Marin. The Tnarg screamed and tried to lash out at him with its talons. Elric's blood cried for revenge as he jumped to his feet and faced the creature.

"Attack me, you worthless piece of dung," Elric growled. "Only the vilest of beasts would dare attack something weaker than they."

The Tnarg snarled and climbed to its feet. "Only the smartest of creatures knows how to outwit their enemies."

"We were no' your enemies. Until now."

The Tnarg cackled and began to circle Elric. "Do you really think you can stop me from killing her?"

Elation pumped through Elric. Marin wasn't dead. Yet. "Aye, I do."

"Even if it means giving up your own life?"

"Aye."

Its red eyes narrowed on him. "I'll kill you first, then her. I only need to kill one of the mates to end it all."

"Why?" Elric asked. "Why would you want to see Drahcir ended?"

"That should be obvious."

Elric gripped his sword with both hands. "If you willna answer my question directly, then let us get on with it."

"As you wish," the beast said, just before it leapt at him.

Elric swung his sword up and then over as he sidestepped. He saw his blade slice into the Tnarg's thick fur, but if he expected to kill the Tnarg, he had been wrong.

The beast looked down at the cut that began to heal and laughed. "Did you really think you could kill me? You? A mere mortal?"

A knot of dread began to form in the pit of Elric's stomach. He realized too late his mistake in thinking he could put an end to the Tnarg. Elric glanced at Marin as she stirred. He had failed her. Neither of them would be able to make it to the gates of Drahcir.

He would not go down without a fight. He turned back to the Tnarg and lifted his sword.

"It's not you that I want," the creature said. "Return to your home."

"If you want to kill my mate, then it is me you want."

"You would die for her?"

"Gladly."

"Then so be it."

When the Tnarg next attacked, it was with much more power. Instead of halfhearted swipes, those deadly talons were now aimed at his heart. Elric managed to keep the majority of the strikes away from him with his sword, but the Tnarg had more strength than he. Already Elric was beginning to wear down, and the Tnarg looked as though its strength only grew.

The Tnarg struck out and hit Elric on the jaw, throwing him backward. He landed hard on the packed snow and ice and struggled to catch his breath. He knew death awaited him. He looked over at Marin to find her watching him. He didn't want her to see him die.

With a grunt, he rolled to his stomach and ran toward her. He wrapped his arms around her and shielded her body from the Tnarg.

"I love you," he said as he waited for the killing blow.

After several moments, Elric raised his head to see that they were alone. He reached for his sword and waited for the Tnarg to attack once again. Yet only the whistling of the wind through the narrow pass sounded around them.

"What happened to it?" Marin asked.

"I doona know." He looked off in the distance and saw two horses thundering toward them as he helped Marin to her feet. "It's Lachlan and Rhonda."

"Can we leave now?"

He shook his head. "First, I need to know if you're hurt."

"No. When it threw me off the horse, it knocked the dagger you gave me out of my hand. I'm sorry."

"Sorry?" he repeated as he pulled her into his arms. "You've nothing to apologize for. The Tnarg must have whistled since I never made it out of the pass. I found you as soon as I could."

"I really need to get out of here."

Elric could feel her shaking. She had his cloak in a death grip, and he knew she could handle very little else that day. "Aye. Now that Rhonda and Lachlan have arrived, let us get through the pass."

Marin expected the Tnarg to jump out at them when they least expected it, but they made it the rest of the way through the pass without any mishap. Elric quickly informed Lachlan and Rhonda of what had transpired, but it wasn't until she saw the tall, gilded gates before her that Marin knew they were truly safe.

"My God," Rhonda murmured.

Marin could only stare. If the gates that enclosed the city were this beautifully decorated with ancient Celtic knotwork, very similar to the mark on her and Elric's arms, she could only imagine what the rest of the city looked like.

"You look impressed," Elric said from beside her.

She nodded. "I am."

"Then wait until you see Drahcir itself. I think you'll enjoy your new home."

Marin took the hand he offered and nudged her horse into a walk. As they approached, the gates opened. She looked around, but saw no one that would operate the gates. Elric stiffened suddenly and she glanced over to see him looking over her head at something. She followed his gaze and spotted the Tnarg atop a mountain watching them.

"Can it get in here?"

"I doona think so," he said, and squeezed her hand.

She turned back to him. "I think we need to find out."

"Later. Right now, I want to welcome you to your new home," he said. "Take a look around."

"It's warmer," she said as she removed the cloak.

Elric smiled. "The Fae bespelled it. The cold doesna reach us here."

"Thank God," she murmured.

Marin turned her head and let her eyes wander over the lush, green valley, vivid blue skies and warm weather. A unique bright blue stone made up the road that traveled down the valley and then up the mountain to the…palace. She blinked at the majestic structure before her. It put Cinderella's castle at Disney World to shame. She had never seen anything so beautiful and grand in her life, never even thought anything of its magnitude existed.

"Wow," she whispered as she tore her eyes from the castle to the structures that dotted the road and landscape. Some were what she would call small cottages while others were on a grander scale and looked like businesses instead of homes. And on each of the all-white structures were symbols similar to the ones on her arm. The atmosphere was one of peace and tranquility. It was all simply stunning.

"What do you think?"

She heard the anxiety in Elric's rich voice. She smiled and said, "I think it's perfect. You never told me it was this beautiful."

"You have to see the city to fully understand."

"I see that," she said as she spotted people walking toward them.

"Prince Elric is home!" someone shouted.

Marin felt as if she'd been punched. She slowly turned her head to Elric. "Prince?"

He shrugged and refused to meet her eyes. "Aye."

"Did he say prince?" Rhonda asked from behind them.

Marin could only nod as she stared at Elric. "Is there anything else I should know?"

"Only that my parents will most likely demand that we marry soon. I'll explain things to them."

A laugh bubbled. "Is that your roundabout way of asking me to marry you?"

"I asked you to marry me the day I invited you to return with me."

Marin's smile died. "I didn't know."

"It doesna matter," Elric said with a small smile. "We made it here. I have no' seen my family in years, and I'm anxious to see them."

"Then let us go to them."

Elric gave her hand another small squeeze before he released it and waved to the people surrounding them. Marin returned smiles and waves as she followed Elric down the road to the palace. Drahcir was larger than she first imagined, but the beauty only increased the longer she was there.

When they reached the castle steps, Elric hurried to her side to help her dismount. As she slid down his body, hers came alive with need. To her pleasure, Elric's green eyes darkened and a low growl moved through him.

"I need you," he whispered.

"Not near as much as I need you."

"Soon, my love," he said, and kissed her forehead. "For now, we must greet my parents."

Marin didn't know what she expected of his parents, but the smiling people before her wasn't it. The king looked regal in his grand purple robes and golden crown, while the queen stood elegantly beside him with her lavender gown and smaller crown.

She stood and watched the couple as Elric raced toward them. The greeting brought tears to her eyes as she remembered her own parents. It was only then she spotted another couple behind the king and queen. It was obvious by their dress and the way the man smiled at Elric that they were kin.

"Lucian?" she heard Elric exclaim.

The two men embraced and slapped each other on the back loudly. Suddenly, five pair of eyes turned toward her. Marin wanted to run and hide. She could only imagine what she looked like after traveling through the mountains and fighting off the Tnarg. She felt something touch her arm and took Rhonda's hand as she and Lachlan came up behind her.

"Marin," Elric called.

Her mouth became dry as she tried to make her feet move. It was worse than a job interview. She forced her feet to move and put a smile on her face as she moved toward the small group. Elric came to meet her and took her hand.

"I love you," he whispered in her ear.

She smiled and gazed up at him as she began to relax. "I love you too."

"Welcome to the family," the king said as he moved forward to embrace her.

Elric watched his mate as she accepted the hugs from his mother, father, brother, and sister-in-law. He frowned. He didn't even know Lucian's wife's name.

"Marin," Elric said. "Let me introduce to you my father, King Urises, and my mother, Queen Morag."

"Please," the queen said, "she mustn't be so formal. You may call me Morag, but I hope you'll eventually call me Mother."

Elric saw Marin blink rapidly to stop the tears that threatened. "It would be an honor."

"And this," Elric said turning to his brother, "is Lucian, my elder brother."

"Pleased to meet you," Lucian said as he bowed low over her hand. "Let me introduce my wife, Isabelle."

Elric was pleased with the brown-haired woman whom Lucian called wife. She complemented his brother well.

"Where are Sorin and Keiran?" he asked.

"They have no' returned," his father said.

Elric sighed and wrapped his arm around Marin. "I thought I would be the last."

"I thought the same," Lucian said.

His mother looked over his shoulder. "Elric, dear, who are those people by the horses?"

"Oh," Marin exclaimed as she waved them over. "This is my very best friend, Rhonda," Marin said as they walked up. "And this is Lachlan."

"You all must be tired," Morag said. "Let us retire in the castle. I'll find Marin, Rhonda, and Lachlan chambers right away."

Elric turned and looked out over his city as his father and Lucian moved to either side of him. "I never thought I'd return."

"Did you have trouble finding her?" his father asked.

Elric snorted and told of how Aimery helped him shift through time and the Tnarg.

"The Tnarg moved through time as easily as you did?" Lucian asked.

"Aye," Elric said. "I thought we were dead in the pass. Nothing I did even slowed it."

"It was the same when I battled one."

"That means it will go after Sorin and Keiran's mates. It

told me that I could return unharmed but that it had to kill Marin."

"What stopped it?" his father asked.

Elric shrugged. "I've no idea. I moved to Marin to protect her and the next moment it was gone. I just wish there was a way to warn Sorin and Keiran."

11

Marin woke to the sounds of birds outside her window. She rolled onto her back and stretched. Her gaze ran over the beautiful cream and dark mauve bed hangings and she thought of Elric. She had wanted to spend time with him last night, but after dinner, he and his father, brother, and Lachlan were locked in the king's study. She knew what they were discussing—the Tnarg.

While Elric had been discussing the Tnarg, she had been with Morag, Isabelle, and Rhonda talking about the wedding. Lucian and Isabelle had returned to Drahcir just a few weeks before. Morag had wasted no time in getting Isabelle and Lucian to the altar, and it seemed she was doing the same to Marin and Elric. Not that Marin minded. She had waited her entire life for Elric, and now that she had him, she didn't want to let him go.

Marin had reservations about being a princess, but Isabelle assured her several times through the night that she would be fine. She just hoped Isabelle was right.

A princess. Never in all her daydreams had Marin ever envisioned herself as a princess, yet that was exactly what she was about to become.

The door to her chamber suddenly opened, and Elric quickly stepped inside. He smiled as he shut and locked the door.

"I missed you last night," she said as he walked to the bed. Her mouth began to water as he removed his tunic and shed his boots and pants.

"No talking," he said as he laid down beside her. "All I thought about all night was filling you with my rod."

Elric's husky voice and desire filled eyes brought Marin's body to life instantly. She opened her mouth for his kiss and ran her hands over his bronzed skin. His muscles moved and bunched beneath her fingers as his hands roamed down her body.

Her breasts swelled and her nipples hardened beneath her thin nightgown as his hand scraped across her sensitive nipples. A moan broke from her lips as his hand massaged first one breast, then the other.

Elric ended the kiss and leaned back on his knees to look at her. His breath came in huge gulps. "I want you too desperately that I doona think I can be gentle."

"I don't need gentle," she said as she ran her finger over his lips. "I just need you."

Large hands gripped her shoulders and pulled her to her knees in front of him. His mouth came down on hers hard and demanding, promising pleasure so intense she shook from it. His lips left a trail of hot desire as he went down her neck to her shoulders.

Vaguely, she was aware of him lifting her nightgown and pulling it over her head, careful of the bandage that bound her injuries, before tossing it to the floor. Marin leaned her head back as his mouth and hands continued to work their magic on her body.

The long, hot length of his arousal throbbed against her stomach. She reached down and took him in her hand and gently squeezed. He sucked in a breath and moaned. Marin moved her hand up and down his length, her blood pumping loudly in her ears as her body pulsed with need.

She kissed his neck and moved her lips across his chest and down to his stomach. When she reached his hips, his hands gripped her shoulders, and for a moment she thought he might stop her. She flicked her tongue over the head of his rod and heard him growl. She didn't give him time to stop her though as she opened her mouth and took him inside.

The salty taste of him was exhilarating and only spurred her passion higher. But she wasn't given long to enjoy her newfound power over him as Elric pushed her back on the bed and entered her with one long, hard thrust.

Marin let out a long moan. He began to thrust within her, building her already growing desire until she thought she would burst. Her world shattered around her as her climax exploded. She felt Elric give one final push and join her as he cried out her name.

As the last of her tremors left her, Elric rolled to the side and brought her against him. "Good morning," he said as he brushed the hair from her face.

"Good morning. I think I'd like to wake every morning just like this."

Elric laughed. "I'm up for the task. Did Mother get the wedding planned last night?"

"Yes. It's going to be very grand."

"As only royalty is," he said. "Does it bother you that I'm a prince?"

"No. It was just a surprise. You never said anything."

"I thought it might be too much for you at once, then with the Tnarg chasing us, I wasna given much time."

"True. But we're here now."

He squeezed her against him and kissed her forehead. "Aye, we're home."

Silence descended upon them and she leaned up on her elbow to look at him. "You're worried about your other two brothers?"

He nodded.

"Is there any way we can help them? Get word to them somehow?"

"Nay. We have no idea where they are, or if the Tnarg has already gotten to their mates. Only the Fae could find them now."

"Then ask the Fae."

He smiled gently. "It may come to that, or the Fae could already have found them. It was Aimery who helped me shift through time, so who is to say he hasna helped Sorin or Keiran."

"I hope they arrive soon. Your mother is very worried."

"So are Father and Lucian. All we can do is hope and pray now."

Marin rested her chin on his chest and grinned. "Your mother has the wedding planned for the day after tomorrow. She's having a gown made for me."

"And she'll get it done, this I promise you. Now, hurry and get dressed," Elric said as he rose from the bed. "I want to take you out to meet the people."

"And I want to see more of the palace."

"Hmmm," he said as he nuzzled her neck. "We might try the palace first. There are many vacant rooms and dark corridors."

Marin closed her eyes and sighed. "I like that idea."

The wedding was a huge affair, one that would have rivaled any modern-day royal wedding. Marin felt every bit the princess, and with the crown atop her head keeping her long veil in place, she looked like one too.

She had met her first Fae. Aimery, the very Fae who had aided Elric in finding her. He was nothing like she pictured a Fae to look. He wasn't small with gossamer wings, but tall, slender, and so beautiful he would have put Adonis to shame with his long flaxen hair and unusual blue eyes.

Aimery hadn't stayed long, but before he left, he assured the king and queen that he would try to locate Sorin and Keiran.

"Princess Marin," Elric said as he leaned down to kiss her lips. "I like it."

Marin smiled. "I do, too. By the way, have you seen Rhonda or Lachlan?"

"I think they went exploring the castle."

"I highly recommend it after the fun we had."

"I think Lachlan plans to ask Rhonda to be his wife."

Marin was floored. She knew they had deep feelings for

each other, she just hadn't realized how deep those feelings had gone. "I'm so happy for them. I know Rhonda will say yes."

"Enough talk of them. We've been celebrating for the past few hours, and I doona think I can wait a moment longer to make love to you."

"Then what are you waiting for?"

He pulled her against him as he claimed her lips in a searing kiss. "I love you, my princess."

"And I you, my prince."

PRINCE OF LOVE

Four brothers, a secret kingdom, and an ancient curse.

As the youngest of the four princes, Sorin waited for his chance to search out his mate. Now, it's his time to fulfill his duty, and he refuses to fail. But the dangerous magical creature tracking his every move is one step ahead of him, and Sorin must reveal the truth of what he is and where he comes from to his mate—or die trying. Will the undeniable attraction they share, be enough to convince her to leave everything she knows and enter a magical kingdom?

Katrina feared she'd never find a man to hold her interests. Until Sorin. He's charismatic, dangerous, and handsome as sin, and she feels alive when she's with him—as if she's waited for him her entire life. Katrina knows in her heart that they're meant to be together, but is the love she feels enough to leave her family behind forever?

Invergarry, Scotland
Summer, 1270

*L*ife had a funny way of turning sharp corners with no warning. Sorin Sinclair thought he had learned to adapt in his search for his mate, but no matter how many times he thought he couldn't be surprised again, he was.

He stared into familiar hazel eyes and wanted to shout for joy. With a smile and a throat clogged with emotion, he looked at his eldest brother and heir to the kingdom of Drahcir. "Keiran? Is that really you?"

Keiran jerked Sorin against him for a hug, slapping him on his back. "Aye, brother, it's me."

Sorin stepped back and looked into a face he feared he might never see again. "How?"

"I doona have time to explain, and it doesna matter anyway," Keiran answered

"I would've thought you'd have returned home by now. Have you no' found your mate?"

Keiran sighed as his smile slipped and weariness settled on his face. "Nay, but no' for lack of searching. It seems, little brother, there are forces working against us."

"What forces?"

"I had a visit from a Fae who warned me the Tnargs are looking for our mates. They're trying to find them before we do so they can kill them."

Sorin loudly expelled a breath and leaned back against the building, feeling as if the wind had just been kicked out of him. As if they didn't already have a heavy burden to carry in finding their mates and returning to Drahcir with them, now the Tnargs.

The alley was deserted, giving them the privacy they needed. Sorin shook his head in disbelief. The Tnargs were beasts who had one mission—kill any mate of a prince or princess of Drahcir. His brothers had used to scare him with stories of the Tnargs when he was small, but it was the ferocity, the strength of the creatures that made a chill run down his spine now.

"This can no' be possible. It's damned difficult enough to find our mates and convince them to leave their families behind. And now you tell me the Tnargs are trying to find them before we do?"

"Everyone thought after all these centuries the angered Fae princess would have forgiven—or at least forgotten— our family. It seems she wants to end it all. Aimery tells me the Fae banished her from their realm for what she did. I doona think even Father knows of this latest news. But that isna important. We need to find our mates, brother."

Sorin ran a hand down his face as he absorbed the news. "Shite. If our mates are killed, we can no' fulfill the curse upon our family. That's why the Tnargs are trying to locate our mates before us. The princess sent the creature," he finished, as he comprehended who was behind it all.

Keiran nodded grimly.

"The Fae who visited you, are you sure you can trust him?"

"Of course. It's Aimery," Keiran said. "You might no' have seen him the times he visited the castle, but I did. He can be trusted."

Sorin accepted his brother's word. "Have you seen Elric or Lucian?"

"Nay, but Aimery helped Elric find his mate. I have to assume that our brothers are home."

"Of course," Sorin said. "We'll make it, Keiran. I know it."

The smile Keiran gave him was forced, tight, and barely concealed the doubt in his hazel gaze. "Aye. Keep your eyes opened for the Tnarg. You willna be able to miss the beast, and it willna hesitate to kill your mate. Once you find her, convince her quickly and get her to Drahcir post haste."

"You're leaving?"

"Our time is running thin, little brother, and I've yet to find my mate. Be safe. I'll see you soon."

Sorin clasped his brother to him, almost unwilling to let him go. It had been so long since he'd seen any of his family, and parting again was torture. He released Keiran, and after one more wave, his brother disappeared into the crowded street.

With a deep breath, Sorin turned to the inn he had been about to enter when Keiran stepped in front of him. Knowing that the dreadful Tnargs were hunting their mates sent a chill of foreboding through him. His family meant the world to him. He would gladly give up his life to ensure their survival, but the curse wouldn't allow that.

The damn curse that sent each of his brothers out of their magical kingdom to search for their mates. They were given until the fifth moon of the harvest year to return to Drahcir with their brides or the kingdom and all who inhabited it would cease to exist. Sorin and Keiran had less than two months to return home.

Two months to find their mates and then persuade them in any way to return to Drahcir.

Two months.

Sorin clenched his hand into a fist as frustration consumed him. He'd crossed Scotland multiple times, but hadn't come any closer to finding his intended than he had the moment he stepped out of the gates.

"I can no' let my family down," he mumbled to himself.

All he could think about was his family and his people who counted on him to bring his mate home. Ever since he learned of the curse when he was six summers, he'd thought about completing his mission.

Lucian had often chided him for thinking more about the curse than of his intended mate. It was true. No matter what his father told him of how he'd feel when he found his woman, Sorin had always felt the heavy burden of not failing the kingdom.

The excitement of finding his mate had never taken hold of him. Was that the problem? Was it because he was more concerned with the kingdom than being happy? Could that be what was keeping him from finding his mate?

For all he knew, he'd stood right beside her but had been too preoccupied with the curse to even notice.

Sorin wanted to punch something. Hard.

He had to get his head on straight and push aside the worry of fulfilling the curse and think more of his mate. With that in mind, he moved through the village leisurely.

His gaze searched every female face of marriageable age. And felt…nothing.

With disappointment hounding him, he began to wonder how Keiran had come to be in Invergarry. Each time they left Drahcir, it was a different year, for time moved much slower in their magical kingdom. The odds of any of them encountering each other were very slim indeed.

As Sorin stood and looked around him, he was amazed at how few people actually saw him. They were so busy with their own lives that few noticed anything other than what was right before them. It was so different than Drahcir, where everything moved at a slower pace and everyone knew everyone else. People in his kingdom stopped and spoke, they did not hurry past without so much as a smile.

The congestion of the village did afford Sorin the time to survey everything. He had been searching for his mate for over a year. Seeing Keiran had given him renewed hope, especially learning that Elric and possibly Lucian had found their women and were in Drahcir at that moment.

Not even the knowledge that the Tnargs were out there could dampen the happiness he felt for his brothers. He couldn't wait to see them and his parents again. A smile pulled at his lips as he thought of the tricks he and Elric had played on each other.

That was when he heard it. A laugh that was musical and sweet, rich and vivacious. It hit him square in the chest so hard that he took a step back from the impact. It was a laugh that made him long to find its owner. He wanted to know what would make a woman laugh so. And he needed to know what kind of woman could gain his attention with such a delightful sound.

It didn't go unnoticed that it was the first time a woman had caught his attention at all in the year he'd been searching. His blood pounded in his ears as he pushed through the crowded street until he came to a group of people who watched a man juggling daggers. All around him people gasped and applauded. Yet none of them laughed.

He moved on, his ears listening for that delectable laugh once more. Just when he thought he might have imagined it, he heard it again. Sorin moved faster through the street until he saw another crowd. He hurried to it, looking over heads to see a man who had a small white dog doing tricks.

Sorin's eyes scanned the throng, searching for the woman whose laugh had called to him. He was about to move on when she laughed again. His gaze jerked back to a woman in a gown of soft yellow. She had gilded hair, flashing blue eyes, and an easy smile.

He knew her instantly.

"My mate."

All his life he heard his father speak of how he would feel when he found her. Sorin hadn't expected the uncontrollable, overpowering lust that surged through his veins. His cock thickened just looking at her.

Relief filled him. One obstacle had been overcome. Now that he'd found her, though, he had to convince her to leave with him. After he wooed her. His father had warned that Sorin might have to make love to her to prove his story, because only then would the marks that would bind them forever appear.

Sorin stayed with the crowd, studying his mate as she watched the dog. She was beautiful, his woman, with her pale skin and lithe body. Her laugh was infectious, and the more the wee dog heard it, the more tricks he did, as if he were performing just for her.

He knew how the dog felt, because Sorin would do anything to catch his mate's attention. He longed to see her bright blue eyes flash with happiness at him. He wanted to see her plump pink lips give him such a welcoming smile. He ached to feel her hands pull him to her.

Sorin walked slowly around the mob, always keeping his mate in sight. Her golden hair couldn't be tamed since it continued to come out of the braid with the softest breeze and hang in curls about her face and long, slim neck.

One such curl lay alongside her high cheek bone, brushing the corner of her mouth. She absentmindedly shoved it aside as she let out another laugh. Her head suddenly turned toward him as she listened to something one of her companions said. Sorin was struck by her beauty. The only thing that marred her complexion was a small mole at the corner of her lips on the right side.

Brows a slightly darker gold curved delicately over her blue eyes, that tilted ever so slightly upward at the corners, giving her a regal air. She had small ears, long, tapered fingers, and a stubborn lift to her chin.

He was instantly charmed, entranced.

Captivated.

When the dog finished and she finally moved off, he followed, noting the older woman with her as well as the man who looked at her as if she were a treat at the end of a meal.

It never occurred to Sorin that his mate might be married or spoken for. His father always said their mates would be waiting for them. Sorin didn't know what he would do if she were married, but there was no use worrying over it now, not until he knew it for fact.

As he followed the small group through Invergarry, his gaze moved around him, watching for any signs of the Tnarg. The only one he had ever seen had been in a book in his father's library. It had scared him so as a child that he hadn't been able to sleep for days.

Even as a warrior, the thought of crossing paths with the creature gave him pause. The Tnargs' only mission was to prevent him from returning to Drahcir with his mate. So far, the Sinclairs had won that battle. How many more times would victory fall on their side before the Tnargs won?

Sorin's hand moved to rest on the hilt of the sword strapped to his hip. He prayed he didn't see the beast, but Keiran wouldn't have come looking for him if the threat wasn't real. He and his brothers had been trained as any Highlander would. They knew how to fight—and how to win.

His gaze saw a flash of yellow turn down another street, and he hurried to catch up. When the man with his mate stopped and bought her a bouquet of flowers, Sorin had the urge to punch him.

Instead, he moved closer to the group. As they began to move off, he noticed a drunk stumbling into their path. Sorin lengthened his strides to warn them, but the drunk ran into his beauty before he had a chance.

Fortunately, Sorin caught her as she fell backward. He looked down into her blue eyes and smiled. Her heart-shaped face was even lovelier up close. He wanted to tug on one of her curls and hear her laugh again.

"Are you all right?" he asked.

Her lips parted as her pulse beat erratically at her throat and her hands gripped his arms tightly. "You caught me."

Sorin's grin widened. He'd wanted her attention, and fate had given him what he wanted. "It's fortunate for you that I did, lest you muddy your pretty gown."

"Release her, sir." The man's voice was hard, irate.

Sorin glanced at the man who had accompanied his

beauty. He returned his attention to his mate and slowly righted her. He wasn't yet ready to release her. She'd felt good, right in his arms.

"I owe you my thanks," his beauty said.

Sorin reluctantly dropped his arms and bowed his head. "None needed, my lady. Though you can repay me with your name."

Her lips pulled up slightly at the corners in a smile that made his balls tighten. "Katrina."

"*Lady* Katrina," the brute added as he moved up beside her.

Sorin ignored the man. "It's been a pleasure, Lady Katrina. I'll be more than happy to rescue you again should you need it."

She laughed, the sound music to his ears.

"I'll see to her," the brute said.

"Oh, Patrick, please," Katrina said. "He's merely being polite."

"As your intended, it is my job to look after you."

Sorin's hands clenched at his side. Just as he'd thought. His mate was already given to another man. It would mean he had to work even harder to woo her.

"I haven't accepted your offer," Katrina said, her lips tight with suppressed anger.

Sorin let one side of his mouth lift in a smile as he looked at Patrick. So, his mate didn't want Patrick. Good. Maybe that would keep him from punching the arrogant fool.

Patrick glared at Sorin before he turned back to Katrina. "You will. Why put it off?"

Sorin watched the exchange with interest. He was about to step in when something out of the corner of his eye caught his attention. Someone, or some*thing*, had been watching him.

"And your name, sir?"

Sorin jerked his head back to Katrina to find her staring at him expectedly. "Sorin Sinclair, at your service," he said with a wink. He left off the "prince" part. For the moment.

"I am here visiting my aunt. You're invited to dinner tomorrow night if you are available. It's the least I can do after you've so gallantly saved me from muddying my gown."

"I'd be honored. Who is your aunt?" Sorin was overjoyed in his luck at getting to spend more time with Katrina without having to force an accidental meeting.

"Lady Beatrice MacDuff."

"Until tomorrow evening," Sorin said.

"Until then," she said, and allowed Patrick to turn her away.

Sorin watched as she walked away, the gentle sway of her hips fascinating. He couldn't wait to plunge inside of her as her hips thrust to meet his.

When she glanced over her shoulder, a smile on her lips, Sorin knew he had definitely caught her attention.

2

Katrina went to her chamber as soon as they reached her aunt's house. She couldn't handle another minute in Patrick's company. It had been a mistake to allow him to accompany her, but she had been in a good mood when he asked and hadn't wanted to get into that same old argument.

Patrick was nothing if not persistent. Once they encountered the dashingly handsome Sorin Sinclair, Patrick had pushed her to the breaking point in asking for an answer to his offer. It was times like these that she wished her father were with her.

All she had wanted to do was think about Sorin and how he'd seemingly come out of nowhere to grab her as she'd fell. His brown eyes were dark, fathomless and held a hint of daring she'd never seen before. His dark blond hair was long and held back in a queue. All in all, he was dashing, handsome, and all-too appealing.

The more Patrick pestered her for an answer instead of allowing her to mull through her time with Sorin, the more irate she became. By the time they had reached her aunt's house, Katrina had had enough. She turned Patrick down as gently as she could, but there was no denying the anger in his gray eyes. He had stormed off, and she knew she would never see him again. She wasn't upset at the prospect.

She was relieved.

Katrina put a hand to her forehead and sighed as she leaned back against her door. As awful as it was, she had put off giving Patrick her answer because she hadn't wanted to hurt him. He had been kind, always eager to help her since she'd come to Invergarry. It was really too bad she didn't like him enough to consider him for a husband.

A smile threatened as her mind once more turned to Sorin. She closed her eyes and sighed as she thought of his blond hair darkened with streaks of brunette, and his eyes of the deepest brown. His skin was bronzed from the sun and a shadow of whiskers darkened his jaw, making him look untamed and lethal. His nose was slightly bent, as if it had been broken. His mouth was wide, his lips thin, and his smile simply devastating.

As soon as he'd caught her, she'd grabbed onto his arms and felt the strength in his muscles through his tunic and jerkin. Just thinking of touching him again sent a thrill racing through her. The thick sinew had flexed beneath her palms, making her heart race and the world begin to fall away.

He'd caught her gaze and held it, refusing to let go. It was as if he'd wanted to say something but held back. And even when he'd righted her, she hadn't wanted to let go of him. For the first time in a very long time, Sorin had made her feel secure. Within his arms she didn't feel the crush of the future upon her or the arguments from her family to choose a husband and get settled.

His touch made it all go away, leaving just the two of them.

Her eyes slowly opened, and she bit her lip as she sighed. Sorin was handsome and gallant. A man she could see herself spending more time with. Suddenly, she was anxious about tomorrow night. What would she wear? Would he come? Would he smile at her again, showing that dimple in his left cheek?

She hadn't felt such anticipation in a very long time, and it was glorious.

***

Sorin stood looking at the modest building Katrina had entered. It was her aunt's home, the very place he would arrive for dinner. He had been more than a little surprised to find her and Patrick discussing something on the front steps, something that Patrick obviously didn't agree with. Was it him?

Sorin hoped it was. Patrick made no attempt to hide the fact he didn't like him, not that Sorin cared. He was here for one thing—Katrina.

Waiting until the next night would be impossible. He'd have to think of some way to get near her tomorrow. Time was of the essence, and he had none to waste. If he could, he'd climb up to her chamber right now.

Instead, he kept to his position until sunset. Then he walked the dark alleys. The shadows hid everything, but what Sorin looked for would be easy to detect, even in the darkness. Many nights he had read of the Tnargs, especially when his brothers left to search for their mates. Grand tales of how the Tnargs would lie in wait as the Sinclairs returned to Drahcir with their mates. The Tnargs would attack mercilessly. Many of the Sinclairs were wounded viciously as they, and their mates, had managed to get inside the gates. Several had died once inside the gates, but by that time the curse had been fulfilled.

It seemed the more years that went by, the more the beasts were closer to achieving their goal. It left Sorin with a feeling of dread he couldn't push aside. Impending doom seemed to hover just over his head.

He refused to be the one to end his family and his people because he wasn't vigilant enough. The books hadn't taught him how to fight, but the journals of his ancestors speaking of the Tnargs had given hints in how to hunt one.

He sniffed the air. The stench of stale urine, garbage, and unclean bodies soaked the night, but there was another smell that drew his attention.

The Tnarg was here.

3

It was the sound of her laughter that woke Sorin from his doze. His body recognized his mate and roared to life, the hunger for her overruling everything. Soon, he'd claim her and take her to Drahcir where he planned to spend the days buried in her sweet warmth. His balls tightened just thinking of sinking into Katrina, but he tamped down his desire and rose to find his mate. He had spent most of the night searching for the Tnarg, but he'd never found the creature.

It had remained just out of reach. Knowing it was in the town unsettled him, put him on edge. Because he knew it would come for Katrina.

Why the mates and not any of the Sinclairs? It didn't make any sense. If a Sinclair died, then the curse wasn't fulfilled. Why attack an innocent woman? Sorin was missing something, he knew it.

He quickly pushed that thought away as he shifted in the shadows hoping for a glimpse of his mate. It sounded as if she'd left the house. He couldn't leave Katrina alone for a moment in case the Tnarg struck. So, when he heard her laughter, he rose from his spot across the street and cringed when he saw her mount a horse.

"Shite," he cursed, and recognized he would have a tough time keeping up with her without a mount of his own.

His gaze quickly scanned the streets until he found an unattended horse. He grabbed the reins to lead it away. Once he was mounted, he spotted Katrina as she disappeared down the street. He cursed beneath his breath and urged the horse into a canter. Thankfully her blonde hair shown in the morning sun like a beacon, leading Sorin through the streets.

His gaze scanned the area for the Tnarg, but there was no sign of it. He was more than pleased when they left the city and rode through the open countryside. Sorin stayed far enough back that he could keep an eye on Katrina, but close enough that he could reach her if the Tnarg attacked. He couldn't tell who rode with her, though he thought it was the girl from the day before. It was the perfect opportunity for him to get to know Katrina a little better.

If his luck held, the situation could turn out better than he'd first thought. And as soon as he could, he would get Katrina back to the house and to safety. Being out in the open would only tempt the Tnarg.

Just as he thought he could keep an eye on the girls, they veered right and headed to a small grove of trees. Sorin leaned over the horse's neck as the animal leapt into a gallop. Whatever luck he had quickly ran out as the girls disappeared into the trees before he could reach them. With the wind whistling in his ears, and the horse breathing heavily, he could hear nothing else.

He slowed his mount to a walk once they entered the forest and listened. Nothing. No laughter, no screams...nothing. He was about to call out when he saw movement ahead of him.

With a slight pressure from his knee, Sorin directed the horse to the right. The steed moved, its ears pricked forward. Sorin shifted his hand to the hilt of his sword as the hairs on the back of his neck stood on end.

The Tnarg was there, waiting to attack.

Sorin's heart drummed in his chest at the need to defend his woman. He wanted to call out to Katrina, to tell her to run to safety. But that would only alert the Tnarg and cause it to attack before Sorin could reach her.

Nay, he had to act carefully. It wasn't just Katrina's life at stake, but every person in Drahcir.

The soft whinny of a horse drew his attention. He turned his mount to the left and looked through the dense growth of the forest. Suddenly, he saw the Tnarg in a tree ready to spring down atop Katrina.

Sorin drew the dagger from his boot as he kicked the horse into a run. Just before the Tnarg dove, Sorin threw the dagger and watched it sink into the creature's chest. There was a loud roar as the creature turned its head of mangy brown fur to him and its red eyes full of hatred pinned him.

"Run!" he yelled to his mate.

Katrina's startled blue gaze jerked from the beast to him. Her horse reared, and Sorin watched in horror as Katrina fell, landing hard on the ground. The Tnarg landed beside her and pulled out the dagger, holding it over Katrina while she put her hand to her head.

Sorin unsheathed his sword as his horse quickly closed the distance between them. He leapt from his mount and landed atop the Tnarg just as it was about to slash open Katrina's chest. The beast flung Sorin off its back with ease and turned to face him.

"You won't stop me," the creature growled.

Sorin got to his feet and grinned while he circled the Tnarg. "You wouldna be after Katrina if my brothers hadna succeeded in reaching Drahcir. You've already failed twice. You'll fail again."

"I doubt it," the beast said. "The women are easy to kill."

"If you want a real challenge, why no' test me?" Sorin hoped the Tnarg would accept the dare and Katrina could sneak away.

He couldn't chance to look at his mate to see if she was all right. One slip and the Tnarg would kill them both. Instead, he kept his gaze on the tall, hairy creature with the foul smell, sharp talons, and long fangs.

The pictures he'd seen resembled the beast in front of him, but the blood red eyes were more frightening face-to-face than on any page in a book. Its claws were longer and sharper, and it seemed to have many more razor-sharp teeth than the drawings had shown. Its face was elongated, and even with its mouth closed he could see nearly every one of the jagged teeth in its mouth.

And it stood a head and a half taller than Sorin.

He ducked as the Tnarg suddenly lashed out with its long arms, its claws narrowly missing Sorin's head. "You move too slow, human."

Sorin laughed. "You have to use magic in order to beat me. In a fair fight, you'd already be dead."

The Tnarg pulled back its lips and growled. "You ought not to taunt me. I can make your death very painful."

Sorin was tired of talking. He couldn't trust anything the creature said anyway. He ducked and rolled, and then in one smooth motion, came to his feet and plunged his sword deep into the Tnarg. The beast roared in pain, but Sorin didn't stop. He pushed the sword through the Tnarg and embedded the blade into the tree.

The beast's eyes blazed with fury, and it slashed out with its talons, connecting with Sorin's arm before he could get away. He bit back a growl of pain and rushed to Katrina, who stared in disbelief at the sight before her.

Neither of the horses were near, and Sorin knew his sword would only hold the Tnarg for so long. They had to get moving.

"Are you hurt?" he asked as he helped Katrina to her feet.

"Nay," she whispered and turned her wide, blue eyes to him. "What is that thing?"

"I'll explain later. Right now we need to leave."

Sorin took her hand and started running to the edge of the trees. He spotted the horse he had stolen earlier and whistled to it. The steed raised its head and galloped to them. Sorin vaulted onto the horse's back and held out his hand for Katrina. Once she was behind him, she wrapped her arms around his waist, her entire body shaking.

He nudged the horse into a flat out run as the Tnarg's roar sounded behind them.

"Where is your friend that was with you?"

"I don't know. One moment she was beside me, and the next she was not. What happened, Sorin? What was that thing?"

"Even though you saw it, you probably willna believe me. I'd hoped to kill it last night, but I couldna find the damned thing."

"It was after me?"

"Aye," he said through clenched teeth. He covered her hands with one of his. "I'm afraid it was."

She said nothing more as she laid her head on his back.

Sorin glanced over his shoulder, but they weren't being followed. Yet. He had no doubt the Tnarg would try again. The sooner he could get her inside her aunt's house the better.

Even with the pain of his arm, the lust wouldn't be ignored. Her feminine curves were pressed tight against his body, her arms wrapped around him. She was frightened, probably injured, but he didn't want to tell her anything atop a horse as they raced away from his enemy.

It would require him to be in front of her so he could see her expressions, anticipate her responses. To make matters worse, her friend was likely dead, and since Katrina hadn't asked about her, he wasn't going to bring her up.

Nothing more was said until Sorin stopped the horse just before entering the city. He needed to explain things to Katrina without others overhearing. And he needed to check on her friend. He lifted his leg over the horse's head and slid to the ground.

When he looked up at Katrina, her face was white, her eyes glazed over as she looked down at him, so trusting, so expecting, that he felt his heart catch. This was his woman, his mate. She'd nearly been killed, and he hadn't even kissed her.

He wasn't sure how he was going to keep her from the creature by himself, but he would do whatever it took. Or die trying.

"I left Amelia."

He took her hand in his and squeezed. Then, he lied. "The beast doesna want her." When Katrina didn't argue, he swallowed. "I'll go search for her as soon as I know you're safe."

"You're bleeding," Katrina said and gently touched his arm. "Why didn't you tell me you were wounded?"

"It's just a scratch. I'll tend to it later."

"You'll tend to it now. I won't have you bleeding everywhere."

He couldn't help but grin. She had just encountered a magical beast and she was worried about his loss of blood. "Ordering me around already, lass?" he teased.

"I am."

To his surprise, Katrina reached under her skirts and pulled off a section of her underskirt, giving him a tempting view of her calf. She slid off the horse before he could help her and began to tie the material around his arm.

"Get used to it. Men hate it, but my father has gotten used to it."

He inhaled as she stepped closer to him. "I like a woman who knows her own mind. My mother is much like you."

"Really?" Katrina said, her blue eyes glancing up to catch his gaze as she finished tying off the makeshift bandage. "I'll clean the wounds later, but we had to stop the bleeding."

Sorin inspected her quick handiwork. The gashes had gone deep, and he'd lost a lost of blood. "Fine job."

"Tell me, please. What was that thing?"

She was still pale, but she had stopped shaking. The stubborn tilt of her chin told Sorin she wasn't going anywhere until he told her what she needed to know. "I need to go find Amelia."

"You think she's already dead or you would never have stood here to let me tend you."

Sorin clenched his jaw, then gave a single nod of his head. "We angered the beast. It'll seek retribution."

"Poor Amelia," Katrina said as she closed her eyes. When she opened them, she blew out a long breath. "Now, tell me what that was."

"It's a Tnarg, a magical creature sent to kill you."

She blinked. "I beg your pardon? Did you say magical? You can be hung for that."

"I know. I'm no' jesting, Katrina. Do you think it was by happenstance that I was in that grove? I followed you, because I knew that creature was out there hunting you."

"You're scaring me," she said softly and wrapped her arms around her middle.

"That's no' my intention." He sighed. "In all honesty, you need to be scared. That thing willna stop trying to kill you."

She stared into his eyes, after a few moments she shook her head and took a step back. "You're serious."

"What you saw back there wasna your imagination. My sword will only hold it for so long. I'm sure it's already free by now. You need to stay somewhere protected at all times."

"Why does it want to kill me?"

Sorin hesitated. He had wanted to ease into his explanation, but she wasn't allowing him to. "You're...special."

"Special how?"

Shite. "My lady, that explanation is much longer than I'd like to give right now. Or right here. Let's get you to your aunt's so I can go looking for Amelia."

"Amelia is my maid," she said. "She never wanders away. Why didn't I realize there was danger?"

"You cannot be blamed for anything when a beast such as the Tnarg is after you."

Sorin took her by the arm and led her to her aunt's. He followed her into the house. One look from the small, plump woman with blue eyes that matched Katrina's and she had him and Katrina ushered into the solar where she could discover what happened.

"I need to go look for Amelia," Sorin said as he turned to leave.

"Sit," Beatrice ordered, one brow lifted as if daring him to say anything else.

Sorin's brows went up at the aunt's tone. She reminded him of his mother. "Someone must look for Amelia."

"And they will," Beatrice said, brooking no argument. "I'll send one of the stable lads. You're wounded, lad, and need to be cared for. Now sit," she said, and motioned to the chair near Katrina.

Sorin thought over all he knew of the Tnarg. It only attacked those the Sinclairs had claimed for their own. It knew Katrina was his mate. If he went out there now to search for Amelia, the creature could attack the house and kill Katrina. The odds of the beast attacking a stable lad who went looking for a maid were slim.

As much as he didn't want to put anyone at risk, he couldn't leave Katrina alone. Not after so close a call.

He looked over at her. Katrina gave him a small nod, as if she knew what he was thinking. Sorin reluctantly took the seat while Beatrice had someone sent for the maid. His gaze returned to Katrina to find her staring at the floor.

"We can't thank you enough," Beatrice said as she unwrapped the bandage Katrina had tied. "Had you not been there, there's no telling what might have happened to our Katrina. My brother would never have forgiven me if any harm befell her. She's all he has left."

Sorin nodded, a knot of apprehension developing in his stomach as he heard of Katrina's father. By the time Aunt Beatrice finished cleaning and bandaging his wound, food and ale had been brought in. Color was slowly returning to Katrina's face, though Beatrice's had gone white as Katrina told her of the attack.

He had been surprised when Katrina left out the Tnarg, instead recounting the attack as a couple of men bent on raping and stealing.

"My poor darling," Aunt Beatrice said as she wrapped an arm around Katrina. Her sharp gaze caught Sorin's. "What kind of weapons did they have to leave four wounds on your arm?"

"They struck him multiple times," Katrina hastily lied.

Beatrice patted Katrina's hand and looked at him. "Of course. I don't know what I was thinking. You must stay for dinner. I know Katrina invited you already, but this will be a family affair now."

After that announcement, Beatrice rose and left the solar. Sorin smiled after the plump woman, missing his mother more than ever.

"You're very fortunate to have her."

"I know," said Katrina with a small smile. "My family is wonderful. We're very close."

Sorin knew in that instant that convincing Katrina to leave her family and never see them again would be near hopeless. Just when he thought he had conquered one hurdle, another jumped in front of him.

Yet his lust burned too brightly to ignore his destiny. His cock hungered to feel her hot, wet sex envelope him and, short of death, nothing could stop him from achieving what he had come to do.

"She'll leave us alone for a while as she sees to things," Katrina said. "It would be a good time to hear your explanation."

Sorin leaned back in the chair, trying to ignore the lust that rode him and the cause of it sitting so near. "I doona know if now is a good time, but, regardless, you need to know. You need to be prepared for everything. It's all going to sound farfetched."

"Tell me."

"A verra long time ago, one of my ancestors did the unthinkable. He angered a Fae princess."

"Fae?" she questioned, her brows furrowed in disbelief. "They don't exist."

"And neither do magical monsters sent to kill you."

She blew out a breath and nodded. "So, how did your ancestor anger this princess?"

"The Fae are extremely beautiful creatures. My ancestor wanted to see if he could make the princess fall in love with him. Unfortunately for everyone, she did. The only problem was, he didna love her."

"Oh, dear."

"Exactly," Sorin agreed. "The princess, in a fit of rage, cursed our family."

"I guess she figured that was worse than killing your ancestor. What is the curse?"

"Each generation, the princes and princesses of Drahcir must leave our kingdom to search for their mates and return with them to the kingdom."

"Drahcir? I've never heard of it."

"You wouldna have," he said. "The kingdom is hidden deep in the Ben Nevis Mountains."

"Those mountains are treacherous."

"Drahcir is veiled, Katrina. The Fae took pity on us because of what the princess did. They keep Drahcir hidden from any outsiders. Only those who leave can find it again."

"I see." She slowly rose to her feet and began to pace the solar. "Your tale is most...unusual. And you're a prince?"

"It's the truth. All of it."

4

Katrina looked at Sorin. His dark brown eyes begged her to believe him, and she wanted to, yet she found it hard to. The Fae, a Tnarg, and a hidden kingdom all in one day? It was too much for her to take in.

She didn't doubt what her eyes had seen in the grove. That beast would haunt her dreams for years to come. And to know it was still out there waiting to kill her made her sick to her stomach.

Suddenly, she stopped pacing and turned to Sorin. "Why is the Tnarg trying to kill me?"

His pause was long as he watched her with his dark eyes for several moments before he said, "We leave Drahcir to search for our mates. The Tnarg's mission is to make sure we doona accomplish that."

Her heart skidded to a halt at his words. "Are you…are you saying…."

"That you're my mate?" He nodded slowly. "Aye."

Katrina released the breath inside of her.

Finally, he stood. "This is no jest."

She leaned against the chair before her as his words

penetrated. "I don't understand how you can think I'm your mate. We only just met."

"I know it's difficult," he said as he came toward her. "I've been searching for you for over a year, moving from village to village. It was your laugh that drew me. You have the most amazing laugh."

Katrina found herself pulled into Sorin's gaze. He was breathtakingly handsome, and each time she looked at him, her knees went weak. She didn't know if it was his chiseled features or the power he exuded, but he certainly called to her. And he had saved her from certain death. How could she not be attracted to him? But his story was so fantastic and unbelievable.

"Each of us was given a way to find our mates by the Fae," he continued. "I was afraid I might fail my family before I heard your laugh. I knew before I'd even seen you that you were the one."

"Have any of your ancestors ever picked the wrong woman?"

He shook his head, a dark blond lock falling into his eye. "Never."

"So you take them to Drahcir?"

He smiled then, one side of his mouth lifting to tempt her. "Aye. Though you must come willingly."

"So I don't need to worry about you kidnapping me?" she asked with a grin.

She had seen her nightmares come to life that afternoon, but with Sorin she felt safe...protected. Almost as if it hadn't happened. She knew, instinctively, that he would keep the beast from her.

He chuckled and shook his head. "No kidnappings, my lady."

Her smile vanished as she looked out the window. "It's

still out there waiting, isn't it?"

"It is. It willna stop until you are dead. Or we arrive in Drahcir."

"My father wants me to marry. He says it's well past the time, but none of my suitors seemed...well, right for me. How do I know you aren't daft and making all this up?"

He shifted on his feet causing her to turn her gaze back to him. He then sank into the chair and crossed his bulging arms over his thick chest. His long legs stretched out in front of him, stopping just short of touching her skirts as he crossed his ankles. His trews molded to his thick legs, and she knew firsthand how wonderful it was to be held in his arms.

And then to be told she was his mate? As upset and frightened as she should be, all she felt was...sheltered. Until his dark gaze captured hers and made her yearn for his kisses, to have his hands caress her body.

"I'm no' daft. There's nothing I can say to convince you otherwise. You'll have to trust me."

"Ah, trust," she murmured and jerked her lusting thoughts back to the present. "It's difficult not to trust a man who has just saved my life."

He rose to his feet, and Katrina found herself inches from the tall, mouth-watering man who had suddenly come into her life and turned it upside down. She could feel his heat, and the strange yearnings in her body only fueled her curiosity. His thumb caressed her jaw as he dipped his head.

Katrina found it impossible to breathe as she waited for him to kiss her. His mouth stopped just short of touching hers.

A slow, seductive smile pulled at his lips as he rose. "I'm glad to hear it, lass."

She blinked as Sorin stepped away a heartbeat before her

aunt walked back into the room. Katrina looked at him to see that seductive smile that made her melt every time. She couldn't predict what he would do one moment to the next, and she loved that.

A stomach full of good, hot food definitely improved Sorin's temperament. He and Katrina hadn't been left alone since that morn, but he learned much about her and the lust that lurked in her eyes. How he stopped himself from kissing her, he would never know. But he had seen the disappointment before he had turned away.

That was almost worth being so close to her and tempting himself.

He wanted her to experience the same level of hunger and frustration he knew. To know she was his but unable to take her yet was maddening to say the least.

It was just after the noon meal when the men returned with the maid, bruised and slightly wounded, but alive. Sorin wanted to hunt the Tnarg, but he couldn't bring himself to leave Katrina, not to mention his sword was still in the forest. At least he hoped it was. Though he had other weapons, he wanted his sword returned.

Now, with supper finished, he found himself alone with his mate again. "Which window is your chamber?"

Her blue gaze jerked to his. "Excuse me?"

"Katrina, I doona want to frighten you more than you already are, but as I've said, the Tnarg willna give up just because you're in your aunt's home."

She studied him a moment, tugging on the end of her blonde braid. "My life has turned upside down. What do you plan to do, sleep under my window?"

"Nay. I plan on climbing through your window and sleeping on your floor."

"You are daft," she whispered, though he saw the excitement in her gaze. "I cannot allow you in my chamber."

"And I willna allow you to be killed when I could've protected you."

She wrapped her arms around her waist and shivered. She was putting on a brave front, but Sorin knew she was terrified. The Tnarg had nearly gotten to her that morn.

"My window is the third from the left corner on the second floor."

Sorin nodded. How he was going to get up to that window, he wasn't sure. Yet.

Katrina sat in the middle of her bed, her legs drawn up to her chest. Every creak and moan in the house made her jump. She was expecting the Tnarg to bust through her door at any moment. The idea of being asleep when that happened made her sick to her stomach. So she sat. Waiting.

When Sorin had said he was coming to her chamber, she had thought him a fool. After all, she should be safe in her aunt's home. But now she kept glancing to her window, wondering where he was. She expected him hours ago.

She climbed from the bed and gazed down from her window. It was a sheer drop to the street with nothing to hold onto to climb up or down. In the silence of the night, a board creaked outside her chamber. She spun around, her heart hammering in her chest. Something was trying to come in her door.

Katrina grabbed the dagger on her table she'd taken from Sorin and rushed to the wall beside the door, prepared to plunge the weapon into the Tnarg and race down the hallway. Her breathing seemed loud to her own ears, but she couldn't slow it no matter how she tried.

The door slowly swung open. Katrina lifted the dagger over her head and prepared to bring it down when strong hands suddenly gripped her arms and pushed her against the wall.

"Katrina?"

She nearly cried as she heard Sorin's voice. Her fear melted away and she sagged against him as her hand loosened and the dagger dropped to the floor. "I thought you were the Tnarg. I've been waiting for you."

His arms wrapped around her, holding her tight, as he buried her face in his neck. "I coulda scale the wall. I had to sneak into the house. Everything is all right now."

But it wasn't. Katrina inhaled his scent of pine, spice...and power. She closed her eyes and buried her face against the soft material of his tunic and took a deep breath. Thickly muscled arms held her steady, comforting her as no one else could.

She wasn't sure what made her want to be near Sorin so. Was it because he said she was his mate? Did she want to believe him so desperately she had started to convince herself?

"You're shaking," he murmured in her hair as he leaned his face close to hers. "I told you I would protect you."

She swallowed and pulled back to look at him. "You're asking me to believe the impossible, and yet, I find myself doing it."

"Good." He smiled and ran a finger down her cheek. "By the saints, it hurts just to look at you. I've never seen a woman so beautiful."

Many men had told her she was pretty, but no one had

meant it as Sorin did. Being this close to him, having his arms around her, made her hunger for him. She yearned to kiss him. Not the chaste kisses her former beaux had put upon her cheek, but a kiss of passion and desire. A kiss that one lover gave to another.

The air closed in around her. Sorin's face was in shadows, hiding his emotions. And just when she was about to step out of his embrace, one of his hands moved to her neck, urging her forward.

Her lips parted and her breathing quickened. Her skin tingled in anticipation, her heartbeat accelerated, and for the first time in her life, she felt like a woman. His head lowered toward hers, and beneath her palm, she felt his heart race.

Then his lips touched hers.

Soft, seductive...and too tempting to resist, Katrina's mouth moved against his. A groan vibrated his chest and his hands pulled her closer, crushing her against him. His lips kissed, licked, and nipped hers, making her yearn for more, to feel more of him.

When his hand braced against the back of her head and his mouth slanted over hers, she wrapped her arms around him. Slowly, his tongue ran over her lips. Her lips parted, and as soon as they did, Sorin's tongue delved into her mouth, touching his tongue against hers. It was the most erotic thing she had ever felt.

And she wanted more.

As he increased the kiss, she followed his example, giving as much as he gave her until her body began to hum with a desire she had never thought to feel. But it terrified her, this irresistible desire, this tangible need.

Katrina broke the kiss and stepped away from him. She used the wall at her back to keep her upright as she gently touched her lips. They felt swollen, just as her breasts did.

"Katrina?"

His voice was barely a whisper, but it sent chills racing over her heated skin.

"Are you a magician that you've cast a spell over my body?"

His head swiveled slowly side to side. "Nay. I'm a man, a man who's found his mate. The desire you feel will grow with each hour we're together until you can no' deny it."

Just then a throb of longing pulsed between her legs. Katrina gasped and squeezed them together, but it only made the sensation return.

"Doona fight it," Sorin whispered. "Let me show you how wonderful our joining can be."

She wanted nothing more than to go to him, to take his outstretched hand and lean against his strength. But the longing in her own body kept her rooted against the wall.

She watched him as he moved to her. His hand brushed her face, moving a lock of hair behind her ear. The heat of him, his seductive scent drove her wild. What was happening to her? It was as if her body wasn't her own, her mind wasn't her own.

For all she wanted, all she cared about was Sorin, of feeling his lips on hers again, of his hands on her body.

And suddenly, she was in his arms. His body pressed her against the wall as his mouth took hers in a fierce kiss that ravaged her like a thief. But instead of making her fear him, it only made her want him more.

Katrina slid her arms around his neck to hold him against her. She heard him moan and a thrill went through her. His body was hard and hot, much like his arousal pressed against her stomach. He was fire and rock, passion and strength.

Intensity and need.

Sorin couldn't get enough of her sweet, intoxicating mouth. Drinking from those plump lips was like drinking the most delightful wine. He'd never get enough of her mouth or of hearing her soft moans as she gave into the desire running through her.

It hadn't been his intention to seduce Katrina that night, but now that he had begun, he knew he wouldn't be able to stop. His father had warned him that the lust would be great, but Sorin hadn't expected it to override everything.

He turned them and slowly backed her to the bed. Her kisses left him breathless, his body on fire for her. The need to sink into her heat, to feel her clench around him was overwhelming. Once they reached the bed, he broke the kiss long enough to lay her down and move next to her. Her lips were wet and swollen, her eyes glazed with desire.

His head lowered and he nipped at her mouth. No words were needed, not now. Not when every kiss, every touch told him it was the right thing to do. Once he had joined their bodies, she would see for herself they were well and truly mates.

And in the meantime, he would get to enjoy her delicious body.

His hand moved from her hip over her stomach to the curve of her breast. She gasped as he cupped her soft breast. It soon turned into a moan as his thumb stroked her nipple into a hard little pebble.

Her body instinctively sought his as her back arched and her hips moved against him. It took everything he had not to rip off their clothes and plunge into her. He reined in his desire as he kissed down her neck. She smelled of wildflowers and innocence, of desire and passion.

And she was all his.

5

Katrina's hands moved over Sorin's thick shoulders and heavily muscled arms. His mouth was doing delectable things to her skin as he moved down her neck to her chest. His hand massaged her breast and tweaked her nipple, sending shivers of delight racing through her to pool between her legs like liquid heat.

Her sex clenched, greedy for more.

And Sorin was more than willing to give it to her. When he settled over her body, his weight made her tremor with anticipation. His cock pressed against her sex, as if seeking entrance through their layers of clothing.

It was too much for Katrina. She clawed at Sorin's tunic as she tried to pull it off him. In one swift motion, he sat up and yanked it over his head before tossing it aside. She sighed and rose up so she could look her fill of him. Her hand reached out to touch him, but he rose from the bed.

Katrina was afraid he was leaving, but then she saw him tug off his boots and yank down his trews. She bit her lip as she got her first real look at a man.

He was...beautiful. Tall and rippled with sinew, Sorin was everything a man should be.

She rose up on her knees at the edge of the bed and let her hands move over his broad chest and down his hard stomach to his narrow hips. His rigid cock jumped every time her hand neared it.

As much as she wanted to touch him, feel him, she was too hesitant to do it. Until he took her hand and placed it over his rod.

"Feel me, feel the desire I have for you," he whispered in her ear, just before he took her lobe in his mouth and sucked.

Katrina gasped at the sensation and closed her eyes. He was hot and hard and velvety smooth. He guided her hand up and down his length while his other hand found her breast. Pleasure spiked through her. Something warm and needful unfurled in her sex. And then he yanked her chemise over her head. She arched her back and let her head drop back as her hips sought him.

His hand came around her waist to hold her as his mouth descended on her nipple, suckling it deep in his mouth. Katrina bit her lip to keep from crying out as her need grew to overwhelming proportions. She wanted...more.

Sorin didn't make her wait. He pushed her back and knelt beside the bed. Katrina lifted her head to look at him when she felt him opening her legs. No one had ever looked at her sex, but the need for him overruled her fear.

His hands caressed the insides of her thighs, placing kisses against her skin. She let her head fall onto the bed, unable to hold back the tide of need that had taken her. Her body gave a slight jerk when his fingers skimmed over the curls at her sex, but at the same time, delicious heat filled her. His fingers parted her and dipped inside her.

Katrina clawed at her bed coverings and cried out his name. His fingers went deeper, stretching her, teasing her. Filling her. The pleasure was intense, but still she wanted, needed more.

And then his mouth touched her.

Her mouth opened on a silent scream as his tongue did things to her she didn't know were possible. He licked, he kissed, and he suckled, sending her spiraling towards something she didn't understand.

And just when she didn't think she could stand it anymore, her world shattered around her. Wave upon wave of pleasure rolled over her, sending her drowning in an abyss of ecstasy she never wanted to end.

Her body still convulsed with her climax when Sorin moved over her. His cock rubbed against her sensitive flesh, and she opened her arms to welcome him. His thick head slid easily into her wet sheath.

Slowly, he pushed his rod inside her and then stopped.

"It's going to hurt," he whispered.

"Don't make me wait," she begged. "I need more of you."

The words were barely out of her mouth when he partly withdrew, then thrust deep. Katrina gave a soft cry and buried her head in Sorin's neck as the pain spiked through her.

"I'm sorry."

"Shh," she said, and moved her head to look at him. "It's the way. It had to be done, and the pain is already receding."

He smiled and kissed her. "How did I live my life without you?"

She couldn't answer him, not when he began to move his hips, sending her desire spiking once more. Her body accepted him eagerly, and the pleasure was blinding. His thrusts were long and deep, short and quick, and each one brought her more satisfaction than the last.

The need began to build again, unfurling in her belly with greater intensity than before. Sorin gave a final thrust and stiffened as his seed spilled into her causing her to peak again, the pleasure blinding her with its power.

Katrina wrapped her arms around him and kissed his neck. "Thank you," she whispered.

A few moments later, he rose up on his elbows to stare down at her. "You're incredible."

She giggled. "Nay, what we did was incredible. I never knew it could be like that."

A frown passed over his handsome, angular face.

"What is it?" she asked.

"There's more I need to tell you, especially now."

A shiver of dread filled her. "What?"

He pulled out of her and sat on the edge of the bed. "Remember how I told you the Fae help us find our mates, and that we're never wrong when we find them?"

"Aye."

"There's something else that happens, to help us ensure we return with the right woman."

She almost hated to ask by the tightening of his jaw. Whatever it was, he expected it to anger her. "What is that?"

He lifted his right arm, and before her very eyes, a pattern began to darken from his elbow to his shoulder. The pattern was unique in its knotwork and beautiful in its swirls.

Katrina sat up and ran her hand over the now black marks. "It's…magnificent. So, once you bed the right woman, this mark appears?"

He grimaced. "Aye, but no' just on me."

She blinked, unable to believe what he was telling her

until she looked down at her arms. The same pattern on his arm now appeared on her left. "By the saints," she said with a gasp.

If she hadn't seen with her own eyes, she'd think it was a hoax. Now, she could only look in stunned silence at the beautiful mark upon her skin. It seemed both odd and appropriate that it be on her arm.

She was shocked to see it, but the sizzle that raced over her skin and through her body as she realized what it meant didn't leave anger. It left her…breathless with the prospect of her future. Because now, more than ever, she couldn't push aside Sorin's words as false. They were as real as the sun that rose every morning.

"Katrina?"

"I'll have it always?" she asked.

"Aye. As will I."

She raised her gaze to his. In his dark eyes was a sadness that made her heart drum sickeningly in her chest. "There is more, isn't there?"

"Aye," he said with a sigh. "I have to return with you before the fifth moon of the harvest year."

"And that is when?"

"In less than two months."

No wonder he was sad. The news meant she had very little time either with him—or with her family. Katrina needed to think. She rose and paced before the bed, heedless of her nakedness. "And the rest?"

"I doona know if now is the time, lass."

She turned sharply to him. "I think now is definitely the time, Sorin. I don't doubt that I am your mate. Especially now. But I need to know everything."

"All right." He ran a hand down his face. "If you doona

return with me, my kingdom and all its inhabitants will cease to exist."

She stopped pacing and her stomach dropped to her feet. Of everything she might have imagined, she hadn't expected anything of this magnitude. "My God."

"You can refuse me if you want. What I ask is a lot, but please know what if you do refuse me you'll never find happiness with another man. Eventually, over the years, the pain at not being with me will grow and turn you bitter and hateful."

"Yet, you can find another?" That hardly seemed fair.

"Nay." He lowered his gaze to the floor. "If you decide no' to return, I'll stay with you for I can no' leave my mate. I'm bound to you, forsaking all others. For you."

Katrina wanted to cry. How had she gotten into this mess? And what could she do other than return with Sorin? His people, his family, counted on him returning. Yet, how could she leave behind everything she knew?

It was a frightening possibility, but the idea of not being with Sorin left her cold. Besides, all women left their families when they married. Her father had never understood why she had been so choosy in finding a husband. Now she knew. She'd been waiting on Sorin.

He'd been searching for her, but she had also been searching for him. The one man she'd known was meant for her the moment she fell into his arms and she looked into his dark eyes. It had been just an instant, but her body, her heart, her soul, had known him.

"I'll go with you to Drahcir." She expected him to show some happiness or excitement. Instead he closed his eyes and clenched his jaw. And that's when she realized what she hadn't understood before now. "If I go with you, I'll never be able to see my family again, will I?"

He slowly shook his head.

Her family meant the world to her, how could she leave knowing she would never see them again? Never have her father hold her children or her children know him. She'd already had her mother taken from her, she wasn't ready to let go of her father as well.

"You ask the impossible," she murmured, and reached for her chemise. She pulled the garment over her head, her hands shaking as her mind and body warred with what each wanted. Her body wanted Sorin. Her heart did as well, but it also wanted to be near her father.

"I know. If I could change things, I would," Sorin said. "Drahcir is kept secret by Fae magic, and though we allow anyone who wants to leave our kingdom to do so, they can never return."

"Yet you can?"

"We doona leave because we want to. We leave because we have to," he said softly. "Time travels slower in our kingdom. Much slower."

"In other words, even if I were able to leave, my family might well be dead."

"You've the right of it."

She returned to the bed and sat beside him, the weight of the world suddenly on her shoulders. "I've waited my whole life to find a man who understood me, who made my blood sing. To find you. I just never expected you to be from a magical kingdom."

He rose and silently dressed. No more words were spoken as she crawled beneath the covers and Sorin took up post in a corner near the window. There was nothing left to say for the moment.

Somehow, despite all she had learned, she was able to

find sleep knowing he was there. Yet, when she opened her eyes with the morning sun, Sorin was gone.

The disappointment she felt was swift and sharp. This would be what it felt like if she refused to go with him. If she remained, so would he. He would never see his family again. And they would die.

"This isn't fair to either of us," Katrina said as she looked at the empty corner where he'd been during the night.

Sorin waited until the streets began to fill before he moved away from his post beneath Katrina's window. He spent the night watching her sleep, replaying their conversation over and over in his head. His body yearned to feel her beneath him again. Her soft cries of pleasure had been music to his ears, and he could easily spend the day making love to her. But she needed time, time they didn't have.

And he needed her.

He had seen her face. The thought of leaving her family forever was not something she could do. He wished he had more time to woo her, to convince her that they were meant to be together. But time wasn't on his side.

Already he could feel the countdown to the fifth moon of the harvest year. He had lied when he said he had two months before he had to return. It was less than a month, but he hadn't wanted to worry her more than she already was.

All he could do now was give her a day or so to think while he hunted the Tnarg. If the Tnarg was dead and she decided to return with him to Drahcir, their way would be considerably less dangerous.

In the light of day, the Tnarg wouldn't venture into the

heart of the city, which is where he prayed Katrina stayed. It would give him some peace of mind while he retrieved his sword. He had numerous other weapons, but his sword was important to him. He and his father had made the weapon, so to lose it would be like losing a part of his father.

Sorin took one last look at Katrina's window and moved off through the streets. The sky was gray with storm clouds. He prayed the storm held off until he could find the Tnarg. The rain would only send everyone indoors and make it easier for the Tnarg to attack Katrina.

He found another horse at the edge of the city. After a quick look around, Sorin untied the animal and vaulted onto his back. A click from him sent the animal into an easy gallop. Sorin's gaze searched the ground for any sign of the Tnarg's tracks. He circled the city twice before he was sure the beast wasn't there. Then, he turned to the grove of trees.

With his thoughts jumbled, he walked the horse to the grove, hoping along the way he could figure out a way to persuade Katrina to return with him. Thunder rumbled in the distance as the wind began to bend the trees and whistle over the ground. Out of the corner of his eye he saw something move. He jerked his head around, but it was too late.

The Tnarg was fast and stayed out of sight as much as possible. But Sorin knew the beast was there. Waiting.

When Sorin walked the mare to the trees, the horse refused to go in. She sidestepped, jerking her head up and down as her eyes rolled wildly.

"Easy, lass," Sorin murmured as he dismounted and patted the horse on the neck. "I doona want to be here either. Go back to your master," he said and turned the horse toward the city. He gave the mare a slap on her rump that sent her galloping away.

Then, with a sigh, he looked into the trees.

Before he could hunt the creature, he needed his sword. He stepped into the wood and noted the absolute silence. No crickets or birds made a sound, for evil was near. He walked as silent as a ghost through the dense trees. The thick layer of pine needles and the wind quieted his steps as he moved to where he had fought the Tnarg the day before.

When he came to the spot, he glared at the tree where his sword was embedded nearly to the hilt. Sorin touched the leather wrapped pommel. At least the beast hadn't broken it. His hand gripped the weapon and tugged.

Just as he feared. The oak was thick, and the sword deep inside it.

A twig snapped behind him. Sorin didn't need to turn to see the Tnarg behind him. Lightning suddenly split the sky a heartbeat before the rain began.

"You'll never get the sword out in time," the beast hissed.

6

Katrina blew out a breath and rose to her feet. She'd been on edge and frantic ever since she had woken to find Sorin gone. He'd left so he wouldn't be discovered in her room, but now she was growing concerned that he hadn't come to see her since.

Where are you, Sorin?

"Katrina, you're making me nervous with your pacing. The storm won't last long," Aunt Beatrice murmured over her needlepoint.

Katrina ran to the window and looked at the dark clouds racing toward them. As her gaze scanned the city, a lone rider traveling to the woods caught her eye. She knew instantly it was Sorin.

"Nay," she whispered, as fear took her heart in a tight grip.

Without a word to her aunt, she raced from the solar to the crossed swords hung in the hall. Katrina gripped the pommel of the sword and tugged.

"Lass, what are you doing?" her aunt asked from the doorway.

"I don't have time to explain. Trust me. I need this sword." Just then a servant rounded the corner. "I need a horse. Now!" she shouted when the servant didn't move.

Aunt Beatrice stepped to her side after the servant went running to do as she commanded. "Katrina, you're worrying me. Come sit down until your father arrives."

Katrina's head swiveled to her aunt. "Father is coming?"

"Aye, my darling girl. I sent word to him yesterday after the attack. He's come to take you home."

Katrina felt as if someone had yanked the earth from beneath her feet. "I'd love to explain everything, and I know it appears as though I've gone daft, but I need this weapon."

"Why?"

"Sorin lost his yesterday battling the beast."

Aunt Beatrice's eyes narrowed. "You mean the men who attacked you."

Katrina shook her head. "Nay. Aunt, forgive me for lying to you. It was a beast, a beast come to kill me. Sorin saved my life, and he's gone to kill it. He needs this weapon."

She waited one heartbeat, two as her aunt debated her words. Finally, Aunt Beatrice nodded and reached up to grip the sword.

"We'll pull together," she said.

It took three tugs, but they finally got the sword free. Katrina could barely lift it, but she would do what she needed to get to Sorin. She walked to the door when her aunt's voice stopped her.

"What do I tell your father?"

Katrina looked back at her aunt as an unusual calm overtook her. "Tell him I love him, and if I haven't returned, send an army to the grove."

"Katrina," her aunt murmured as she covered her mouth with her hand.

But Katrina couldn't wait a moment longer. She had to get to Sorin. With the help of a servant, she mounted the mare and settled the sword across her lap. She didn't glance back at the door as she nudged the horse into a run.

The rain came before she made it out of the city. In a matter of moments her clothes were plastered to her skin. The howling wind made hearing anything difficult, and the lightning spooked the mare each time it forked across the sky.

Katrina blinked against the blinding rain and saw a shape come at her. Her heart jumped into her throat as she thought it might be the Tnarg, until she saw it was a horse. A riderless horse.

"Sorin," she whispered, urgency making her blood pump quicker.

She tried to nudge her horse faster, but the mare refused to move forward. She turned in circles, trying to get Katrina to go back to town.

"Just a little farther," she urged to the mare.

The horse snorted and grudgingly walked to the grove, though its body began to tremble.

"I've lost my mind," Katrina mumbled to herself. "Only a daft person would be out in this storm to face a magical beast that wants me dead."

But she knew she wasn't daft. Sorin brought her there. She knew next to nothing about the man other than he quickened her blood and made her feel whole. It wasn't something she could explain, but there was truly a connection between them that even that mark on her arm couldn't compare with.

She wiped away the rain from her eyes to see she reached the trees. With her hand wrapped around the hilt of the heavy sword, she had begun to dismount when a loud roar filled the air. Katrina managed to descend from the mare before she reared and bolted back to the city. Katrina turned to the trees, her entire body shaking with cold and fear.

She lifted the sword with both hands and kicked at her wet skirts as she walked into the grove. All she had to do was follow the roars to find Sorin and the Tnarg. She just prayed she wasn't too late.

———

Sorin clenched his jaw at the Tnarg's voice. The sword wouldn't budge, so he'd have to fight the beast with something else.

The rain, wind and thunder muffled all sounds, but Sorin knew the creature would strike fast. He released his grip on his weapon and dove to the side to roll away. He wasn't as quick as he should have been, for the beast's claws caught him on the back. Sorin hissed in pain and rose to his feet, brandishing the daggers he had pulled from his boots.

The Tnarg laughed as it looked at the daggers. "I'll cut you in half before you get close enough to put those small blades in me."

Sorin knew the beast was right, but even though he would most likely die, he wouldn't go down without giving a few wounds himself.

"If you kill me, you'll leave Katrina alone?"

The Tnarg laughed and shook its oblong head. "I could've killed you a hundred times over as I followed you here. Nay, my target is your mate. Whether I kill you or not, she dies."

Sorin's gut tightened. How had he not known the Tnarg was tracking him? How could he have been so careless? The

Tnarg tilted back its head and roared. Its red eyes narrowed on Sorin, and its claws extended as it prepared to strike.

Sorin crouched on the balls of his feet, ignoring the rain and the near constant lightning as he began to circle the Tnarg. The beast was taller, faster, and deadlier, but Sorin had a slight advantage. He'd been raised with the intent of battling anything that might get in his way of returning home. He'd learned to be light on his feet and think quickly.

He'd been preparing for this day his whole life.

Sorin smiled and turned the long blades of his daggers against his forearms. The Tnarg raised its arms and leapt at him. There was no way Sorin could get out of the way quick enough, so he stepped into the beast and sunk both daggers into the Tnarg's sides.

The creature screamed in fury and backhanded him. Sorin managed to hold onto his daggers as he flew back against a tree, hitting it so hard his head slammed against the bark. He shook off the pain and rolled his shoulders as he stepped away from the tall pine. He ducked and lunged to his right just as the Tnarg swung a massive claw at his head. As Sorin turned, he raised his arm and slashed the beast's stomach.

The Tnarg bellowed again, but this time he sunk his claws into Sorin's back. Sorin bit back a yell as he jerked away from the beast.

Blood ran in thick, sticky trails down his back and into his trews. He leaned against a tree to catch his breath and shook his head to move his hair, which was plastered to his face from the driving rain.

This time, he decided he would be the one to attack. He rushed the Tnarg, but before he could get close enough to use his daggers, the beast punched him in the gut. Sorin reeled backwards and crashed into a tree again.

The slick pine needles slipped beneath his feet and he fell to the ground. He tried to keep upright with his fist, but he fell to the side and on his back. His entire body ached, but he couldn't give up. Not yet.

Something smooth and warm touched the back of his hand.

"Sorin."

Hope blossomed in his chest at the sound of Katrina's sweet voice. He wanted to thrash Katrina the same time he wanted to kiss her. But there wasn't time for him to chastise her, not when the Tnarg didn't know she was there.

"I brought you this," she whispered.

He struggled to open his eyes. Her hand opened his and removed the dagger only to have something heavy and hard replace it. Sorin wrapped his hand around the pommel of the sword and turned his head to her. His eyes cracked open to see her smile.

"Kill it," she urged.

Sorin slowly rose to his feet, no longer feeling the pain that had overtaken him just moments earlier. Katrina was there. He would end the Tnarg once and for all so Katrina could be safe.

"You want more?" the Tnarg taunted.

Sorin grinned and lifted the sword. "I want more."

"Poor choice," the beast said as it flew at him.

Katrina choked back a scream as she watched the Tnarg and Sorin slam together. Her hands bit into the rough bark as they battled. Time and again the Tnarg attacked with deadly swiftness, playing with Sorin as it slashed his arms, chest, and stomach before hitting him.

And every time Sorin would climb back to his feet and challenge the Tnarg again.

He hadn't spoken to her, but Katrina knew he wouldn't want her witnessing the battle. Yet, she wasn't about to leave him. Not now.

Not ever.

The realization made tears prick her eyes. To live the rest of her life without him wasn't an option. She had to have him. She wished she could give what little strength she had to Sorin as he tried to lift the sword several times before he managed it. He was weak from the blood loss and his injuries, and it infuriated her to see him being played with by the creature. The Tnarg just laughed and swung a mighty fist at Sorin's head.

Sorin tried to duck, but he wasn't fast enough. He landed several feet away on his back, his sword flying from his hand. His eyes were closed as he lay unmoving. Katrina bit her lip as the Tnarg walked to him. It leaned down and looked Sorin over. She had to listen carefully over the rain to hear what the beast said.

"You should've left. There was no way you could win."

Sorin chuckled defiantly as his eyes opened. "I'll battle you until the last breath leaves my body."

"It won't stop me from killing her. And now it's time for you to die."

The world slowed to a crawl as the Tnarg raised a claw. Katrina didn't think about what she was doing as she put herself between Sorin and the Tnarg.

"It's me you want!" she yelled over the driving rain at the Tnarg. "Leave him alone."

"Katrina, nay," Sorin bellowed and struggled to sit up.

She kept her gaze locked with the red eyes of the Tnarg. It studied her a moment before it grinned. "Stupid wench."

Katrina shut her eyes and waited for the blow that would strike her, but the only sound she heard was the howl of the Tnarg. Her gaze flew open to see a group of men racing for them on horseback with several crossbows aimed at the Tnarg. It screamed and turned in the direction of the riders. Katrina took one look at the arrows sticking out of its back before she fell atop Sorin.

"How badly are you hurt?" she asked him.

"No' badly enough that I can no' wring your pretty neck for putting yourself before that beast."

She smiled into his dark eyes and kissed him. "We're safe."

"For now," Sorin said and tried to sit up again.

Katrina helped him to lean back against a tree. By the time she turned around, the Tnarg was gone and the men were nearly upon her. The wind suddenly stopped and the rain halted to just a drizzle.

"Katrina!"

She leapt to her feet at her father's voice. "I'm here, Father," she said and ran to his horse as he dismounted. His strong arms came around her.

"Lass, I thought I'd lost you," he said into her hair.

She leaned back and smiled. "Aunt Beatrice told you where I was?"

"Aye, though I still doona believe what I saw."

She sighed and took his hand. "I'll give you an explanation, but first I need you to help me get Sorin back to Aunt Beatrice's."

When she turned back, Sorin had gotten to his feet and used the sword and the tree to keep himself standing. She rushed to his side and let him lean against her. "You're badly wounded."

He chuckled and winked at her. "Nothing that a few kisses willna heal."

"Katrina?" her father asked.

She moved her gaze from Sorin to her father. "Father, I want to introduce you to the man who has stolen my heart, Prince Sorin Sinclair."

"Prince?" her father repeated.

Sorin grinned. "It's nice to finally meet you, my lord. I know you have many questions, and I have all the answers."

"Not until you are cleaned up," Katrina told them.

She took a deep breath and said a prayer of thanks as Sorin was helped onto a horse. Her father wanted answers he most likely wouldn't appreciate.

Especially the one where she explained that he would never see her again.

Sorin's throat was dry from all the talking he'd done with Katrina's father. He still wasn't sure who was more surprised at Katrina's announcement, him or her father. She had chosen to return with him to Drahcir. It almost seemed like a dream he waited to wake from. Yet the pain from his wounds told him he was more than awake.

"How are you feeling?"

He inhaled her sweet fragrance. "Much better. How is your father?"

"He's upset about never seeing me again, and he's having a difficult time believing everything. I think seeing the Tnarg convinced him."

Sorin laughed. "Aye, it does have that effect on people." He looked deep into her blue eyes. "Are you sure, Katrina?"

"I've never been surer of anything in my life. I want to be with you, always, even if that means I have to leave everything I know behind."

He pulled her against him to claim her lips in a kiss that promised passion beyond her wildest dreams as soon as night fell. Her hand reached between them and grasped his cock, wringing a moan from him. Not to be outdone, he cupped her breasts and tweaked her nipple. Desire flared, and the yearning to take her washed over him. He angled her toward a chair.

But the clearing of a throat broke them apart.

Her father walked slowly into the solar. His tall, lean frame made him a man to be wary of, a man you didn't want as an enemy.

"There's no way I'll ever be able to see her again?" he asked.

Sorin hesitated. "I can speak to my father once we return. We doona tell anyone of our location for fear of it being discovered, but maybe something can be worked out."

"I've always wanted grandchildren," he murmured.

Sorin exchanged a look with Katrina. "I give you my word I'll do everything I can to make sure you can see Katrina and our children, but I can no' promise anything."

"I understand. And thank you," he said, his faded blue eyes misting. "When will you leave?"

"As soon as possible." He glanced at Katrina to see her looking down at her hands. "I doona know if the Tnarg will attack us again, and I need to return before time runs out."

Her father nodded. "I can spare some men to travel with you for as long as you need them. They will offer protection."

Sorin appreciated the offer, especially since they would need as much help as they could get. "Thank you, I would appreciate it."

"Where will you marry?"

Sorin shrugged. All his ancestors had been married at the castle, but nothing said they couldn't have two ceremonies.

"My parents will want a ceremony at the castle, but we can have one before we leave."

"Wonderful," Katrina said with a relieved grin. She rose and hurried from the solar.

Her father eyed Sorin. "All I ask is that you make her happy."

"I will," Sorin vowed.

Katrina stood at her window and looked out over the moon-drenched city. The Tnarg was still out there somewhere, though she didn't fear it quite as much as she had the night before.

There was a small grunt behind her. She smiled and turned to face her husband. A soft sigh escaped her lips. Her husband. She would never get used to saying it. To have such desire for a man she barely knew was surprising but also wonderful. It was still difficult to believe, but she'd never been happier.

"Do your wounds still ache?" she asked as she moved to the bed where Sorin lay. Soft candlelight made his naked skin glow golden.

He nodded with a grimace. "Aye. The beast has sharp claws. I'll be happy to never feel them again."

"I agree. You told me earlier that you saw your eldest brother before you found me?"

"I did. I doona know how he was here, but he was. He's still looking for his mate, and I pray he finds her."

"And your other two brothers? Have they already returned?"

"I have to believe they have. I willna know until we're back in Drahcir though." He grinned. "I'm anxious to see my family. It's been over a year since I stepped out of our gates."

"That is a long time." She moved to rub some healing cream on his wounds. "Did you really mean what you said to my father?"

He tilted her chin up until she looked at him. "About visiting? Aye, I meant every word. As I told him, I can no' promise anything."

Katrina smiled and leaned up to kiss him. His arms came around her and pulled her against his chest. He hissed in pain and she pulled back.

"We can't. I'll hurt you."

A wicked gleam entered his dark eyes. "Oh, but we can, lass."

"How?" she asked, excitement growing in her belly.

His hands yanked her chemise over her head and to the floor before he pulled her atop him, her legs straddling his hips. Katrina gasped at the feel of his cock against her sex. His hands rocked her hips forward, rubbing his rod against her pearl.

Katrina sighed with pleasure that began to heat her blood. When Sorin's hand touched her sex and parted her women's lips, she sucked in a shaky breath. His finger moved softly over her clitoris, stroking it, teasing the tiny bud until she felt herself grow damp.

She wanted him inside her, to feel his heat and his hardness, but he held her still. The pleasure was intense, blinding and felt oh, so glorious. She never wanted it to stop.

But she wanted more.

More of Sorin.

Her hips moved against his hand seeking fulfillment. She was close to peaking, so close to going over the edge and experiencing those wonderful emotions. But Sorin moved his hand and gripped her hips. Her gaze snapped to his to see one side of his mouth lifted in a grin and his beautiful brown gaze darkened with desire. Before she could ask him what he was about, he lifted her.

Katrina's mouth opened on a gasp as he slowly lowered her atop his shaft. He filled her inch by delicious inch until he was fully sheathed. For a moment she couldn't move, the pleasure was so beautiful. But she knew what awaited them both.

The need to rock her hips, to feel him within her, was too great to ignore. She pushed against his hands and sucked in a breath at the friction and the exquisite shot of desire that traveled through her.

She rotated her hips again and heard him groan as his fingers dug into her hips. Katrina couldn't stop the grin that pulled at her lips. She felt powerful, knowing it was her movement that caused him to feel such pleasure.

After the beautiful experience he'd introduced her to the night before, she wanted to do this for him. To give him the same joy, the same pleasure he had given her. Her own desire spiked, and she moved her hips faster. She heard Sorin whisper her name as his hands moved to cup her breasts. His thumbs stroked her nipples, making them into hard little buds.

Katrina's head dropped back. She moaned and her sex clenched around him. A low groan tore from his throat and he pinched her nipples. She gasped and moved her hips faster, needing more of him with each heartbeat. He seemed to sense her need and moved his hips in time with hers.

Her desire built rapidly. She could feel herself reaching the pinnacle, knew it was close. And then it hit. She screamed his name as she fell forward and braced her hands on his muscular chest. Her body spasmed around him, her breath locked in her throat. Sorin gripped her hips and thrust deep inside of her. He gave a shout and she felt him spill his seed.

Her chest rose and fell rapidly as she slowly opened her eyes to see Sorin watching her.

"You're going to be the death of me," he groaned.

She laughed and leaned over him for a kiss. "I'll gladly die a little death every time we make love."

His hands moved over her back, caressing her skin as only a lover could. "You've made me the happiest man in the world."

She laid her head on his chest, careful of his wounds, as he blew out the candle. They had a long journey ahead of them that began at dawn.

***

Sorin checked the saddle on Katrina's mare once more as she finished her goodbyes to her family. She blinked back tears all morning, but no one could blame her for shedding them now.

He took her hand as she walked to him. "I'm sorry you have to leave them."

She shook her head and wiped away her tears. "All women must leave their families when they marry."

Sorin said no more as he lifted her atop the horse. After a brief nod to her father, Sorin mounted and they were off. He wanted to run his horse all the way to the gates of Drahcir, he was so excited about returning, but he somehow kept the horse at a walk.

The perfect plan would be to travel during the day in open spaces so the Tnarg couldn't sneak up on them then bed down at an inn. But Sorin knew they wouldn't get that lucky. Their journey would take them through deep forests and high into the mountains.

The Tnarg would most certainly attack. Sorin just wished he knew where.

Katrina was so tired of looking between her mare's ears that she almost didn't even feel the cold anymore. They had been traveling for nearly two weeks with no sign of the Tnarg.

Though Sorin wished they didn't need her father's men, he'd been glad to have them in the darkest hours of the night. Katrina herself had been protected. Had the Tnarg attacked, it would have had to go through six men and Sorin before it got to her.

Their horse's hooves were muffled in the deep snow, and she tried not to feel frightened now that her father's men had departed.

"I couldn't chance them finding the way," Sorin said for the second time.

"I understand," she said, though half of her really didn't.

Sorin sighed. "I would've liked the protection for you."

"Maybe the Tnarg has given up."

A snort was her answer. "Doona ever think that, love. It willna give up until Keiran has returned with his mate. Until then, it'll be after us."

"Wonderful," she murmured bleakly. She blinked several times to rid her eyelashes of the new snow that had begun to fall. She couldn't see two strides in front of her, it was so thick. "Are you sure we're headed in the right direction?"

Sorin chuckled. "Aye. If we're lucky, we'll reach the gates of Drahcir by nightfall. I doona want to spend a night without the guards your father loaned us."

"Nay, I'd rather not do that either." A chill raced down her spine. She was bundled in a heavy fur-lined cloak and matching thick gloves her father had given to her just before she left, but still she shivered. Every breath she took burned her lungs, and all she wanted was the feel of a soft, warm bed.

And Sorin.

"What are you smiling at?" he asked.

"I'm thinking of once again having you in my bed. We haven't had any privacy since we left Invergarry."

Sorin laughed. "I told you I'd have given you pleasure any time you wanted it."

"Aye, but not with the men there." She shook her head. "They would have stared."

He reached over and squeezed her hand. "Even a monk couldna look away from your face or ignore your cries as you peak, my love."

"You're only saying that because you're my husband."

"Hm," he growled. "I love the sound of that, wife."

She giggled. "And I like the sound of that."

"I'm going to enjoy having you as my mate."

"Is that so?" It was then she realized she had no idea what was expected of her. "I'm really going to be a princess?"

He smiled. "Aye, with all the privileges that goes with it. Be prepared though. You'll be Princess Katrina in Drahcir."

She bit her lip at his words. "Princess. It's still difficult to believe that you are a prince and I'll be a princess. I thought royalty was only allowed to marry royalty."

"If our mates were royalty, then that's who we would marry," he said with a shrug. "Our kingdom doesna care that you are no' royalty. What matters is that you're the best woman for me. There is a bond between us that can only be broken with death. Nothing and no one can come between us."

She took a deep breath and smiled. "I like hearing that. I imagine most women would like that kind of assurance with the men they marry."

"Now, that's no' to say we willna have our share of arguments," he cautioned. "I can be a bit obstinate at times."

"A bit?" she asked with a laugh. "At times? That's putting it mildly. But I may as well tell you that I have a bit of a temper myself."

They shared a laugh and linked hands. Katrina couldn't wait to meet her new family. Every day on their journey to Drahcir, she and Sorin had exchanged stories of their families and childhoods.

She knew secrets about him he hadn't even shared with his brothers. She had been an only child, so she was anxious to meet Sorin's brothers and their wives. She prayed they got along well.

"Doona be nervous," Sorin said, as if reading her thoughts. "Everyone will welcome you."

"How can you be sure?"

"Because I love you."

Her gaze jerked to his as she pulled on the reins to stop her mare. "What?"

"Is it such a surprise, wife? I'd have thought you knew how I felt already."

"I...I had no idea," she mumbled. "I knew you cared for me, but I just assumed our love would grow over the years."

"Not mine." His gaze refused to let hers go.

And she finally admitted to what she knew had been growing in her heart since the first day she met him. "I love you."

"I know," he said with a wickedly charming grin. "I've just been waiting for you to realize it."

"Oh, you're impossible," she said, and turned her head away. "What's that?" she asked, and pointed ahead of them.

Sorin blew out a loud breath. They had finally reached the pass. "It's the pass to Drahcir. Sheer snow and ice walls line each side. It's narrow. You'll have to ride in front of me."

"In front?" she echoed.

He nodded. "I doona want you behind me where I can no' protect you."

"It's a perfect place for an attack, isn't it?"

He hadn't wanted to tell her, but he should have known she'd see it. She was smart and intuitive. "Aye," he admitted reluctantly.

"Then let's go. I'm tired of fearing for my life."

He grinned at his little warrior wife. Every moment he was with her he loved her more, if that were possible. "Here," he said and handed her a dagger from his boot.

She looked at the weapon then back up at him.

"I'd rather know you have a weapon to defend yourself with. Please, Katrina."

She took it from him and stuffed it into her boot. "We're not going to need it," she said confidently. "It's left us alone. It'll continue to do so."

He let her lie to herself but couldn't help but hold out the same hope as she did. They were so close to Drahcir, so close to fulfilling the curse. A few moments later they were traveling through the pass. Sorin kept his gaze above him, looking for any signs the Tnarg was following them. But he saw nothing.

Yet, he couldn't shake the feeling it was near. Very near.

As they moved slowly through the pass, it seemed much longer than it ever had. Part of him wanted to kick the horses into a gallop, but the snow was too deep for them to do anything more than walk.

Then he saw it—the end of the pass. Excitement rushed through him. He was so close to home he wanted to shout. He looked over his shoulder once more but saw nothing. When they neared the end of the pass, he let out a breath. If the Tnarg had thought of attacking, it would have already done it.

Once they reached the end, he nudged his horse beside Katrina's and smiled at the large gate to their left. "We're here."

Just as expected, the gates swung open, welcoming them into Drahcir. Sorin saw his parents and Elric and Lucian with their mates. He had made it, he was home.

His family's smiles faltered as they began to shout. Sorin's heart dropped to his feet, for he knew of only one thing that would make his family react so. Elric and Lucian both drew their swords, but Sorin knew they wouldn't be allowed to leave Drahcir to help him.

"Katrina, listen to me," he said calmly. "Get off the horse and run as fast as you can to the gates. Doona stop, and whatever you do, doona look back."

"Sorin, nay," she said. Her hands shook as she gripped her reins.

"Remember, I love you," he said and spun his horse around to find the Tnarg behind them. "Run, Katrina!" he yelled and unsheathed his sword for an attack.

The Tnarg's long claws ripped open the horse's chest. The horse screamed in pain, and Sorin leapt from it just before the mount collapsed into the snow. He got to his feet and tried to push thoughts of Katrina and their future from his mind.

Sorin knew he couldn't win against the Tnarg. Nor did he think he could make it to the gates in time. He didn't relish his family seeing him slaughtered either.

He had precious few choices.

"You should've just let me have her," the Tnarg said. "You could have saved your family seeing you sliced into little pieces."

"Just get on with it," Sorin said.

He had just begun to recover from his other wounds, so he knew he wouldn't move as quickly as he normally did. But he did have his sword back.

Unlike before, he waited for the beast to attack. As soon as it did, Sorin went down on one knee and slashed with his sword. The Tnarg howled and gripped its arm as blood dripped into the snow. Sorin grinned and rose to his feet.

"As I said, get on with it," he taunted.

He knew he wouldn't get away with that move twice, but he also knew it was essential that he continue to wound the creature without letting it get him. That in itself would be a miracle.

Sorin waited. The Tnarg bared its teeth and growled, its red eyes glowing. It was angry now. It flew at Sorin, knocking him to the ground and straddling him. His sword flew from his hand just out of reach. The Tnarg wasted no time in using its claws.

The Tnarg held up a claw and lengthened its talons before slowly raking them down Sorin's chest. He clenched his jaw, determined not to cry out.

Surely, Katrina had made it safely to the gates by now. At least Sorin prayed she had. He knew he wouldn't last long without a weapon. He turned his head and saw his sword just out of his reach. He stretched his hand for it and a cry of pain escaped his lips as the Tnarg pushed its claws into Sorin's side.

Sorin could feel his hot, sticky blood pool from his sides into the thick snow. His life drained from him just as quickly as his blood did.

Katrina.

Suddenly, the Tnarg's claws vanished from his side as the creature threw back his head and bellowed in pain. Sorin opened his eyes to find Katrina behind the beast.

The Tnarg clawed at something in its back as it fell off him. And then Katrina's arms wrapped around him.

"We have to get into the gates, Sorin," she said.

He stumbled to his feet and leaned against her. The gate was so far away that Sorin knew they wouldn't make it.

"You should've gone to my family."

"You're being stubborn. I'm not going to stand by and watch you die. Now, move those feet," she demanded.

Sorin grinned and moved faster. He looked over his shoulder to see the Tnarg had managed to pull the dagger from its back.

"We've got to hurry," Sorin whispered.

He gritted his teeth and pushed aside the pain as he grabbed Katrina's hand and sprinted to the gates. His family stood at the entrance yelling at them to run faster. Sorin didn't need to look behind him to know the Tnarg was gaining on them. They were nearly to the gates, just a few more steps and they'd be safe.

And then Sorin landed on his face in the snow only to be pulled out of Katrina's arms.

"Nay!" she screamed and started after him.

"You're mine!" the Tnarg bellowed, as it raised its claw to slash open Sorin's chest.

Instead, Katrina kicked it in the face. Sorin jumped to his feet raced to the gate with his wife. As soon as they were over the Drahcir threshold, they collapsed on the ground in each other's arms.

"Well," Katrina said. "That was eventful. I don't think I want to do that again."

Laughter sounded around them and Sorin raised his head to see his family surrounding him. He leaned down and kissed Katrina, and despite his injuries, despite the crowd around him, all he wanted to do was bury himself inside of her. And he would, too. Just as soon as they got to the palace.

"We made it," he whispered.

"Aye," she said, and cupped his face. "We did, you stubborn man."

The first thing Katrina noticed about Drahcir was the warmth. She was helped to her feet by a beautiful woman with auburn hair and hazel eyes.

"You won't be needing that," she said and took Katrina's cloak. "By the way, I'm Marin, and this is Isabella."

Katrina turned to the dark headed woman with the striking blue eyes next to Marin and smiled. "It's a pleasure." She glanced over at Sorin to find two men kneeling beside him stripping him of his tunic and jerkin and quickly bandaging him to stop the flow of blood.

"I'm fine," Sorin said, and grinned up at her.

"Nay, you are no'," said the man with black hair and eyes. He finished tying off the bandage and looked up at her. "Welcome to the family, Katrina. I'm Lucian. The idiot on the other side of Sorin is Elric."

Elric with his dark brown hair and green eyes punched Lucian in the arm before helping Sorin sit up. "Forgive him," Elric said. "He has no idea how foolish he is."

"You've done enough for now. Stand me up so I can

introduce my mate to our parents," Sorin demanded of his brothers.

Katrina was relieved to see the blood flow stemmed, and especially comforted when Sorin's strong arms wrapped around her, giving her more pleasure from his simple touch than she thought possible. "You're injured. Again."

He chuckled. "Now, let me introduce you to my parents. Urises and Morag."

Katrina started to curtsy when the queen took her arm. "No need, dear," she said with kind brown eyes. "We're so blessed and grateful to have you in the family."

"Thank you," Katrina said. Her mother had died when she was but a small child, and her father had never remarried, so the thought of having a mother again brought tears to her eyes.

"Welcome, daughter," King Urises said as he took her hand. "You were very brave to help Sorin the way you did. We were unable to do so. You've shown your worth as only a mate of Drahcir can. It is a privilege to have you in our family."

"Come," Queen Morag said. "We need to clean up Sorin before he falls on his face. He's putting on a brave face, but we all saw his injuries."

Katrina moved aside as Lucian and Elric walked to Sorin, each taking one of his arms and draping it over their necks as they helped him to the carriage that was waiting to take them to the castle. She turned and saw the castle atop the mountain with bright blue skies dotted with puffy clouds. The road beneath them was made of the most unusual, beautiful blue stone that seemed to capture the color of the sky in its depths.

The white buildings and homes on either side of the road were each decorated with knot work similar to what was tattooed on her arm. It was then she noticed the people of Drahcir lining the road waiting for their first look at her. Their welcoming cheers and waves helped to ease her.

A grating sound behind them drew her attention and she turned to watch the giant iron gate close on its own.

It was truly a magical kingdom.

"What do you think?" Sorin asked.

She grinned up at him. "I think it's magnificent."

"Can you be happy here?"

"I'll be happy anywhere you are."

He squeezed her shoulder and sighed. It wasn't until that moment that she realized he had been worried.

"I love you, Sorin Sinclair."

He stopped and looked down at her. "And I love you, Katrina Sinclair."

EPILOGUE

Sorin watched Katrina talk to his mother and two sisters-in-law. It had been a relief to know both Elric and Lucian had returned, but they all worried about Keiran. More so now than ever since it was just a few weeks until the fifth moon of the harvest year.

"Everything rests on Keiran's shoulders," Elric said, as he moved to stand beside Sorin.

"Aye, but if anyone can get to the gates, it's Keiran."

Elric and Sorin exchanged a grin. "True enough," Elric admitted. "It's good to have you home, little brother."

"It's good to be home." He shifted his shoulders and felt the pull of the stitches in his side.

Elric chuckled. "I know your new wife will be taking excellent care of you. Just lock your door."

"Why?"

"Mother hasna quite gotten used to us having brides yet."

Sorin threw back his head and laughed. "Did she walk in on you and Marin?"

"Nay. She walked in on Lucian and Isabelle. It took a few days for Isabelle to be able to look her in the eye again."

"Thanks for the warning," Sorin said. "I'll be sure to do that."

Their smiles died as a guard came running into the palace.

"What is it?" King Urises demanded.

"It's the Tnarg, sire. He's sitting outside the gates."

Lucian sighed as he moved to join them. "He's waiting for Keiran."

"No' if I can help it," Sorin said.

"You can no'," Elric ground out.

Sorin's gaze moved to Katrina's. "I'll find a way. I refuse to let my brother die."

He turned to his brothers. "That beast has tracked us all over the country. It has attacked our mates and tried to kill us. I know what the curse says, but I'm no' just going to sit back and watch it kill Keiran."

Elric and Lucian exchanged a glance.

"I agree with him," Elric said.

Lucian blew out a breath. "What do you suggest?"

"We use some magic of our own," Sorin said with a grin, as he took Katrina's hand.

Elric rubbed his hands together. "I've got the perfect plan then. Curse or no, I agree with Sorin. I'm no' going to let the Tnarg prevent Keiran from returning home."

Sorin glanced at Lucian before he turned to Elric. "Let's get prepared then. Keiran can return any time now."

And they all needed to be ready to kill the Tnarg. An entire kingdom's life rested on their shoulders. For too long the Sinclairs had lived with the curse. It was time to do something about that, and Sorin knew that time was now.

They just had to wait for Keiran.

PRINCE OF PASSION

Four brothers, a secret kingdom, and an ancient curse.

Keiran has always allowed his passions to rule him—for both good and bad. But as the eldest and heir to the throne of Drahcir, he acutely feels the weight of the family's ancient curse and knows that time is running out. When Keiran gives in to a night of desire and discovers his mate, the fire he feels shifts course. He must convince her to return with him in time to save his beloved kingdom before evil destroys everything he loves.

Senga has loved Keiran from afar for ages, living to catch glimpses of him in the streets. When one of the famed Fae urges her to leave the kingdom to await Keiran, she's surprised to discover that she is his mate. Unfortunately, when Keiran finds her, it's not as she'd hoped, but that doesn't stop the passion that flares to life between them. Even as their attraction cannot be denied, the evil hunting them will stop at nothing to destroy them and fulfill Keiran's family's curse—obliterating the kingdom and all within. Will Senga's love be enough to end it all once and for all?

1

Winter, 1270
Foothills of the Ben Nevis Mountains

*L*ike the wings of a raven, night swept the land, drenching the small Scottish village in darkness. Keiran Sinclair welcomed the obscurity, for it matched the growing weariness inside him.

He sighed heavily and leaned upon the wooden table before the hearth. The inn was small but clean, and though he should be out searching for his mate, exhaustion and the cold had driven him indoors. He liked the village because it was near the pass that would lead him home.

Home.

The fire warmed the chill that settled into his bones from the frigid temperatures that had fallen two days ago. He missed the warmth of Drahcir. He pined for the gentle, loving smiles of his mother and the way his father asked his opinion as heir to the throne. But most of all, he missed his three brothers.

As eldest, he'd left Drahcir first. He expected to be the first to return. Yet he was destined to be last.

Keiran rubbed the heel of his hand into his eye, sending red flashes behind his lid. His eyes felt as if sand was embedded in them from the sleepless nights, and his body was drained down to his soul.

For so long he'd searched for his mate, moving from town to town, and even from time to time with the help of the Fae. When Aimery had sent him to his youngest brother, Sorin, with a warning, it had taken everything Keiran had inside him to walk away from his brother and not help as he yearned to.

Seeing Sorin had been wonderful. But parting had cut Keiran deeper than any blade.

All he could hope for was that Sorin made it back to Drahcir with his mate.

Keiran snorted as he lifted a mug of ale for a long drink, letting the liquid burn a trail down his throat. It was the damned curse that sent the brothers from the safety of their magical kingdom to search for their mates, a curse from a spoiled, selfish Fae princess who had been toyed with by one of his ancestors.

His hand clenched around the mug. If only Keiran could find his ancestor and strangle him before he could damage the entire Sinclair line.

Each brother had left Drahcir. They had until the fifth moon of the Harvest year to return with their mates. Since time moved slower in Drahcir than anywhere else, the time was different in Scotland when they stepped from their gate.

If only finding their mates was easy, but the task was complicated by the Tnargs, vicious beasts with one task in mind—kill the Sinclair mates. When Keiran's ancestors managed to locate their mates and elude the Tnarg, the Fae princess had stepped in and moved future mates throughout time in her attempt to destroy the Sinclairs.

Fortunately, there was Aimery, a Fae commander and friend to Drahcir. It was Aimery who helped the Sinclair brothers, but there was nothing he could do for Keiran.

Keiran tossed back the rest of the ale and slammed the mug on the table. Anger and frustration threatened to drown him. He turned to gaze into the fire and blew out a shaky breath.

I've failed. I've failed everyone—Drahcir, but more importantly my family.

His family and all of Drahcir would cease to exist if he didn't return with his mate, and it looked like that was exactly what would happen. All because he hadn't been able to find the woman destined to be his.

The fifth moon of the Harvest year was in *days*. How could he locate his mate and convince her to leave her world and family behind to travel to a magical kingdom in such a short time? It was impossible, which is just what the princess had wanted.

As heir to Drahcir, it had never entered Keiran's mind that he would fail. For over four years he had been searching for the woman that would match him completely, the woman he would be bound to for eternity. Surely, he should have found her by now.

"Would you like another?"

The melodic, soft voice reached him through his musings. He blinked and turned from the fire to find a woman beside him. Her hair was the color of honey streaked with gold. Ringlets had come loose from her thick braid and framed her face. He wondered what her hair would look like falling around her, and if it would feel as smooth and soft as it appeared.

"My lord?" she asked.

Keiran cocked his head to the side as he gazed into her unusual gray eyes. There was something almost familiar about the girl, as if he should know her.

Finally, he nodded. "Aye. I'd like another."

The corners of her mouth lifted in a smile before she turned on her heel and moved to the bar. Keiran watched her hips sway as she walked and felt himself respond to her curves. She walked with the grace of a queen and the command of a general, a heady mix for a man who had been without for too long.

But there was something in her face that told Keiran he had seen the girl before. But where? He had ventured near this village when he'd left Drahcir, but not once had he stopped at the inn.

He looked more closely, noting the way her honey-colored brows gently arched over her large eyes that tilted upward ever so slightly at the corners. Her cheekbones were high, her determined chin telling him she was from good breeding. His gaze lowered to her mouth, marveling at the full, dusky lips that begged for attention.

She was of average height and had an easy smile, as though the world hadn't yet beaten her down. Her soft curves in all the right places made Keiran take notice. Her skin was the color of cream, glowing warm in the firelight as she approached.

"Here you go," she said, and set down the mug.

Keiran flipped her a coin, amazed as she caught it deftly in her hand. "What's your name?"

She refused to meet his gaze. "My name?"

He hadn't missed the way her brows had furrowed before she questioned him. "Aye. Your name?"

"Senga, my lord."

He liked the sound of it. "Well, Senga, why are you no' at home tending your husband?"

A slow smile spread as she briefly met his gaze. "Because I have no husband, my lord."

He was more than surprised. Senga was a very comely girl, the kind most men would marry in a heartbeat. Keiran glanced around the nearly deserted dining area. "I find that difficult to believe."

"Not so difficult actually," she said, and turned her gray eyes to him. "I won't settle for just any man."

Something inside Keiran roared to life at her words. He sat up and held her gaze. It had been a long while since he had eased his body with a woman, and he was certainly up for the challenge.

"And what kind of man is that?" he asked.

She lifted one slim shoulder in a shrug. "One who loves me and doesn't want me simply to birth his children so he'll have someone to tend the fields with him."

Keiran chuckled. It had been so long since he'd felt like laughing. "I gather that's a problem here?"

"More than you could imagine."

He sat forward in his chair, intrigued. "Sit with me," he urged, and scooted out the chair opposite him with his foot.

Her eyes twinkled. She glanced at the chair and licked her lips. "I cannot."

There was something about her accent that wasn't quite right. He could hear the Scottish brogue, but he didn't think it came naturally. "Sure you can. There are few of us left, and if someone needs you, they can give you a shout. Sit with me. Please."

She twisted her white apron in her hands and glanced around the room before she sat.

Keiran leaned his forearms on the table. "Where are you from?"

"A village near here."

His gaze narrowed. The more he spoke with her, the more he thought he knew her. *Impossible.* "You've only lived here?"

"I've moved around," she confessed.

"Often?"

She leaned back and raised one brow at him. "Why the interest in where I've lived?"

"Because I'd swear, I've seen you before."

She sighed, her smile gone as she blew out a soft breath. "That's because, Prince Keiran, you have. In Drahcir on the day you left. I was the girl by the gates," she said, before she rose and walked off.

Keiran felt as if he'd been kicked in the stomach. His mind reeled with her revelation. There were some people of Drahcir who left the magical kingdom, but once they walked through the gates, they could never return.

He watched as she wiped down the bar and carried a tray of dirty mugs into a back room. He remembered vividly the day that he'd left his beloved Drahcir to seek his mate. Since it was the entire kingdom at risk, everyone turned out when a prince departed. The blue stone streets of Drahcir had been lined with his people throwing flowers at his feet and chanting his name, all the while wishing him success.

He had stopped at the gates and turned to bid his family one last farewell. Just before he left, he had spotted a girl staring at him. She hadn't smiled, nor had she cheered. But her gray eyes had held him immobile as she watched.

By the gods!

2

Senga wanted to kick something she was so irritated. Over four years she'd waited for Keiran, holding onto the prediction Aimery had given her—a prediction that had made her leave Drahcir.

Aimery made her pledge not to tell anyone, not even her family, why she left the magical kingdom. Her family hadn't understood and had tried everything but tying her to the bed to make her to stay. Leaving Drahcir had been the hardest thing she'd ever done.

It wasn't until a month ago when Aimery had suddenly shown himself that she knew she hadn't taken his word for naught. But what he'd told her left her with ice in her veins.

The Tnarg had found her.

She had rarely ventured from the inn for a month. If she did, it was in daylight with several people around her, and she never strayed from the village. The Tnarg might be vicious, but it wasn't brave enough to barrel through a village and chance being hunted by the men.

Still, every night, she would lay awake wondering if it would get through the shutters she'd reinforced with iron.

Aimery had been positive the Tnarg would arrive any day, and she knew the beast was nearby, waiting for her. The fact Keiran now sat before the fire was proof of it. She had longed for Keiran to come for her, to claim her as his mate, but now…now she worried they'd never get past the Tnarg to save their people.

Senga glanced at Keiran. He sat hunched over the table, hair so dark it was nearly black hung to his shoulders. His hazel eyes held so much sorrow and self-doubt that she longed to tell him who she was.

But she couldn't. Aimery had forbid it. He had taken a chance sharing the information with her.

Keiran's face didn't hold the youthful exuberance it once had. In its place was a man hardened by this new world and his responsibilities, but it only served to make him more mysterious, more handsome, if that were possible.

Even before Aimery had told her of her destiny, Keiran had caught her eye. As heir to the throne, every female from child to crone wanted him. The fact he was more handsome than sin only made things worse.

She shook her head and walked to the back room where dishes awaited her. When she reached for the bucket she was sure she had filled just an hour ago, she found it empty. The dishes couldn't wait. She had to have them cleaned before morning and the arrival of her employer, because if he let her go, she had nowhere to live.

Senga picked up the bucket and opened the back door. The music of crickets filled the cold, clear night. The moon was only a sliver in the night sky and the stars glistened from above. It looked to be a beautiful setting, but she knew what lurked in the shadows.

She peered into the night, straining her ears to hear any sound of a Tnarg. Other than the crickets and an owl in the distance, there was nothing. She lifted her foot to step outside when hands grabbed her by her shoulders and spun her around to land roughly against the wall.

Senga looked into Keiran's troubled hazel eyes. His face was inches from her, his legs braced on either side of hers. The heat from his body made her breath catch in her throat.

"What are you doing here?" he asked in a strangled voice. "Why did you leave Drahcir?"

She opened her mouth to answer but glanced outside and swore she saw something move in the shadows. Before she could lean over to look, Keiran slammed the door shut.

"I need an answer," he demanded.

"And I can't give you one." She wanted to tell him, but a vow was a vow. Especially to a Fae.

Keiran leaned closer, his warm breath fanning her cheek. "Why did you leave?"

His voice was as frigid as the temperatures. Since few ever left their kingdom, he would not stop until he had an answer. Beneath her hands, arms of steel held her immobile. His body was hard, like a wall of granite that she would never get past.

His thick muscles had been honed since he was a young lad, and he'd filled out even more since he'd departed Drahcir. The boy had become a man—a man who would stop at nothing to get what he wanted.

She swallowed and let her eyes drift over the hard planes of his face, from his cheekbones, to the hollows of his face, to the small indent in his chin. His brows were thick and slashed low over his hazel eyes that watched her like a hawk with his prey.

His lips, wide and full, were flattened in a hard line that told her his patience had reached its breaking point. She gave a slight push against his solid chest and wide shoulders, but she didn't even budge him.

"It was my destiny," she finally admitted as her eyes took in the way his tunic was open at the neck, revealing a large swatch of bronze skin and black hair.

His gaze searched her before he closed his eyes. "You're lying."

"Nay. I'm not."

His eyes flew open, flashing in anger. "You left the magic and beauty of Drahcir for this? You expect me to believe that?"

"I left because it was my destiny. We all have things we must do that we'd rather not. Yours was to fulfill an ancient curse. Mine was to leave Drahcir."

He released her and paced away. His body was stiff, and dark circles shadowed his eyes. Senga stepped toward him and put out a hand to still him. Heat met her palm as she came in contact with his chest again. A muscle twitched beneath her hand, and she had the desire to push away his jerkin and lift his tunic to touch his skin.

"Please, your highness. I've a chamber you can use. You need rest."

He snorted. "Rest? Senga, if I doona find my mate, all of Drahcir will vanish."

"I know," she answered softly.

"And doona call me 'your highness'. I'm just Keiran here." He ran a hand down his face and leaned against a wall. "By the gods, I've never been so exhausted."

She took a step closer, bringing her near him again. She couldn't seem to stay away. He'd always drawn her, and after finally seeing him again after so long, she was powerless to resist his pull. "Come. You need rest."

Somehow, he allowed her to take his hand and pull him

from the room. Once in the main room, she dropped his hand, but he continued to follow. She would give him her chamber. It wasn't large, but it was safely tucked between others, so it would be difficult for the Tnarg to get to him without alerting them it had arrived.

Though every man, woman, and child of Drahcir knew of the Tnargs, only the royal family and their mates had ever encountered one. Stories of how the beasts would try to kill the mates were legendary, but worse were the stories of the Tnargs turning on the Sinclair family if the mates couldn't be killed.

Senga refused to allow Keiran to die so near his home.

He climbed the stairs slowly, and when she stopped inside her chamber, he halted beside her.

"It's your chamber?"

"There are no other empty rooms," she lied. "You need to rest."

One side of his mouth tilted in a smile. "Will you be joining me?"

Senga's stomach fluttered at the sexy baritone of his voice. The teasing lilt had deepened his voice, making chills race over her skin. She couldn't meet his eyes, not when she knew the future already. "Rest, Keiran."

She tried to step away when his arm halted her. His hazel eyes trapped hers as he leaned toward her, swarming her with his heat and his scent of pine, snow…and power.

"You're verra beautiful," he whispered. "Too beautiful for this world. You should've stayed in Drahcir."

And not gotten you? Never.

His hand moved to her neck, then upward to cup the side of her face. It became impossible to breathe as she waited…hoped…for his kiss. She had dreamed of it for years, wondered what he would taste like against her.

She fisted her hands to keep them from shaking as his gaze lowered to her mouth. Her lips parted of their own accord, her heart pounding so fast she knew it would burst from her chest.

All she had to do was lift her face and their lips would meet, but fear kept her immobile.

And then his head dipped.

The first contact of his lips against hers was like lightning through her body, and she was powerless to resist. Yet, he didn't stop with the simple brush of his mouth.

Soft, supple, and insistent were his lips. A small sigh escaped her when his tongue slipped between her lips. Her heart stopped when his mouth slanted over hers, his tongue pushing inside her mouth. He moaned low in his throat, rumbling his chest as he brought her closer.

It was the most exquisite pleasure, the most intense sensuality. And she never wanted it to end.

As soon as she opened for him, he deepened the kiss, bringing her up against the hard planes of his body. Unable to stop herself, her arms wound around his neck, and her fingers threaded through his thick, dark locks.

Aimery had cautioned her to wait until they had returned to Drahcir before she let Keiran claim her, but the kiss awakened something deep inside of her. Something that wanted only Keiran.

Gods, aye. I've waited so long.

When the kiss finally ended, she found she couldn't step away from him. Being in his arms made her forget everything but him.

"Look at me," he urged her.

Reluctantly, Senga opened her eyes.

"I've no right to ask, but stay with me."

She could walk away. She knew he'd let her. But the

stark loneliness in his gaze made her heart catch. If she stayed, he'd claim her. Aimery had made it clear they should wait. But how could she, after such a kiss? Already her body longed to feel his lips again.

It was simply asking too much of a mere mortal.

She forgot about the dishes and the few patrons still below. All she cared about was the man in her arms.

"Aye," she answered.

With a shove of his foot, Keiran closed the door and took her in a fierce kiss that left no doubt what he wanted to do to her. The promise, the passion, had begun as a slow ember, but it had been fanned, and the embers were now a roaring blaze.

Her bed was narrow and there was no hearth in her small chamber, but none of that seemed to matter as Keiran led her to the bed. Slowly, as if he had all the time in the world, he began to undress her. The cool air met her exposed flesh and caused chills to rush over her skin as, piece by piece, her clothing was discarded.

When she stood naked, he reached around for her braid and released her hair until her curls cascaded around her.

"Exquisite," he murmured.

No man had ever seen her nude, but Keiran's gaze warmed her, making her feel beautiful and sensual—the woman she'd always wanted to be.

His hands caressed down her arms to her hips. Achingly unhurried, he began to move his hands upward to the indent of her waist, stopping just below her breasts.

Her breath came in great gasps as she waited expectantly, anxious to feel his hands touch her. Her breasts swelled and her nipples puckered in the cold air beneath his heated gaze. When he finally cupped her breasts, her eyes slid closed.

When his thumbs moved over her sensitive nipples,

Senga sucked in a breath, her senses whirling. The pleasure was so intense, so wonderful that it became almost too much. She gripped his shoulders to keep herself steady as something new and amazing blossomed within her, spreading from deep inside outward until she was panting with it, all the while aching for more.

Her head fell back as she began to drown in the pleasure. Keiran's mouth was everywhere. He kissed her neck and the sensitive skin behind her ear; when his lips moved to her breasts, her legs refused to hold her. One of Keiran's arms wrapped around her for support a moment before his mouth latched onto her nipple.

Keiran laved the pert little bud in his mouth, luxuriating in the sound of Senga's soft cries. Her other pink nipple cried for attention as he shifted his mouth to the waiting peak. Her breasts were firm and filled his hands perfectly.

He suckled her deeply, dragging her nipple far into his mouth before running his tongue over the bud. His cock throbbed, begging him to fill her and ease the longing within him. But he wasn't yet ready to stop his exploration of her magnificent body. Her flawless, creamy skin was smooth as silk and soft as down.

He gripped her hips and thrust his rod against her. Her answering moan and shift of her hips only made his desire burn brighter. To find someone from his home had been just what he needed, even if she wasn't his mate. He didn't feel so alone with Senga in his arms.

His clothes became a hindrance, a nuisance that prevented him from feeling her flesh against his. He wanted skin to skin, to have her softness, her supple curves against his hardness. The irresistible, crushing need intensified each moment she was in his arms.

Never had a woman felt so good. Never had Keiran felt such urgency to take her. He didn't question it, simply gave in to the sensations that swept through him.

Before he lifted his head, he lightly bit down on her nipple, causing her to gasp and grind her hips against his. Keiran turned and laid her on the bed before he jerked off his clothes. When he was at last free, he stood frozen as her hungry gaze raked over him.

Deep in his heart, Keiran knew he shouldn't even be thinking of bedding Senga, not when he still had his mate to find. But there was something alluring about her, something he couldn't turn away from. Whether it was her exquisite beauty, her calming influence on his soul, or the simple attraction between them, he couldn't—and wouldn't—walk away from her.

His balls tightened when her gaze stopped at his cock. He groaned when she licked her lips, making him think of how her tongue would feel on him, of sliding his rod into her hot, wet mouth.

When he could stand it no more, he crawled atop her. Her soft body cradled his as her gray eyes devoured him with the same desire that pumped through his veins.

It was going to be one heavenly night.

$\mathcal{S}$enga felt as if she was floating on clouds. For so long she'd waited to be held in Keiran's arms, even before Aimery told her of her destiny. And now, her greatest desire was being fulfilled.

His body was hard and warm. The delicious weight of him atop her was unlike anything she'd ever experienced. She would be content to lie beneath him for all eternity. Especially while he kissed her as he was now.

The kiss was hypnotic, making her limbs liquid and her body heat. The tiniest movement of his hips and she felt his thick arousal against her, tempting her…teasing her. With his mouth pulling her under with the very expert way he nibbled, licked and kissed her lips, Senga was barely able to contain the pleasure within her.

Then his hand touched her breast again.

Desire, quick as lightning, shot through her, centering at her sex and giving her the uncontrollable urge to rub her hips against him. She gave in and moaned as intense pleasure flooded her. Her hands glided over his bulging arms to his wide shoulder then over the muscles of his neck that flexed and bunch beneath her hand.

"By the saints, you're beautiful," he whispered, just before he nuzzled her neck.

Senga sighed and closed her eyes as his body shifted downward until his face was even with her breasts. She waited expectantly for him to take a nipple in his mouth, to rub his tongue over the bud. She watched, mesmerized, as he circled first one areola then the other with his finger, making her nipples pucker. He tweaked one peak the same instant his mouth descended on the other.

A soft cry tore from her throat as she arched her back with the pleasure that consumed her. He shifted slightly, his hand skimming over her waist and hip to her thigh. Her lips parted, a low moan issuing from her throat when his fingers parted the curls of her sex and cupped her. The heel of his hand pressed against her, making her grind her hips against his him.

She wanted more, *needed* more. But she wasn't sure what it was she needed. Her body searched for something, moving her toward some goal, and all she could do was lay there and experience every blissful moment of it.

When his finger dipped inside her, pushing deep within her, her nails dug into his shoulders. In and out, his finger moved, driving her wild with each thrust. She moaned as his finger brushed across her clitoris. Urgency built within her as his thumb stroked her nub and his fingers readied her. His hands knew where and how to touch to make her writhe with need.

The sensations wracking her body were intense, beautiful, and addictive. Her hips moved in time with his hand, matching his rhythm as the delicious pressure continued to build until…she shattered.

Senga cried out as her first climax ripped through her body, sending her drowning in the waves of bliss. Time ceased while she soared upon this new pleasure that awakened her body—and her soul.

She opened her eyes to find Keiran leaning over her, his eyes darkened with desire. She gasped when he rubbed his rod against the sensitive flesh of her sex. Instinctively, she opened her legs wider. A muscle worked in his jaw as he stared down at her. With one arm holding him, he guided the blunt head of his cock to her opening.

When he hesitated, she urged him forward. "Don't you dare stop," she whispered.

"Never," came his velvety reply.

With her gaze caught in his, he entered her. He filled her slowly, stretching her inch by inch. His hips shifted slightly and he slid deeper. Senga knew he would feel good, but she hadn't expected this exquisite pleasure.

"I can no' wait," he said. "You feel too damn good."

Senga wrapped her arms around him. "Don't. I want to feel you. All of you."

And with that, he pulled out of her, only to give one hard thrust to bury himself to the root.

She stiffened, burying her face in his neck while trying to overcome the pain of him breaching her maidenhead. When he didn't move, she looked up at him to see him staring at her with shock and surprise.

"Senga," he started, but she quickly placed a finger over his lips.

"It was mine to give, Keiran. Don't think. Just feel."

When he still wouldn't move, she raised her legs and wrapped them around his waist so her ankles locked together. He moaned as it brought him deeper inside of her.

He gave her a hard kiss and began to thrust. Long and

slow, short and quick, each movement left her panting for breath and eager for more. Her body floated, encircled by the strength of Keiran's arms as he took her higher and higher. She gave herself over to him readily, knowing she was binding her heart to his.

His thrusts quickened as he pumped deeper, faster. Her body awakened again, eager and willing to be touched and kissed by Keiran. Their breaths mingled and sweat glistened their bodies as he continued to drive into her. Time and place were forgotten. All that mattered was each other and the pleasure surrounding them.

He whispered her name before he gave one final thrust that buried him to her womb as he threw back his head and poured his seed into her. She gasped as she peaked a second time. Senga held onto him as their bodies climaxed together. When he collapsed on top of her, she eagerly held him, comfortable in the knowledge they were together.

She didn't know how long they lay there before he gently pulled out of her and rolled to his side. His face was turned to her, his breath evened into sleep. Unable to resist, Senga rolled to her side and ran a finger down the face that she'd been dreaming about for years. She hated the dark circles beneath his eyes and the lines of worry around his mouth.

Her finger caressed the dark brows that slashed over his eyes before moving to his square jaw and wide mouth. A lock of his hair fell across his wide forehead. She moved it away and smiled down at the man who had claimed her.

Tomorrow would lead to questions and explanations, but tonight was theirs to enjoy.

Keiran awoke to see the first rays of sunlight filter through the shutters on the one window in the chamber. He smiled down at the woman who slept facing him, her lovely honey hair with its golden highlights curled around them. He couldn't remember the last time he had slept the night through. He felt more rested than he had in months, and all because he'd given in to his passion.

His cock stirred at the sight of Senga's exposed breast and nipple. He was just thinking of various ways he could wake her when she turned over in her sleep.

Keiran's body jerked as he stared in shock at Senga's left arm. From shoulder to elbow, an intricate melding of knots and swirls announced to the world what she was.

His.

He inhaled a shaky breath as his stomach felt like he'd been punched. Slowly, he rose up on his elbow and looked down at his right arm. Just as he expected, the same markings adorned him.

Keiran ran a hand down his face and tried to wrap his mind around the fact he had actually found his mate. Without even trying to. But was it by coincidence, or had there been something more at work?

Drahcir had no choice but to allow Senga to return, since she was his mate. If she wanted to return.

He swung his legs over the side of the bed and leaned his elbows on his knees as he dropped his head into his hands. His mind reeled with questions, but he wasn't sure if he had time for them.

The Tnarg was out there, waiting for them. As soon as they started the journey to Drahcir, it would attack. That was if Senga agreed to return with him. She might have found a good life outside of Drahcir. As her mate, Keiran couldn't return without her.

A soft hand touched his back, causing him to jerk in surprise. He turned and looked at Senga over his shoulder. "Look at your arm."

She licked her lips and glanced from his marked arm to hers. Her nervous swallow told him more than any words could.

She had known.

"Why did you no' tell me?" he asked, confusion and relief mixing together.

She dropped her hand and sat up, clutching the blanket to her chest. "I should have, I know. It was selfish, but I wanted you to want me for me, not simply because I'm your mate."

"It explains the instant and deep attraction," he admitted, and turned toward her. He wished she would have told him, but the release he felt in finding her overrode any other emotion. "I've never felt anything like it in my life. I should've recognized it for what it was."

She played with the blanket in her hand, her eyes downcast. "It was everything I had ever dreamed of and more."

"How long have you known you were my mate? I must know."

She blew out a breath and shrugged, her curls wild about her face. "I suppose I can tell you now. The day you left Drahcir, Aimery visited me."

"What?"

She raised her gaze to his and nodded. "He told me I was your mate, and that if I stayed in Drahcir, you'd never find me since all mates are outside the gates."

"Shite," he murmured. "No' a single Sinclair has ever found their mate with one of our own."

"I'm not sure how it happened, but I'm not sorry that it did."

Keiran reached out and took her hand. "I'd almost given up hope of finding you. I came here because I wanted to be as close to Drahcir as I could."

"What do we do now?"

He glanced at the window. "We need to get to Drahcir. That is if you want to return."

"I only left for you."

Her words, soft and unwavering, made his chest ache with some peculiar emotion. Lust and desire he'd expected. But the warm, tingling feeling he felt just being near her wasn't something his father had warned him about. As to what it was, he'd have time to determine that after they were inside the gates of the kingdom.

Keiran stood and paced to the window. "There's also the Tnarg. It's here. I know it. I'm surprised it didn't try to kill you before I arrived."

"Aimery told me it would hunt me. The last month I've kept to the inn, only venturing out during the day surrounded by people, and I've never left the village. It was difficult for it to get me."

"Why didna it attack you in here?"

She pointed to the shutters. "Rather difficult when they're reinforced with iron."

He chuckled. "Brilliant."

"Aye, I am," she said with a smile.

His own grin faded. "Senga, are you ready for what's to come? It willna be easy."

There was no missing the way her gaze darted to the window. "Of course."

He let her lie. She put on a brave front, but she had

every reason to fear for her life because the Tnarg would stop at nothing to kill her.

"We need to leave immediately. We have precious few days to reach the gates, and the weather will slow us."

She slid from the bed. "Not to mention the Tnarg."

He clenched his jaw and began to dress. He was elated to find his mate, but that euphoria combined with a bone deep fear. If his other three brothers had made it to Drahcir, then the Tnarg would be relentless in trying to kill Senga. Just thinking of her dead made him feel sick to his stomach.

Keiran glanced up to see her slide her gown into place. She was so beautiful he could stare at her all day. Her eyes, a most unusual gray, could capture him with just one look. And the wealth of beautiful honey hair that curled to her waist made him want to tug the curls and see how many different colors he could find with the sun shining in her hair.

He looked down at the tattoo on his arm just before he pulled on his tunic and jerkin. He and Senga were branded to each other forever now. He barely knew anything about her, but it didn't seem to matter. They had the rest of their lives to learn all there was to know.

Yet, he was anxious to begin their life together. How he wished the Tnarg would disappear and the Fae princess would release the curse. Centuries had passed, but she was never satisfied, no matter how many times the Sinclairs beat the curse.

Keiran didn't think he could stand to see his children leave Drahcir to search for their mates. It wasn't right to ask them to do it, and it must be stopped. How, he wasn't sure, but he was going to see about doing it.

"Keiran?"

He looked up to see Senga standing in front of him. He

pulled her into his arms, loving the way she felt against him. He should have recognized her as his mate, and he might have had he not been so immersed in looking so hard. "I've waited for you my entire life."

He'd been raised as the heir and loved deeply by his family. He'd learned to lead justly and with honor, but always there was a part of him that longed to find his mate. Now that he held her in his arms, he felt complete. Truly whole. There was no denying the feelings of protection and desire she inspired, but that other, unknown emotion was growing each moment they were together.

"If only we could've had the years in Drahcir with each other," she said, and raised her gaze to him.

"We'll have years together, Senga. I'll get us to the gates. I promise."

Her brow furrowed as her head suddenly cocked to the side. "That's odd."

"What?"

"There are no sounds coming from below as there should be this time of morning."

Keiran's stomach knotted. Something was wrong.

She smoothed her hands on his chest. "The Tnarg is here, isn't it?"

"Aye, but I'll protect you."

And he would—to his dying breath.

4

Keiran adjusted his weapons, checking them twice before he reached for his cloak. Senga's hands fisted, searching for warmth, though it wasn't the chill of the chamber but fear of the Tnarg that had driven the heat from her flesh. She knew how skilled Keiran was, but the creature that hunted them wasn't just any beast. It was one made of magic by the Fae.

She touched the dagger at her hip. It had been a parting gift from her father, one she always kept with her. It wasn't much, but it would be something against the Tnarg. "What does it look like?"

Keiran's gaze snapped to hers. "The Tnarg?"

She nodded.

"It's big and covered with thick, dark coarse hair. Its eyes are blood red. Its teeth are long and many, and its talons are sharp. It's supposedly fast, but I've no' seen one in all my time searching for you, so I doona know exactly what to expect. It knows we're coming, though."

She snorted. "Quite an unfair advantage."

"I agree. We can no' outrun it, and it has the strength of ten men."

"We'll never make it."

He was beside her in an instant. "Every one of my ancestors made it. So will we. The Tnarg has a weakness. We just have to find it."

Her heart thumped wildly when he leaned in to kiss her. A thrill shot to her stomach and spread to her sex, heating her blood. Her hands came around his neck of their own accord as the kiss deepened. She was reluctant for it to end, but they could waste no more time.

"By the saints, I want you again," he murmured.

Senga couldn't help but smile. She had Keiran, at long last. She would have waited an eternity to hold the man she loved in her arms. And those four years had felt like four lifetimes. They were so close to the gates, yet the weather and a magical beast lay in their path.

He held out his hand. "Ready?"

She wasn't anywhere near ready, but if she was going to be his wife and the future queen of Drahcir, she had to have courage. She took his hand and stood beside him. "Our future awaits."

One side of his mouth tilted upward. "You're going to make a magnificent queen."

"I don't care about being queen as long as I have you."

Keiran saw the truth of her words shining in her clear gray eyes. "Queen or no', you'll always be by my side."

"That's all I can ask for."

He cupped her face and gave her a quick kiss before he pulled her from the small chamber. He unsheathed his sword and kept her behind him as he walked stealthily down the corridor to the stairs. Not a sound was made below. Keiran descended the stairs one slow step at a time, his sword at the ready. When he reached the bottom and saw the main dining room he halted and heard Senga's quick inhale behind him as they halted.

Every table and chair was torn to pieces, the floor littered with splinters of wood that had once been furniture. Senga's hand began to shake in his, for they both knew what had done this.

The Tnarg.

"Is it still here?" she whispered.

Keiran backed them to a wall. "I doona know. If it came in here, why no' up to your chamber?"

"I'm just glad it didn't."

There was a bump from the back room. Senga tugged on his hand, trying to get his attention, but Keiran didn't want to look away in case it was the Tnarg.

"Keiran," she murmured.

He looked to where she pointed and found the three dead bodies. The Tnarg had never killed innocents before. At least, none that they knew of.

"To your chamber," he whispered and urged her up the stairs.

He walked backward as he followed her, his gaze on the doorway to the back room. It wasn't until they reached the top two stairs that one creaked. The noise in the back room stopped instantly.

Shite!

"Get inside your chamber," Keiran told her as he spun around.

They raced to her chamber and shut the door behind them.

"The chair," he said as he leaned against the door.

She hastily brought the chair that he propped against the

door. It wouldn't hold the beast, but it would give them time.

He gave her a gentle push to her window. "We'll be leaving another way."

"We're on the second floor," she said, her eyes wide.

He gripped her shoulders. "Trust me, Senga."

Keiran released her and stalked to the window. He lifted the iron latch holding the shutters together, then threw open the shutters that had been reinforced with iron. The ground below was packed with snow, which would break their fall. He'd prefer to go first and catch Senga, but he couldn't chance her not getting out in time.

He lifted her onto the windowsill, her legs dangling outside. "The snow will catch you. Doona wait on me. Run to the stables and hide. I'll be right behind you."

"And if you're not?"

He smoothed a lock of hair from her face and wished he could wipe the worry from her puckered brow. "I will be. Now go."

She stared at him a moment longer before jumping. He held his breath until she rose from the snow and ran to the stable. Nothing followed her. The eerie silence of the town told him something was very wrong.

He couldn't worry about that now. He had to get to Senga. Keiran put first one leg, then the other out the window. Just as he was about to jump something banged against the door hard. The fall was quick. He jumped to his feet as soon as he could and followed Senga's tracks to the stable. Their chance to pack food for the trip was gone, and as long as the Tnarg was this close, they weren't safe.

He closed the stable doors behind him and let out a breath. "Senga?"

"Here," she called and rose to her feet in a stall. "I'm here, Keiran."

"We doona have time to waste. There's something wrong with the town."

She walked from the stall and dusted off her hands, her brow furrowed. "I think they're all dead."

"How could we no' have heard anything?"

She shrugged. "The village is usually bustling by now. There is no one about. It's the only explanation."

"Unless they sense the creature and are keeping to their houses."

"Let's hope," she said and looked around her. "Should we take horses?"

He shook his head. "They willna move any quicker in the deep snow."

Keiran saw her shaking and drew her into his arms. If only he'd recognized her as his mate last night, they could've departed then and saved the town.

"How come we didn't hear the beast inside the inn? And why didn't it come to my chamber?"

Keiran briefly squeezed his eyes shut. "It's toying with us. It wants us to think we're safe, that we can escape."

"Or it wants us to know just how quick and deadly it is."

"Aye, love, that too." He took her hand. "Come. We need to make haste."

The quickest way to Drahcir was up the mountain path, and the only way to the gates of Drahcir was through the pass. As he passed a horse, he stopped and looked at the large dark eyes of the animal.

"What is it?" Senga asked.

He patted the horse on the neck. "I've got an idea. It might help to slow the Tnarg."

"Anything to give us an advantage," she murmured. "What do you need me to do?"

"Grab another horse," he said as he opened the stall door and led the big black mare out.

A few moments later, Senga stood beside him holding a gray. He gave her a nod and walked to the back of the stable.

"I'm sorry, girls," he said to the horses. "It's cold out there, but you could save our lives."

He opened the stable doors and slapped the horses on their rumps, sending them running off into the snow. Keiran wanted to watch them to see how far they would go, but they needed to get to the pass as quick as they could. First, they would see if their plan worked.

"Come," he said as he took Senga's hand and led her to the ladder.

They climbed into the upper area and hid in the hay on their stomachs so they could see down into the barn. It seemed an eternity sitting in the itchy hay as they waited, but finally they heard a noise below.

Keiran squeezed Senga's hand when she began to tremble. The Tnarg walked below them sniffing the air. He prayed his plan worked, for if the Tnarg found them, it was over. He held his breath as the beast walked slowly around the stable sniffing the air as it searched for them. Hope swelled within him when the creature found each of the empty stalls.

But then it stopped and smelled the ladder they had climbed.

Keiran gripped his sword in his hand, ready to defend Senga as she ran to freedom if need be. Yet, to his relief, the Tnarg continued on to the back of the stable and followed the hoof prints into the snow.

They waited until the Tnarg was well enough away

before they hurried down the ladder. Keiran clasped his mate's hand and raced out the front. The new fallen snow from the night before was so thick in places they could only manage a slow walk.

"Keiran," Senga whispered and pointed to her left.

He followed her gaze and found someone peeking between the shutters of their home. "I doona think the Tnarg harmed them. I think maybe everyone knew it was there, so they stayed in their homes."

"I hope you're right."

He did, too.

Every once in a while Keiran would look over his shoulder to see if the Tnarg had realized it had been duped yet. It wouldn't take the beast long, but Keiran wanted as many leagues between them as he could get.

It took them longer than he'd have liked to put the small village behind them. The cold soon numbed him, and though he hated the knee-deep snow, when the snow began to fall once more, covering their tracks, he rejoiced.

"Where are you taking us?" Senga asked through chattering teeth.

He pulled her cloak tighter around her. "When I first left Drahcir, I spent a few days learning the mountain. It's how I discovered an alternate route to the pass."

"Thank the gods you did."

He chuckled and helped her through a deep patch of snow. She was winded, as was he, but he couldn't chance a rest. Not now. Not yet.

"Aye," he nodded. "I like to be prepared. Taking this route will add another day, though."

Senga stopped and jerked her head towards him. "Keiran, we don't have another day. Already we are five days away from the fifth moon of the Harvest year. We must be through the gates of Drahcir to fulfill the curse."

He sighed and started walking again. "You are no' telling me anything I doona already know. We doona have much of a choice, no' with the Tnarg having found us already. Time isna on our side, but I'll fight it."

"As will I," she vowed. "No one else has waited this long to return. I cannot help but worry."

He couldn't either, but he wouldn't add to hers by admitting it. "We'll make it."

"Yes, of course." She wiped at her face to remove the snowflakes from her eyelashes.

Keiran glanced at his mate, eager to know more about her, but already enjoying what he had seen. She was frightened out of her wits, frozen solid, unsure if she would see the morrow, but she kept her faith in him.

He couldn't—and wouldn't—let her down.

5

Senga tried to clench her jaw to keep her teeth from chattering, but nothing worked. She could no longer feel her fingers, and though she knew Keiran held her hand, she couldn't feel his.

Her boots had long since been soaked from the snow, making it impossible for her to move her toes or feel anything, even with the thick wool stockings. She stumbled so many times she had lost count, but always Keiran was there to steady her.

She silently cursed the weight of her skirts as they became hampered and soaked in the thick snow. How she wished for a fire, a warm bed, and a hot meal. The people of Drahcir took their mild climate for granted, but never again would Senga make that mistake. If she made it back home.

It was easier than she expected to say farewell to the village she had lived in for four years. If it wasn't for Keiran and their future together, she could have easily lived her life in the small, sleepy town. The people were good and decent, but it wasn't Drahcir.

It wasn't home.

She missed the magic and the majesty of Drahcir. She missed seeing the imposing structure of the palace high above them, where the towers mingled with the clouds, and the beautiful blue stones that lined the road.

Most of all, she missed her family.

"Senga!"

She jerked her head to Keiran. "What is it?"

"I've been calling your name. Are you all right?"

"Aye."

"Liar," he said with a smile. "I'm frozen."

She chuckled despite herself. "I can't feel my feet or my hands. And I don't even know if my nose is still attached or not since I quit feeling that long ago."

"It's still there." He winked at her, warming her from the inside. "Tell me about yourself."

She shrugged as they moved to more packed snow, giving her aching legs a break. "There's nothing to tell really. I was no one special in Drahcir."

"I doona believe that."

A smile pulled at her chapped lips. "It's true."

"I'd never have noticed you before I left if you hadna been special."

His words warmed her heart. "You noticed me?"

"Oh, aye. You were the last thing I saw before I walked through the gates."

"My family owns a horse farm," she said. "We always had coin but had to work for it. We're not nobles, just a hard-working family who has a love of horses."

"As if it matters if you're nobility or no'. There have been very few instances where any prince of Drahcir has returned with a royal mate. As soon as we claim you, you're royal."

"And my family? Will they be an embarrassment to you?"

He shook his head. "No' at all, though as far as I know, no' a single Sinclair has married a member of Drahcir. There will be some differences, but I doona see how that matters."

She sighed. Until that moment, she hadn't realized how fearful of his answer she had been.

"What is your family like?" he asked.

She inhaled the frigid air and felt it freeze her lungs. "They're wonderful. When I asked them to trust me, that I had to leave Drahcir, they did it though they weren't happy about it."

"Nay, I imagine they were no'. Do you have siblings?"

"A younger sister and an older brother."

He nodded, his lips pressed together. "I miss my family. I'm close to my brothers and having not spoken to them in so long is…."

"Painful," she interjected.

He glanced at her. "Exactly. I can no' wait to meet their mates."

"It'll be a glorious reunion." She could only imagine how their return would be. The Sinclairs were well-loved in Drahcir, and the deep loyalty and love of the family was known throughout their kingdom.

Yet, she had to wonder if his family would approve of her. Would she get along with them? She was the future queen, after all. Just thinking it made her stomach pitch.

"Is it wrong that despite being frozen, I still want to kiss you?" Keiran asked with a devilish grin.

Senga laughed, her breath billowing around her. "If you can desire me when I look this bad, then I think we'll be all right."

"You look delicious to me," he whispered into her ear.

Despite the temperature, the falling snow, and her soaked boots, she didn't gripe when he stopped her and turned her to face him. His warm breath fanned her cheek just a heartbeat before his lips descended on hers.

He was like a ray of sunshine, and she basked in his glow. His kiss set her afire, his lips moving over hers slowly, seductively, heating her blood. Her sex clenched hungrily, and her breasts swelled. Had he wanted her right then in the snow, she'd have gladly lain down and offered her body.

She heard the stories of the uncontrollable desire, the throbbing need and vast hunger a mate of a Sinclair would feel, but experiencing it herself was more intense than she imagined, she was left panting with a need so deep and immense; a lifetime with Keiran would never be enough.

It wasn't just the desire while in his arms. She couldn't quite explain the pleasure at just being near him, of knowing she was his. It was almost as if she had become whole when he had claimed her. In marking her arm with the ancient symbol of the Sinclairs, he had also marked her heart and soul.

She had wanted to stare at the tattoo on her arm this morning. The small glimpse she had gotten sent a chill across her body, for despite Aimery's prediction, she had doubted the end result. Yet, there was no doubt now, not with her arm, as well as Keiran's, marked for eternity. She ran her hand over his right arm.

"I still can't believe it," she whispered when he raised his head. "Even knowing I was meant to be yours, I can't believe it. I used to watch you in Drahcir when you rode through the city atop your mount. You were so handsome, so skilled."

He rubbed his nose with hers. "I'm all yours now, love, even if you doona want me. I have horrid quirks that will no doubt drive you daft in short order."

Senga burst out laughing, her strength renewed. "I don't believe that for a moment."

"Doona say I didna warn you," he told her as he continued walking.

———

The snowfall turned into a vicious storm with winds that howled around them, driving them backward even as they trudged through the snow. Keiran stood in front of Senga, taking the brunt of the wind as well as shoving aside the knee-deep snow to make it easier for her to walk. She held onto his cloak, letting him know she was still there. He was exhausted. His thighs ached and his entire body hurt from the cold.

By the gods, why couldn't it have been summer?

It was always cold on the mountain, but winter storms were the worst. No one in their right mind climbed the mountain in winter, but he and Senga didn't have a choice. They had to reach Drahcir.

Keiran glanced behind him. Senga had her head ducked, her chin to her chest against the bitter wind. She clasped her cloak together, but still the wind yanked it away from her. He sighed. They couldn't stay out in this. She'd die for sure.

Keiran looked through the quick-falling snow for a hint of a cave, of anything, to get them out of the wind for a while. He squinted and turned his head to the side when he caught sight of something. It almost looked like the glow of a fire through a window. But that couldn't be. No one lived this far up the mountain. At least none whom he knew of.

However, it was worth checking out, especially if they found shelter for the night, since it had begun to grow dark in the past hour. Keiran took them toward the trees. Senga followed with nary a sound. As soon as he reached the first tree, he put his back to it and pulled Senga in his arms.

"I think I found us shelter," he shouted over the wind.

She nodded her head in answer.

He wasted not another second out in the storm but hurried to the cottage, one arm still around Senga, guiding her toward their shelter. Smoke poured from the chimney, urging Keiran faster. If they could just have time to dry out their clothing and warm up, it would be enough. There had been no sign of the Tnarg, and with the storm, there was little chance the beast would find them soon.

By the time they reached the small cottage, he all but held Senga up. Keiran pounded on the door, sending a violent ache down his frozen arm.

A moment later, the door opened to reveal a middle-aged woman with kind blue eyes. "Oh, goodness," she said when she spotted them. "Come in out of that storm."

Keiran didn't hesitate as he pulled Senga into the cottage. Immediately, warmth surrounded them.

"Both of you are frozen," the woman exclaimed. "Get by the fire and remove those wet clothes before you freeze to death. I'll get some blankets."

"Keiran?" Senga whispered.

"It's all right. Come warm yourself," he said as he settled her near the fire and began to remove her boots and cloak.

He glanced at her face to find her eyes closed and her hands stretched towards the roaring fire. He knew exactly how she felt. He could cheerfully dive into the fire he was so cold. Instead, he pulled off his own boots and set them near the hearth beside Senga's to dry.

"Here, dear, let me help you," the woman said as she began to help Senga remove her gown.

Keiran turned his back to the women and hurriedly got

out of his wet clothing before wrapping a blanket around himself and turning back to the fire. Senga was already nestled in a blanket on the floor, her bare toes near the fire.

"I don't think either of you has frostbite," the woman said. "No one in their right mind comes up on this mountain in winter."

Senga's gray eyes met Keiran's before he looked at the woman. "The storm caught us by surprise. We appreciate you sharing your blankets and fire with us."

The woman smiled and touched her dark hair streaked with a few gray hairs. "Think nothing of it. I rarely get visitors, so this is a treat. I've made some soup. Are you hungry?"

"Aye, please," Senga whispered.

Keiran's own stomach had been growling for hours. There hadn't been time for them to eat before they had left the village. "That would be wonderful."

"Good," the woman said. "Call me Molly. My husband and I settled here years ago to get away from everyone. I've been without my Fergus for nearly five years now."

Keiran watched as she stirred the soup over the fire. "I'm sorry for your loss. I'm Keiran and this is my wife, Senga."

Molly shrugged. "Such is life, I suppose. It's nice to meet you both."

"You live up here alone then?"

"I do," she said with a smile.

Keiran wondered how she did it all, but she looked as though she had everything she needed. Some women could hunt, and he guessed Molly had learned from her husband how to keep food on the table should something happen to him.

The soup was dished out and tasted delicious. Keiran had two helpings before he set aside the bowl. Between the food and the warmth, he could already feel his body begin to thaw.

He glanced at Senga to find her watching him. Her cheeks had a soft glow to them again. "Feel better?"

"Much," she admitted. "I've never been so cold. I'd do fine without ever seeing snow again."

He couldn't agree more. He wondered what she thought about him calling her his wife. In Drahcir, even without a formal ceremony, she was considered his wife as soon as they had been marked. Still, it was the first time he had spoken of her as his wife, and he felt a swell of pride at having her by his side.

His brave woman. She would make an excellent queen.

Molly handed each of them a mug of hot tea. "This will help, as well," she said. "The storm should break overnight, and both of you are welcome to stay. I wouldn't suggest venturing out into the storm again."

Keiran's met Senga's gaze, silently asking her what she wanted to do. She gave a very slight nod of her head.

"If you doona mind," he said. "I think we'll take you up on your kind offer."

6

Senga flexed her fingers and toes as the feeling returned to them. Keiran scooted closer to her and rubbed her feet to help bring the feeling back. She smiled at him. He was a good man, sacrificing so much for his people. She knew of his kindness, of the wisdom he'd seemed to possess even at a young age. Drahcir would prosper under his reign as it had in the generations before him.

"What are you thinking?" he asked.

Senga glanced at Molly to find her out of earshot. "I'm thinking you'll make a great king."

"With you by my side, I can do anything."

She touched his cheek, rubbing the stubble of his beard beneath her hand.

"Tell me your greatest desire," he asked.

She shrugged and licked her lips. "I've always wanted children. I love the innocence in babies' eyes when they look up at you, the trusting way they grip your finger in their tiny hands. And a child's laughter has to be one of the best sounds in the entire world."

"You'll make a wonderful mother."

She let out a deep breath. "As much as I want sons and daughters with your dark hair and hazel eyes, I'm afraid. I don't know how your parents could stand to let the four of you leave, knowing there was a chance they would never see you again."

"It's a chance each Sinclair has made since the curse came into being. I long to break the curse, to end this wretchedness once and for all. Yet, I doona know how to do it. I used to comb through Father's library, hoping to find something in those tomes that would give me some hint, but I never found anything."

"Did you ask Aimery?"

He shook his head. "I was so worried about finding you, I forgot."

She entwined her fingers with his. "Then that is what we'll do once we reach Drahcir. We'll find a way to end it. I don't want our children suffering through the frustration and anxiety of looking for their mates and trying to outrun the beast."

"The weight of an entire kingdom is on my shoulders, Senga," he murmured. "I can no' tell you how heavy it weighs upon me."

She could only imagine. Despite his broad shoulders, no one should have to carry such a load. She simply refused to have her children suffer as Keiran and his brothers had suffered. Keiran's arm wrapped around her shoulders, drawing her against him as his warmth surrounded her. Her body responded instantly to his nearness. The need to feel him between her legs, thrusting deep within her was overwhelming.

He nuzzled her neck. "I love the smell of your skin," he whispered in her ear. "I could lick you from head to toe and never get enough."

She shivered at his words. By the gods, how she wanted him. "I could lick you as well."

"Ah, doona tempt me, love."

"But I want to tempt you."

His eyes twinkled devilishly. "You can tempt me each day for the rest of our lives."

"Then I shall. Should I start tonight?"

He groaned into her hair. "I want you with a ferocity I find exhilarating and a tad alarming."

Senga bit her lip to keep from moaning when Keiran's hand slipped into her blanket and cupped her breast while he thumbed her nipple. The pleasure shot to her sex, making her squeeze her legs together. She wanted to throw off the blankets and scoot into his lap to slowly lower herself atop his cock and ride him until they both screamed in ecstasy.

Only the presence of their hostess stopped her.

"Keiran, please," she begged.

"Please what? Do you want more?"

"You must stop. We cannot, not with Molly so near," she whispered.

He reluctantly removed his hand. His mouth, however, continued to drive her wild with his soft lips and hot tongue as they scrapped across her flesh. His breath fanned her neck, sending chills across her skin. "I want to bring you to release again," he whispered. "I want to hear you scream my name."

Senga's resistance was wearing down. Her body was in such a state of need that she was nearly to the point of uncaring who watched as she made love to Keiran. Her eyes closed as she titled her head back to grant him access to her neck. His teeth grazed her skin a heartbeat before he ran his tongue over the spot. It was too much for Senga.

"By the gods, how I want you," Keiran said, his voice husky and deep.

The sound of feet moving closer to them made Senga lift her head and open her eyes. "Molly is coming."

"Ah, I wish I was," he said.

She choked back a laugh and straightened her blanket around her. Her body pulsed with need, desire strummed through her veins demanding she seek the release and pleasure only Keiran could give her.

And she would. Just as soon as Molly went to sleep.

Molly leaned down to add another log to the fire before she dusted off her hands and faced them. "There is a loft where the two of you can bed down for the night, or I can make you a pallet in front of the fire."

"The loft will be fine," Keiran answered.

"Help yourself to anything you need, then." Molly moved past them to her bed, which sat directly behind them.

Senga rose and started for the ladder that would take them to the loft. Keiran was right behind her. It took a while to navigate the ladder while holding her blanket closed, but by the time she and Keiran were in the loft, Molly was in her bed.

When Keiran pulled at her blanket, she let it fall from her shoulders to puddle at her hips. His warm hazel eyes caught and held hers as he cupped the side of her face. "You're mine."

She nodded and glanced at the mark on his arm, a mark that let all the world know he was mated. "I'm yours. For always."

His kiss, when it came, held all the desire, promise, and love she had seen in his eyes. Again and again his tongue swirled around hers. She pushed at his blanket, exposing his muscled form to her view. With a flick of her wrist she pushed him onto his back and straddled his hips. His thick cock nestled between her legs, hard and hot.

Though she longed to hold him in her hand, she made herself wait. Instead, she spread her hands over his chest, feeling his heart beating beneath her hand. Slowly, she moved her hands down his torso and over his rippling abdomen and tight stomach.

His cock jumped in anticipation as her hand neared him. A glance at his face showed her he was watching her intently, silently wondering if she would take him in hand.

When Senga could stand it no longer, she grasped his cock, amazed at the smoothness of him. Her thumb rubbed over the tip to the bead of moisture the pooled there.

"Senga." His voice was strained, rough.

Her hand moved up and down his length, learning the feel of him. Several times he moaned, his hands fisting in the blanket, yet not once did he stop her.

"I need you too desperately," he whispered.

Before she could argue that she wasn't done, he leaned up and took her in a kiss that stole her breath. She clung to his shoulders, her body quivering with each rub of his rod against her sex. He reached between them and cupped her, running his finger through her moist curls until he pushed inside her. Senga gasped at the sensation and tore her mouth from his.

In and out his fingers moved. She felt her own wetness, the desire coiling inside her. As if he understood her need, Keiran laid back and lifted her by her hips until she knelt over his cock. She sank onto him, his length, his heat, his hardness, filling her inch by delicious inch.

His hands cupped her breasts and gave her nipples a pinch before his thumbs began to move back and forth over the tiny buds. Shivers of delight raced through her, causing her to shift her hips, and the most delectable pleasure consumed her.

She moved her hips, causing Keiran's fingers to dig into her skin as his own pleasure mounted. Just when she thought she couldn't take any more, his hand moved to her sex and stroked her pearl with the barest of touches, sending her higher.

Her climax took her almost instantly. With her hands on Keiran's chest to hold her up, Senga bit her lip to keep from crying out and rode her orgasm. Keiran gripped her hips, sliding her up and down his length, and he plunged deep inside of her. He buried his head in her neck a moment before he stiffened beneath her, his body jerking with his own climax.

Keiran caught Senga as she fell atop his chest, their ragged breaths filling the air around them. Though they had tried to be quiet, he was sure Molly hadn't slept through their lovemaking.

He ran his hands over his mate's back, learning the wonderful, silky feel of her skin. He couldn't wait to return to Drahcir with her by his side. They would enter the gates to the cheers of their people. His family would be there to greet them with hugs, tears and laughter.

Much rejoicing would fill the kingdom as the curse would be fulfilled once more. Keiran knew his mother would waste little time in getting a ceremony together for their wedding. It was just a formality, but one he knew Senga would enjoy immensely.

He couldn't wait to see the crown sitting atop her beautiful honey curls, the bright sun shining down upon her and highlighting her golden strands.

A gift. He wanted to give her a gift, something to

celebrate their return to Drahcir and their future together. He had a magnificent teardrop shaped sapphire he could have set in a necklace.

Though he would gift her with it, it wasn't exactly what he had envisioned. In his mind, he went through the jewels he had purchased over the years, as well as the ones in the royal vault. And that's when he recalled the amazing yellow diamond ring he'd stumbled across before he'd left Drahcir.

It was perfect. Just the gift for his wife. He couldn't wait to see it on her hand. It would be a sign of their love.

Love? Do I love her? I lust after her, but love?

Keiran pushed a strand of hair from her face to find her sleeping. Her lips were parted slightly and her hand was curled on his chest. She was beautiful, brave, loyal and courageous—everything a future queen of Drahcir needed to be. Being with her made him feel whole, and there was no question he cared for her. The emotion that made his heart beat faster every time he looked at her could be love.

He suspected it was love. But he couldn't say for sure. Not yet, anyway.

Gently, he rolled to his side. Senga shifted and curled on her side away from him. He ran his hand over the swell of her hips to the indent of her waist. Even now, as exhausted as he was, he wanted her again. He wondered how long before she swelled with child. And then he recalled the curse.

By the gods. I doona want my children to suffer through this.

But there wasn't another way. Or was there? He had never thought to question Aimery on it. Could the Fae have held the answer all the years? Surely Keiran wasn't the first Sinclair to wonder about ending the curse.

He leaned up and pulled the blanket over himself and Senga before he snuggled up against her. Whatever the price that needed to be paid, he would do it if it ended the curse forever.

A smile pulled at his lips as he drifted off to sleep and dreamt of his kingdom with Senga by his side and their children playing around them.

7

Senga wasn't sure what woke her. She yawned and sighed against Keiran's chest. His arm was draped over her with his hand cupping her breast. Even in sleep, her mate had a need to touch her.

"My mate," she whispered, loving the sound of it.

It was still difficult to believe Keiran was actually hers and they were on their return to Drahcir. If only the Tnarg wasn't trying to kill her.

Her mood now shattered, Senga sat up and clutched the second blanket to her chest as she moved to the edge of the ladder. She glanced over the side to find the fire roaring and Molly sitting at the table smiling at her. Senga returned her smile and started down the ladder.

"I trust you slept well?" Molly asked.

Senga nodded. "I did, thank you. You have our gratitude for offering us shelter."

Molly waved away her words. "Nonsense, child. I'm happy to have the company. I've been alone for so long now."

Senga grew uncomfortable in the silence that followed as

Molly looked into her cup. There had been something in Molly's words and tone that set off warning bells in Senga's mind. She started towards their clothes. They were nearly dry, which meant they could leave soon. Suddenly, she wanted out of the cottage as soon as she could, even if it meant stepping back into the snow.

"Come sit with me a moment," Molly beckoned.

Senga had no choice but to do as Molly requested. She glanced up at the loft, but Keiran slept on. Senga walked to the table and accepted the cup of tea Molly offered. "Thank you. Is there anything I can do to repay your kindness?"

"Ah, no need, lass," the older woman said. "Where are you and your husband traveling to?"

Senga hesitated. No one was supposed to know of Drahcir.

Before she could respond, however, Molly continued. "You must be newly married."

"Aye," Senga admitted.

Molly ran her finger over the rim of the mug. "Where will you make your home? In the village at the base of the mountain?"

"Nay. We've other plans."

"Good. Good." Molly licked her thin lips and turned her blue eyes to Senga. "I've a confession to make."

Senga shuddered, that odd tone back in Molly's voice. Why couldn't Keiran wake? "What would that be?"

"My name isn't Molly. In fact, I'm not even human."

Senga's heart began to pound a slow, sickening tempo. She'd known there was something odd about the woman, but it had come to her too late. "Who…what are you?"

"I shall show you." With a wave of her hand, a bright light infused the cottage.

Senga lifted her arm to shield her eyes as she watched the

plain, older woman transform to a young, gorgeous Fae before her very eyes. There was no denying the swirling blue eyes or the flaxen hair.

"This is the real me," the Fae said. "My name is Saynarra."

Instantly, Senga knew who she was. "You're the Fae princess who cursed the Sinclairs."

Saynarra shook her head. The wealth of flaxen hair that fell past her waist shimmered in the firelight. Her swirling blue gaze stared daggers at Senga. "I'm not a princess, though I am Fae. It was a Sinclair who labeled me a princess, the stupid fool. The Sinclairs weren't meant to fulfill the curse. They were supposed to fail."

"But they didn't. So you sent the Tnargs."

"Of course," Saynarra said, her smile malicious. "I succeeded in killing a few Sinclairs."

"Only because of their wounds, yet they managed to make it through the gates."

Saynarra's lips flattened. "Don't remind me. It will all end with Keiran. I've made sure of it."

Senga looked to the loft, wishing Keiran would wake and join her. She was uncomfortable speaking to the Fae alone. Not to mention the Fae frightened her. She knew just how powerful a Fae could be, and one that was angry was the most dangerous of them all.

"He won't wake."

Her head jerked to Saynarra. Her heart thundered in her chest and constricted, as if a steel band had wrapped around it. "Did you kill him?"

"Nay. Not yet anyway."

Senga closed her eyes in relief. She took in a steadying breath and looked at Saynarra. "What do you want?"

Her flaxen head tilted to the side. "Maybe it should be I who asks you that question, Senga of Drahcir."

Senga's stomach fell to her feet in dread. "I don't understand."

"Aye, you do. What do you want most for your mate and all of Drahcir?"

"I want the curse lifted," she said. If this was her one chance to remove the curse, she would take it. "Is there anything I can do to lift the curse?"

A slow, sly smile pulled at Saynarra's pink lips. "As a matter of fact, there is. I will lift the curse."

Senga wasn't fooled. The Fae had just said she wanted to kill Keiran. She had to have an ulterior motive to offer to lift the curse. Since Senga knew how much Keiran suffered, and she didn't want any other prince or princess of Drahcir to have to leave the kingdom, she was willing to see what the Fae would say. "What would you ask of me?"

"You must give up Keiran."

Senga jerked, unable to breath. This she hadn't expected. The mere thought of being without Keiran made her heart feel as though it had been ripped from her chest. To live without him after knowing his body, his touch, his kisses? She wouldn't be able to do it. "You ask the impossible."

"Not so," Saynarra said as she rose to her feet. She was tall and lithe. Her blue and silver gown was made of sheer material that hung straight to the floor and floated around her feet. The Fae turned to Senga. "I ask you to give up Keiran in return for lifting the curse. No more Sinclairs would need to leave Drahcir to find their mates. No more would the Tnarg hunt you or any Sinclair."

With the blood pounding in her ears, Senga looked at Keiran sleeping soundly in the loft. She had worried so of their children having to leave Drahcir, but if she agreed,

Keiran's children would be safe. She didn't think beyond that, for to think of Keiran with anyone else made her stomach roll.

She swallowed and faced the Fae. "And the mark upon his arm that brands him as mine?"

Saynarra shrugged. "It will be gone, as will any memory he has of you and your time together. He will return to Drahcir safely to live out his life. The idea of him finding a mate will have never been."

Senga gripped the arms of the chair and rose on shaky legs. Her every instinct screamed to tell Saynarra nay, but how could she be so selfish? She was being offered a way to end the curse, to give the Sinclairs, as well as all of Drahcir, a fresh start.

Keiran wouldn't remember her, he wouldn't know he had already found his mate. There wouldn't be that connection that prevented him from finding a new queen. She would be the only one to feel it, the only one to suffer.

Because she loved him so, she would endure a thousand deaths for him.

She moved to the fire and turned to look up at Keiran again. He was on his side facing her. A lock of his hair had fallen over his forehead, and she longed to smooth it back and feel his strong arms wrap around her one more time. They'd had just a few short hours. It seemed so unfair, but in those hours, she'd found contentment and love.

"Will he be happy?" she asked.

"Aye. He'll marry in a few years and have children, children I should mention who would never have to worry about fulfilling my curse."

With a sigh, she turned to Saynarra. "If you vow that he'll never remember me or the thought that his mate is waiting for him, then I'll do it. But he must never remember anything about me or our time together, because to separate mates is to kill us both."

Saynarra stepped towards her. "My magic is strong. As long as he lives, he'll never recall you."

"What will I do? Will I return to the village and live out my life?"

"Nay. You can't be anywhere near him. I'll take you somewhere far, far away. Somewhere where you can rest peacefully."

"All right," Senga agreed before she changed her mind. "I agree to your conditions."

Saynarra smiled, triumph in her swirling blue eyes. "A wise choice, Senga. You wouldn't have liked dying by the Tnarg's hand."

A shiver raced down Senga's spine at the mention of the beast.

"Now," Saynarra said, as she held out her hand palm up and a shiny cup of silver appeared. "All you have to do is to take a drink. It'll seal our deal."

Senga reached for the beautiful cup, but hesitated for just a second when she recalled the taste of Keiran's kiss. With one last glance at Keiran, Senga lifted the cup and drank. A strange sensation stole through her. It grew difficult, painful to breathe.

Her gaze rose to Saynarra as the silver cup fell from her hand. She could feel her heart slow and sleep pull at her down into a deep, dark fog.

"Don't fight it, Senga," the Fae urged as she wrapped an arm around her. "Let the poison take you. The more you fight, the more painful it will become."

Keiran. Keiran, please help!

The last thing Senga saw before the darkness took her were the swirling blue eyes of Saynarra.

Keiran woke slowly. He was warm and rested and hated to leave the soft bed. He rolled onto his back and slowly sat up to look around. Molly was nowhere in the cottage, but a fire roared and a loaf of bread with cheese sat on the table awaiting him.

He hurried from the loft and pulled on his now dry clothes. After a peek through the window to see the storm had indeed passed during the night, Keiran tore off a chunk of bread and ate it with the cheese.

Finally, he would return home this day.

Once he was finished with his morning meal, he called out for Molly. When she didn't answer, he put on his cloak and went outside. The day dawned bright and clear, but still he couldn't find Molly.

He wished to say farewell before he left. After another thirty minutes of looking, he gave up and started for the pass that would lead him home with long, determined strides. At midday he stopped to eat the rest of the bread and cheese before continuing on, his excitement of seeing his family making him forget the cold.

Two hours later, the pass came into view. Keiran quickened his pace as he wrapped his cloak tighter around him when the snow began to fall once more. The sheer ice and snow walls of the pass rose up around him. He glanced at the beauty of it.

The first time he had come through here it hadn't been a place he enjoyed but knowing that once he was out of the narrow space, he would see the gates of Drahcir, he pushed himself harder.

He was all but running the last few hundred yards of the

pass when the gates of Drahcir came into view. A laugh bubbled inside of him.

"Mother! Father!" he yelled. "I'm home. Open the gates!"

As he neared, his people begin to line the streets their cheers deafening. And then, he saw his parents running toward him. His mother cried, and his father's eyes swam with unshed tears. Behind his parents he saw his three brothers and their wives.

At long last he was home!

Keiran stepped through the gates and into his parents' arms.

"I thought you would never return," his mother said through her tears.

Keiran smiled at her before he turned to his father.

"Son, we're so proud of you," King Urises said.

He stepped around his parents to be enveloped in his brothers' arms, their hugs and pounding of his back brought laughter to everyone. He rejoiced in every second of it. There had been a time he feared he'd never see any of them again, but that was in the past. Now, he was home.

When he could finally stand again, he looked to the women next to his brother and for just a heartbeat, felt as though something was missing.

"Keiran, where is your mate?" Elric asked.

Keiran shrugged. "What are you talking about?"

"Your mate?" Sorin repeated, worry lines bracketing his mouth. "Where is she? You are no' supposed to return without her."

"And yet here I am," Keiran replied, and tried to turn away, yet Sorin gripped his arm and kept him still.

Queen Morag clasped her hands in front of her. "This can't be happening. Urises, the curse."

Lucian shifted feet. "Did the Tnarg attack? Did it kill your mate?"

"Of course no'," Keiran said, but once more that uneasy feeling stole over him. Why was everyone asking about his mate? "I never found my mate, but it doesna matter. I'm here."

Elric snorted. "Of course it matters, you dolt. Did you bang your head or something? You can no' return without your mate or Drahcir and all its occupants will disappear."

Keiran crossed his arms over his chest. "Least you forget, brother, I'm the eldest. I know more about the curse than any of you."

"That's debatable," Lucian murmured.

Keiran slid his gaze to his brother. "I didna hit my head, and the Tnarg didna kill my mate."

"Keiran."

The deep voice behind him was familiar, the note of urgency and warning sending a ripple of apprehension down Keiran's back. He turned and found Aimery standing just outside the gates.

"You're wrong," the Fae commander said softly. "The Tnarg did take your mate."

8

For several heartbeats all Keiran could do was stare at Aimery. Surely the Fae commander was wrong. Wouldn't Keiran know if he lost his mate? He would be screaming in agony over the loss, dying himself.

All around him, the silence was deafening. He could feel the stares of his people, the unspoken questions of his family. And all Keiran could do was stand with his heart pounding in his chest.

No longer could he deny the unease that nudged at his brain. He looked at his brothers' wives and then down beside him. Someone was supposed to be with him.

"There's something wrong," he murmured.

Aimery took a step toward him, the Fae's swirling blue eyes intense as they regarded him. "More than you know. You've had a spell cast upon you. You did find your mate. You were both on your way to Drahcir when you encountered trouble."

"Impossible." *Is it?* "I'd know. I'd know!"

"Listen to your heart," Elric said from behind him.

Keiran ignored his brother and pushed his cloak away

from him. He would be able to know who was lying if the tattoo was on his arm. With one vicious jerk, he yanked the sleeve of his tunic off.

To find his arm bare of any tattoo.

He raised his gaze to Aimery. "See? I never found her. There's no mark."

"The mere fact you looked is because you know it was once there, right?" Aimery asked softly.

Keiran raked a hand through his hair, his frustration and confusion growing by the moment. He began to pace. "This doesna make sense."

Every time he tried to think of the day before, his head began to pound. He gripped his head between his hands.

"That's the spell keeping you from remembering," Aimery said.

This couldn't be happening. *This isn't happening.* Keiran had waited too long to return home to discover he had failed. He dropped his hands and turned to Aimery. "How am I able to step through the gates? If my mate isna with me, why is Drahcir still here?"

Aimery sighed, a look of utter sadness reflected in his swirling blue eyes. "Your mate ended the curse, releasing you and all future Sinclairs from it."

Keiran's knees threatened to buckle as Aimery's words penetrated his mind. He felt as if someone had just kicked him in the bollocks. A flash of a woman's beautiful smile rushed through his brain. He closed his eyes as he saw another image, this one of long curls of honey gold wrapped around his fingers.

"Keiran."

Her voice was soft and sweet as wine, her hands tender as they caressed his back before she urged him over her.

And then he knew.

By the gods!

"Senga."

Keiran fell to his knees, threw back his head, and bellowed. A pain so intense, so violent ripped through him that he thought his abdomen had been ripped apart. He put his hand on his chest and closed his eyes as the ache tore through him, a vast hole of nothingness that consumed him.

"Keiran, your arm," Lucian said from beside him.

He glanced to find the tattoo was once again visible. Where was Senga? Who had done this to him? Senga had ended the curse, but that no longer mattered. He'd walk the entire breadth and width of the Earth five times over if it meant he could hold her in his arms again.

"Aimery?" he asked, his jaw clenched as rage filled him.

The Fae held up a hand. "Before you demand revenge, understand what your mate did."

"I do," Keiran said. *All too well.* "Where is Senga?"

Aimery closed his eyes, his body suddenly stiff. "Saynarra. Show yourself."

Almost instantly there was a flash of light and another Fae, this one a stunning female, appeared. She glanced at Aimery, but her attention remained on Keiran.

"How does it feel?" she asked Keiran, her smile one of gloating. "Do you enjoy knowing you will have to live your life without the one you love? Had Aimery not interfered, you would've married in a few years to a nice Drahcir girl and had many babies."

"I. Want. Senga," Keiran ground out as he climbed to his feet. His hands itched to wrap around the Fae's neck and squeeze the life from her.

Saynarra shrugged a slim shoulder. "She made a deal. It cannot be broken, nor will I relinquish her unless you'd like the curse to once more enthrall Drahcir."

Keiran could no more do that than he could forget Senga.

"You forget something, Saynarra," Aimery said. "The deal you made with Senga is broken."

The Fae woman rolled her eyes. "Nothing could break that pact."

"You went back on your word to Senga," Aimery continued, as if she hadn't spoken. "You swore to her that Keiran would never remember a single thing about her."

Keiran clenched his hands into fists. "I remember *everything* about my mate."

Saynarra's swirling blue eyes moved from Keiran to Aimery and back again. "You did this, Aimery!"

"You've had your revenge," the Fae commander said. "For centuries you put the Sinclairs and their mates in danger. Senga willingly gave her life for the curse to be broken."

Keiran could hear the murmurs of his people, but it was the sound of his brothers pulling their blades from their scabbards that had him reaching for his own sword. Humans couldn't win a battle with a Fae, but the Sinclairs weren't going to stand idly by while one held Keiran's mate.

"Give me Senga," he demanded.

Aimery smiled, his lips peeled menacingly over his teeth as he looked at the Fae. "She has no choice but to do it. Saynarra. Return Senga. Now."

Keiran waited with bated breath for his beloved. Yet nothing happened. He glanced at Saynarra and found her beginning to laugh.

She threw back her flaxen head and cackled. "You want Senga returned?" she asked Keiran. "Then you can have her."

There was a blinding flash. Keiran looked at his feet to

find Senga laying half on the snow and half on the blue stones of Drahcir.

He went to his knees instantly and dragged her to his chest. "Senga," he called. "Senga, I'm here, love. Open your eyes for me. You're home now. We're home."

But she didn't stir.

Nay! I can no' lose her. I willna lose her.

Keiran shook her. "Senga! Wake up, love."

"You'll never wake her," Saynarra said, the glee evident on her lovely, evil face.

"Aimery," Keiran begged.

There was movement behind Keiran as his family gathered around. Their comfort helped, but it wasn't him in need, it was Senga.

"Help her," he pleaded with the Fae commander, when Aimery knelt in front of him.

Aimery pressed his lips together in a flat line and ran his hand over Senga. He inhaled deeply and sat back. "Saynarra has put her into a deep sleep where she will stay for eternity."

"Nay," Keiran said, with a shake of his head. His throat tightened with emotion and the...love he had for his mate. "How? You said the pact was broken."

"It is, which is why you have her with you now. The other wasn't part of the pact."

Keiran caressed Senga's cheek, silently begging her to wake so he could look into her gray eyes and see her beautiful smile. He refused to live without her. A Sinclair never lasted long once his mate was gone.

A hand grasped his shoulder. He turned his head to find his father above him. "Bring her to the palace, son. We'll figure out what to do, but you can no' stay here."

He knew his father was right. "What will happen to Saynarra?" he asked Aimery.

"I'm taking her back to the Realm of the Fae. She'll be punished for what she's done to your family and Senga."

Keiran turned his gaze to Saynarra and lost his breath as he watched her turn into the Tnarg. The once beautiful Fae was now the hideous beast every Sinclair had tried to kill.

"Gods," Sorin exclaimed behind him.

Lucian took a step toward the creature. "I want a piece of her hide."

"Lucian," Keiran said, in a flat tone he knew would halt his brother. When Lucian stopped, Keiran lowered Senga to the ground and rose to his feet.

He longed to plunge his sword into the creature, but instead, he kept the weapon in the scabbard at his hip and walked to the Tnarg. "It's been you all along. You no' only cursed us and moved our mates to different times, you hunted them."

"And nearly succeeded in killing us and our mates," Sorin stated angrily.

Keiran took in a steadying breath. "Why? Just because my ancestor didna return your love? Are you really that petty?"

"I'm Fae," the beast ground out, in a voice unrecognizable as Saynarra. "No one chooses a mortal over a Fae. No one."

"No' without consequences, aye?" Keiran asked. "After all these centuries when we've beaten the odds and returned to Drahcir with our mates, even escaping you, you won in the end. Senga did the most courageous thing a person could do. She sacrificed herself for the happiness of the people of Drahcir."

"Exactly!" the Tnarg shouted. "She wanted the curse lifted for the people, and she didn't care that she left you."

Keiran didn't believe her for a moment. "She wouldna have made you promise to wipe all my memories of her if that were the case. Right now, she could be carrying the future heir to the throne, but you doona care. Now you've gotten your final revenge and hurt the Sinclairs like never before."

He raked his gaze over the ugly beast. "This form you take, this is what you truly are, no' the Fae you claim to be. You want to know why my ancestor toyed with you? Because he saw this inside of you, he saw what you really were. And you paled in comparison to the women we are bound to."

Without another word he turned and walked to Senga. He gently lifted her in his arms and stepped past his brothers to his parents. "Senga is from Drahcir," he said to them. "Aimery bade her leave days after I did to await me in the world beyond our gates. Her family is here."

His father gave a nod. "I'll send for them immediately."

Keiran looked at his mother to see her beautiful eyes full of sadness. He held Senga tighter. "I'd hoped to be celebrating this day and planning our wedding, no' to be mourning her loss."

"Oh, son," she whispered as more tears spilled down her face.

Keiran let her shed the tears he was unable to. In the short time he had with Senga, he had experienced the most joy in his entire life. He glanced down at her as he started down the long, winding road to the palace high in the cliffs. He could almost imagine she was simply sleeping and would wake at any moment, embarrassed that he was carrying her.

Gods, how can I live without her?

9

For three weeks Keiran sat beside Senga, barely eating, refusing to leave her side. The entire kingdom mourned the loss of their future queen, but none mourned her more than Keiran. He had talked to her, yelled at her, and begged her to wake, but she never moved. Not even a flinch to let him know she heard him.

It was the worst kind of torture imaginable.

Movement behind him drew his attention. When he looked over his shoulder it was to find all three of his brothers standing shoulder to shoulder. They were good men, his brothers. Good, strong, loyal, and the best warriors he knew.

"I can no' lead Drahcir without her," he finally spoke into the quiet. He'd come to the decision just days after returning to Drahcir, but he knew it was time to voice it to his brothers. Already he'd spoken to his parents. They didn't agree with his decision, but they stood by him nonetheless.

"I'm abdicating the throne tomorrow. Lucian, as the next oldest, you'll be heir."

Lucian shook his head. "I doona want it, Keiran. It's yours. You're meant to be king of Drahcir."

"I'm meant to be king with my queen beside me. If I can no' have Senga, what good would I be to our people? It's for the best, Lucian. Trust me in this."

Elric's shoulders sagged as he let out a sigh. "I understand why you think you can no' rule, but I think you can. What would Senga want you to do?"

Keiran looked to his mate and fingered a lock of her honey curls. He felt the stirrings of a smile for he knew exactly what she would say. "She'd tell me to do my duty, regardless." As quickly as the grin began, it disappeared. He turned to his brothers. "I pray that none of you has your mate taken. The pain is…unbearable."

Sorin elbowed his brothers to get their attention and walked from the room as soon as Keiran had focused once more on his mate. Sorin turned to his brothers when the door closed behind Elric.

"What is it?" Lucian asked.

Sorin crossed his arms over his chest. "Katrina and I have been up most of the last two nights trying to think of a way the spell can be undone."

"I've already looked into it in the first week," Elric admitted as he leaned against the wall. "Only the Fae who cast the spell on can remove it."

Lucian snorted. "Wonderful. Where does that leave us now? I'll lead if I must, but Keiran was born to that position. It's his."

"He's already set things in motion," Sorin said. He turned and walked to one of the arched windows in the hallway that overlooked their kingdom. "All we ever wanted was for each of us to return with our mates."

"We thought that would be enough," Elric admitted softly. "I can no' imagine losing Marin."

"Nor I Isabelle," Lucian agreed. "Has Aimery found Saynarra yet?"

Sorin shook his head. "Nay. I wanted to go looking for her, but Aimery said if she could elude the Fae, I'd be useless."

"He's right," Lucian said with a chuckle.

Sorin threw him a black look but ruined it with a grin that soon faded. "If we could find Saynarra, we might be able to talk her into releasing Senga."

Elric pushed away from the wall. "It willna happen. Even if Aimery and his army find her, she's to be sentenced in their realm immediately. There willna be time for her to aid us."

"Shite," Lucian cursed.

Sorin couldn't agree more.

Keiran was surprised to find night had fallen. The last time he had noticed the sky out the many windows of the chamber it had been day. How had he lost so many hours?

He'd relived every second of every moment he and Senga had been together. If only he'd known then what he knew now, he would never have stopped at the cottage. When Aimery had told him of the trick Saynarra had played on them, Keiran's stomach rolled in disgust. He knew it had been odd to have a cottage on such a mountain, but he had been so relieved to see it he hadn't thought more about it. Now he knew why.

"I'm so sorry, Senga," he said and entwined his fingers with hers. "I was supposed to protect you. I failed, love."

"Do you love her?"

Keiran spun around at the sound of Saynarra's voice to find the Fae standing behind him. He thought about calling out to his brothers or Aimery but couldn't work up the notion. There was nothing she could do to him now that would hurt worse than what had already been done.

He sighed and turned back to Senga. "Aye, I love her."

Maybe it was when he'd realized she had been taken from him that he'd known the emotions inside of him were love, not just lust. Senga was his everything, the other part of his soul. Without her, he was nothing.

"You should've just killed her," Keiran said as the rage began to build inside him once more. He released Senga's hand and stood to face the Fae. "What you've done to her, to me, is needlessly cruel. It wasna us who damaged your pride. You have bespelled someone so beautiful, so good, that our entire kingdom mourns her loss."

Saynarra's calm features never moved. "As you mourn her?"

He threw up his hands in defeat. He didn't know why he was talking to her. Nothing would change what she had done. "Of course, I mourn my mate!"

"Word has spread that you are abdicating as heir and passing it on to Lucian."

His gaze narrowed. "I have. I'm worthless to Drahcir without Senga. She still lives, so I can no' die, but I'm dead inside."

"A mate will die without the other?"

"Aye," he said, and turned his back on Saynarra. He couldn't look at her stunning Fae features without seeing the

Tnarg. It disgusted him. She disgusted him. No wonder his ancestor never fell in love with her.

Though he should probably be on his knees begging for Senga's freedom, Saynarra had shown her true self. She cared for nothing other than herself. She couldn't comprehend the extent of his pain, and to try to make her understand would be fruitless.

"Why did you come here?" he asked.

When there wasn't an answer, he looked over his shoulder to find her gone. Keiran shrugged and resumed his seat next to the bed, and once more took Senga's hand in his. He scratched his whiskered jaw and laid his head upon the bed, letting exhaustion take him.

Saynarra gazed down at Keiran and Senga, much as she had done when they had been at the cottage. Her all-consuming need to hurt someone as she had been hurt had led her down a path that was as far from the Fae way of life as any. The Fae were supposed to watch over the humans and aid them, not injure them.

She felt Aimery's presence before she saw him. She was tired of running, tired of hiding from the Fae that had hunted her for centuries. It had been two thousand years since she had seen her own realm.

The Fae drew their magic from their realm, but she had been able to feed her magic with her hatred. And any Fae knew that would turn one evil.

"I didn't expect to find you here," Aimery said softly.

She shrugged and glanced at the handsome Fae commander. Aimery had a long list of admirers, but he had yet to find his mate, as far as she knew.

"When I was younger, I used to dream about the day I would fall in love, of the family that would soon follow and the years of happiness ahead," she confessed. She wasn't sure why she told him such a secret when she hadn't shared it with anyone before.

Aimery regarded her with his swirling blue eyes. "What happened?"

"I never expected to fall in love with a human."

They grew quiet as they both stared at the sleeping couple.

"Did you ever find your mate, Aimery?"

He hesitated for so long she thought he might not answer. "Nay," he finally said.

"Do you think you will?"

"In time," he answered.

She took a deep breath and faced him. "I'm ready."

"So be it," he said, and grasped her wrist a moment before they transported to the Realm of the Fae.

Aimery wanted to hit something. Hard. He couldn't believe that even when he begged before Saynarra had been put to death, she still wouldn't release Senga from the spell.

And now he had to tell Keiran all hope was lost.

After everything…he hadn't been able to do anything for the Sinclairs. Failure wasn't something he was accustomed to, ever, and he didn't like the feeling that threatened to choke him.

If only he had known what Saynarra had become. If only he had been there to warn Keiran and Senga beforehand, none of this would have happened. The curse might now be lifted, but Keiran's pain was Drahcir's pain.

Keiran opened his eyes to see a wren sitting on the window. He lifted his head and the bird flew off into the new day. Keiran shielded his eyes from the bright sun and yawned. He stilled when Senga's fingers moved against his.

His gaze jerked to her face. Beneath her lids, he saw her eyes moving.

"Senga? Love, come back to me," he begged. "Please, Senga."

A half laugh, half sob burst from his lips when her eyes fluttered open, and she took a deep breath. He waited anxiously until her gaze met his.

"Keiran?"

He smiled. "Aye, love. It's me."

"You look awful. What…" Her words trailed off as her eyes widened as she began to recall what had taken place. "How?"

"I doona know, and I doona care," he said and brought her against his chest. He wrapped his arms around her and kissed all over her face. "I'm just glad to have you back."

When she wound her arms about him and nuzzled his neck, Keiran knew true bliss. He leaned back enough to claim her lips in a kiss that began gentle and soft but soon turned heated and passionate as their desires soared.

Though he wanted to lay her down and pleasure her body for hours, it would have to wait. He ended the kiss and leaned his forehead against hers.

"We're in Drahcir," he told her.

She grinned, her eyes round. "Truly? You did it, Keiran. Just as I knew you would."

"Nay, love. You did. You ended the curse."

She glanced away. "It was the hardest thing I've ever

done, leaving you. She had bespelled you to sleep through our conversation, but she swore you wouldn't remember me."

"I didna at first. Aimery helped me realize that I had found you, and once I remembered you, it broke the pact you and Saynarra had. You returned to me, but she used her magic to make you sleep for eternity, never waking."

"She's the Tnarg," Senga said.

Keiran nodded. "She showed all of Drahcir. Aimery caught her and brought her back to their realm for trial. She was put to death for her deeds against humans."

Senga bit her lip. "Is that what broke the spell?"

"Nay," said a voice behind them.

Keiran glanced over his shoulder to find Aimery. "Then what broke the spell?"

"Saynarra did it," Aimery said. "I begged her to lift it, but she refused to answer me. I think she had already removed the spell before I asked."

"Had she agreed, would it have saved her life?" Senga asked.

"Aye."

Keiran frowned. "Then why did she no' admit it?"

"I think she wanted to die," Aimery said, and walked to a window. "She turned from our ways. Evil had sunk into her soul, and she was tired of it. She wanted freedom. The only way to do that is death."

Keiran wrapped his arm around Senga. "I'm sorry she's dead, but I'm glad she released Senga."

Aimery turned to them and smiled, his hands clasped behind his back. "I suppose this means you'll be keeping the crown?"

Keiran chuckled at Senga's furrowed brow. "Aye, I will."

With a nod, Aimery walked to the door. "I'll inform

both sets of parents. Prepare for an invasion of the family," he said, before he walked from the room.

"You were going to give up your rightful place as heir?" Senga asked.

He nodded and kissed her again. "Without you, I'm nothing."

"Can this wait?" Lucian said as he strode into the room with a bright smile. "I saw Aimery in the corridor and he told me the news."

Keiran groaned. "Can you come back in a bit?"

"Nay," Lucian said with a chuckle. "I want to meet my new sister-in-law and the future queen of Drahcir."

Keiran rolled his eyes but couldn't stop the laughter that bubbled up. Just the day before, his life had been filled with despair, and now as he gazed at his beautiful mate, the future stretched ahead of them, leading them who knew where.

EPILOGUE

Two weeks later...

Senga's hands fisted in the covers, her back arched as she moaned. "Keiran, please," she begged.

He didn't lift his head from betwixt her legs as he continued to lick her sex, teasing her clit until she was writhing and breathless. Every time she neared to peaking, he would stop and fondle her breasts or kiss her.

"I need release," she cried out.

He chuckled, the sound vibrating against her sex and making her grind against him. His finger pushed inside of her, stroking her slowly at first then increasing his tempo as he added a second finger.

"It's too much. Ah, gods, Keiran," she moaned. She was so close to orgasm, the tension inside of her strung tight as a bow, aching for release.

Just when she thought he might give in, he flipped her onto her stomach then lifted her to her hands and knees. His large hands rubbed over her bottom, cupping and spreading her cheeks as he rubbed his cock against her.

"I love your bum."

Senga was beyond words. She tilted her hips, making her bottom rise in the air. When he moaned, she smiled, knowing he ached as she did.

Finally, his cock rubbed against her damp sex before sliding into her. She cried out as he gripped her hips and buried himself to the root. He gave one hard, quick thrust that sent her blood to boiling.

It was exactly what she needed. He began to pump inside of her, making her breasts sway as she closed her eyes and drowned in ecstasy.

The faster he drove into her, the quicker her body rose. When her orgasm finally washed through her, she screamed his name and her body clenched around his rod.

Yet, he continued to thrust, his fingers biting into her hips as he ground into her. She knew he was close by the way he quickened his tempo. After the pleasure he had given her, she wanted to return the favor, so she began to move against him.

"Senga!" he shouted as he plunged deep inside of her and spilled his seed, his body jerking with his climax.

Their ragged breathing filled the room as they fell as one onto the bed.

"I think I'm done for," Keiran whispered.

Senga chuckled and wiped a strand of hair from her damp forehead. "You said that an hour ago."

"Give me another hour then."

She turned her head to look at him. "The ceremony was beautiful."

"And long," he said with a frown.

The ceiling glittered with each movement of her hand from the beautiful yellow diamond he had given her that now caught the rays of the sun. "I love the ring."

"It suits you," he said, and kissed her temple. "I doona think I'll have to wait another hour. My cock stirs for you again."

Senga rolled over and grasped his hardening rod. "You are needy."

"Only with you, love. We keep this up and you'll be swelling with child soon."

"Hmm. That would be nice."

Keiran tossed her onto her back and rose up on his elbow while his other hand cupped her sex. "Shall we make sure of it, then?"

"Oh, yes," she moaned when he slipped a finger into her.

"Never say I'm no' willing to please my queen."

Senga knew for a fact he was most willing to please. And she was very glad of it.

With the curse broken, the Sinclairs and Drahcir would remain hidden for all time. No more would the princes have to leave and battle the Tnarg. All was as it should be.

She had found her mate, a man who would fill her days with love and light and laughter. Truly a dream come true.

Thank you for reading **THE ROYAL CHRONICLES BOX SET**. The series has finished, but there is a connecting story featuring none other than the enigmatic Fae, Aimery. Read his story in **MYSTIC TRINITY** right now!

She's the only one who can pull him from the darkness…

As Commander of the Fae army, Aimery is used to tracking evil and putting an end to it. When one of the rare and treasured blue dragons is killed and an egg stolen, Aimery is ordered to find the murderer. He never expects it to be one of his closest friends…

Kyndra is a priestess of the Dragon Order sworn to protect all dragons in the Realm of the Fae. She is sent by the high priestess to accompany Aimery and return the killer for execution. Aimery is instantly drawn to the sword-wielding priestess, but he knows he cannot have Kyndra.

Her life is sworn to the dragons, to be touched by no man. Neither expects to find desire and unyielding passion in the other. Yet when they track the killer to another realm, Aimery's life is at stake and Kyndra gives herself to him and the love she cannot deny in order to save him…

MYSTIC TRINITY IS NOW AVAILABLE!

Donna Grant
www.DonnaGrant.com
www.MotherofDragonsBooks.com

ABOUT THE AUTHOR

New York Times and *USA Today* bestselling author Donna Grant has been praised for her "totally addictive" and "unique and sensual" stories. She's written more than one hundred novels spanning multiple genres of romance including the bestselling Dark King series that features a thrilling combination of Dragon Kings, Druids, Fae, and immortal Highlanders who are dark, dangerous, and irresistible. She lives in Texas with her dog and a cat.

Connect with Donna online:
www.DonnaGrant.com
www.MotherofDragonsBooks.com

facebook.com/AuthorDonnaGrant

instagram.com/dgauthor

bookbub.com/authors/donna-grant

goodreads.com/donna_grant

pinterest.com/donnagrant1